London
Has
Fallen

Samantha Barrett

First Edition.

Cover art by Leah

Formatting by Formatting and Design by Jaye.

Editing Elizabeth Gardner

𝕎arnings!

This book contains sexual acts that may be triggering for some, forced proximity, Dub Con, torture, murder, rape and explicit scenes as well as language that may offend.

Please note, if there is a trigger that isn't listed please let me know as what I may not find triggering may be a trigger for you. I endeavor to ask the help of my alpha and beta team to point out triggers but some can be missed.

If this book isn't for you then close the page and find another amazing as fuck book! But, if this book is for you, then hold the fuck onto your panties and get ready for a wild ride because these characters are about to turn that pussy into a slip 'n' slide!

For my dad,
Thank you for always being my rock, my best friend, my ride till the fucking wheels fall off guy. I wouldn't be where I am or who I am without you, old boy. You gave me the gift of showing me how a man should love a woman and how I should be treated. Because of your teaching, I found the love of my life and never settled for less.

GODFATHERS OF THE NIGHT CODE

- *All who hunt the white rabbit and garner the kill shall be the chosen ruler of the sanctum, this law is final and will be upheld by all or they shall risk the wrath of the forefathers before them!*
- *All who are inducted shall fall beneath the rule of the Godfather, only blood shall rise within the organization.*
- *The winner of the challenge to rule the family will face the trials, if they fail, they will be met with a slow and painful death.*
- *No woman shall be allowed to enter the meeting chamber or the trials of the white rabbit, the society is ruled and governed by all male heirs.*

Prologue

I refuse to go back to that godforsaken school—he can't make me!

All those pussies do is moan and drone on and on about how much money they fucking have. I have spent three long ass years there. I'm eighteen, I should be able to make my own choices, but my father won't let me. If I drop out, the rules of the families state I can never take over for my dad. I am his only heir—he and Mom have been trying for a child for years. She has suffered many losses and Dad refuses to keep putting her through the pain of more miscarriages. I know my birth will be a factor in other families protesting me taking over the *Memento Mori* with my cousins *and* the Murdoch mafia by myself, but I am a Murdoch and have been since I was ten years old.

Royal and Erika Murdoch are my parents, maybe not by blood but in every way that counts, they are.

"London!" I cringe and turn away from the TV in the living room to see my dad standing in the doorway, looking pissed the fuck off. At nearly twenty-nine years old, the guy still looks good, but I would never tell him that. He likes to fuck with my grandpa and call him old, so I help my grandpa out by giving his son shit about looking old.

"Yeah?"

His pale blue eyes burn with rage. "Why the fuck did another headmaster just hand in their resignation?"

I balk and place my hand over my heart batting my lashes. "Daddy, how could you think I had anything to do with Mrs. Thompson quitting–"

"Cut the shit, she said she refused to continue working at Blackwood Academy as long as you were a student there."

I manage to catch myself before I roll my eyes. The old hag is too uptight and constantly has me in detention after school, so I may or may not have played a little prank on her.

"Well, simple then, I quit and she can have her job back."

"You are not dropping out!" he shouts, now I do roll my eyes. He should know by now that yelling at me never gets him anywhere. All it does is piss me the fuck off and forces me to fuck with him, like right now. As soon as he leaves to go find Mom so she can *talk sense* into me, I plan to take his new G-Wagon for a joy ride.

"Why the hell not? Who are those old bastards to tell me that I have to attend a fucking school I hate?" I never went to a normal school growing up, I refused so my mom home-schooled me and I passed with flying colors. Well that, and the fact since the knowledge of my father's identity became public to other families, it meant he was receiving death threats about me.

"They are the heads of each fucking country. Your grandfather happens to be one of the people who voted yes for the school. Why don't you call him and scream at him while I go find your mother to help talk some damn sense into you." I smirk when he turns his back and mumbles how much he hates that I'm exactly like him. The second the coast is clear, I dash out of the living room and snag his keys off the counter, then run out the front door. Climbing behind the wheel of his car, I don't fuck around, starting the beast and burning rubber as I floor it out of the driveway.

Two minutes.

I count the time in my head as I race down the street, passing by Aunt Nelly and Uncle Chaos's houses. Seeing his house brings that same feeling of guilt brimming to the surface inside me. I snuff that feeling out before it can send me into a spiral, again. I make it half a block away before my phone rings. I answer on the second ring and place it on speaker.

"Hey, Dad."

"You little shit! Bring my fucking car back here now."

"What? You're cutting out, Dad, it's really bad service," I lie.

"London, I am–"

"*Warning you,*" I say, mocking him.

"Erika!" he screams for my mom as I fight back laughter, this must be hard for him since he pulled these types of pranks on his own father. I round the corner and have to jerk the wheel to the right when someone darts out in front of me. I'm too late, I scream when I feel the person hit the front of Dad's car. That isn't the worst part. When I feel the tire roll over the guy's body, I know without a doubt I just killed him, or at least I hope I did so I don't have to reverse back over him to put the fucker out of his misery. I slam the car into park and jump out, racing around the back of the truck—the sight of the guy's mangled body has bile rushing up my throat. This is so fucking inconvenient and is going to delay my plans from going to pay that bitch Mrs. Thompson a visit for snitching on me.

"Fuck!" I shout. I look around, the street is empty and I think I will be able to flee without anyone knowing what I did and then my dad can't blame me for this. The only lighting is from the street lamps. I hedge toward the guy and stop a couple steps away, leaning forward to get a better look. Eww, the vacant look in his eyes is gross, this fucker is so dead and has just ruined my freaking plans for the night. His head is cracked open and I'm pretty sure that is brain matter on the pavement beside him. His arm is twisted in an *S* like shape but it's both his legs that have me screwing my face up, one is bent up toward his body and the other has a bone sticking out of it. I didn't think I hit him that hard to cause this amount of damage!

"Who the fuck are you?" I spin around to find three guys around my age standing behind me, each holding a Glock and immediately I'm on high alert—fuck, I left my phone in the car!

"Who the hell are you?" I snap, making sure to stomp my foot like a petulant child. I feel my knife in my boot and relax. Dad says never bring a knife to a gun fight but believe me, these fuckers have no idea who I am and how good I am at wielding a blade.

The boy on the left peers around me at the body on the ground. "Ares, she killed the rabbit." I frown and look back to make sure it was a person I hit and not a fucking bunny.

"No fucking way," The one on the right says as he steps forward to get a better look.

"Ares, he's right, she did kill the rabbit," The one in the middle says. Ares eyes me warily.

"Apollo, get back here," Ares snaps. The three of them

stand there eyeing me with accusation in their gazes. "I'm Ares, these are my brothers Apollo and Adonis."

"Cool, how the hell do you know him?" I ask, jabbing a finger over my shoulder toward the body. I play this whole thing cool trying to gauge their reactions, we already have one dead body here, I would fucking hate to have three more to clean up if they felt they need to get froggy.

"He was ours to capture, we were supposed to be initiated but you claimed that right."

"What?" When headlights shine toward us, the three of them turn ready to flee. Fuck, I have no doubt that's my dad and his men and I am so going to be in shit for this. The asshole is tracking my fucking phone again!

"See you soon, goddess," Apollo winks and says before he races after his brothers. Three cars come to a screeching halt and within seconds my dad is in front of me checking me for injury.

"Are you okay?"

"Yeah, I'm okay," I answer, annoyed at his coddling.

"What the fuck happened, London? Marco, check him for a pulse and ID," Dad barks.

"Dad, he came out of nowhere. You can't blame me for his stupidity, the dude ran in front of my car, like come on it's not my fault he wanted to die!"

"Boss." Dad darts his gaze over my head.

"What is it Marco?" Dad snaps.

"No ID but he has a brand on his neck." At the somber tone of Marco's voice, I turn around and find him looking panicked.

"Show me," Dad growls as he steps around me to inspect the body. Marco tilts the guy's head to show my dad the brand on his neck. I can't see it clearly from where I stand and I don't want to get closer and risk my dad focusing on me. I see the raised skin from some scarring but I can't make out what the brand is. "Get rid of the body and clean the scene now," Dad barks. All the men rush to do as they are told.

"Dad?" I ask, suddenly feeling the shift in his mood from anger to worry.

"Get rid of the car and scrub any video evidence. I want no witnesses—"

"Too late," I mutter, drawing their attention to me.

"What do you mean?" Dad clips out.

"Three guys, Apollo, Ares and Adonis, were here, they took off when they saw your lights."

"Fuck!" he roars.

"Dad, what the hell is going on?" I shout, getting pissed off that they all know something I don't!

"The guy you just killed was marked by the Greeks. I allowed Costa to host his hunt here as a show of goodwill because of all the trouble you are causing at Blackwood."

I shake my head not following what he is saying. "What does that mean?" I shout.

"It means you just killed the fucking *white rabbit*! The Greeks are beholden to their laws, London, they will try to come for you!"

"So fucking let them come for me, I'll run their asses down too!" I rush to say.

He shakes his head and pins me with a stern look. "You don't understand what the fuck you have just done!" he roars.

"Don't understand what?" I scream.

"A new headmaster has been appointed, Artemis Argyros."

"I don't know him," I say.

"You're about to. He's the son of Costa Argyros, the leader of the Greeks. We need to meet with them now before Artemis comes for you. The school is the first place he will look and if he can't find you, he'll send the fucking triplets you just met after you. I'd kill them all if I could, but I can't."

"Dad, what's going to happen to me?" I whisper, the fear in his eyes has me suddenly feeling like this is a huge deal and this wasn't just some random guy I ran down.

"If I can't work something out with Costa, you will be forced to go through a series of trials to be initiated into the *God Father's Of The Night*, it's a secret society led by Costa and his son Artemis."

I shake my head. "No, I'll kill them all," I say with conviction.

"London, Artemis was trained from birth the same way me and your aunts and uncles were. To hunt, track, kill—you name it, he can do it all. There is no escaping him if he comes and we'll wage a war against them if we have to, because I won't allow them to take my daughter from me."

"But, if you go to war with the Greeks, that means the end of the peace treaty you worked so hard for."

"Then let's hope I can con my dad into backing me when I meet with Costa to try to right this wrong."

I have a sinking feeling it's already too late. They know what I did and they will come for me... Well, guess what, motherfuckers, I'll be ready and waiting for you to try and take me out.

Chapter One

London

With great power comes great responsibility.

I snort to myself, that is the worst fucking statement I have ever heard come from my father's mouth. He stole that line from a freaking Marvel movie thinking it made him sound wise! I don't bother replying to his text as I walk through the halls of this prestigious school that is supposed to inspire us to want to learn everything we can to lead our families. They want us to broker peace among the top families and make sure no one can ever come between the seven families, Russian, Canadian, Irish, Greek, English. My Grandpa and Dad claim the other two seats at that table. Blackwood Academy is supposed to shape the minds of the young heirs from powerful families —I call bullsheeet!

Don't get me wrong I have always hated this fucking pathetic excuse for a school and managed to get numerous amounts of staff relieved of their positions. It's not my fault they can't take the fucking heat. My dad is at his wits end with me. I know I haven't been an easy child to raise but what the hell did he expect? I never asked to be shipped off to some poor ass excuse of a prison, I mean school. My uncle Chaos only came up with this stupid idea to protect his twins, Storm and Halo. I will admit, I may have agreed to pull my head out of my ass for the time being until my dad can arrange a meeting with Costa—the leader of the Greek family. No one knows much about the Greeks, only that they run a whole ass secret society and *never* allow outsiders in.

I walk lazily through the halls, letting these sorry excuses for heirs get their fill of me, they all know exactly who I am and I relish that. I've made sure to stamp my mark on this place and rule it with an iron fist. Many doubted me because my lack of a cock but I made up for it by rearranging their faces and showing them. I don't need a dick or balls to be the top dog, this is a eat or be eaten world and I am no one's fucking prey!

I hold my head high the whole way to my dorm room. Unlike most schools, our dorms are located in the four corners of this castle-like fucking palace, it's a mix between a gothic church and a castle. We also don't use keys, I stand in front of the retina scanner and wait for the green laser to scan my left eye. The door clicks open, and the moment I step inside and slam the fucking door I take my first full breath since stepping foot on the school grounds ten minutes ago. I pull my phone out and text my dad back.

ME

In my room like a good girl.

I wasn't supposed to return back here for another week but Dad caught me trying to run to prevent a fucking war from breaking out and shipped my ass back early. The bastard! I was sandwiched between my Uncle Chaos and Uncle Kacey on the fucking plane, I wasn't even allowed cutlery to eat my food because neither of them trusted me not to use it as a weapon against them. Apparently, my maiming and stabby behavior was cute as a kid but now that I'm older, Uncle Chaos thinks it's lost its appeal and I should go to weekly therapy. My phone rings and I scowl at the screen, debating if I should ignore my father or not, but the looming threat over my head prompts me to accept the call.

"Yes, *Your Royal Highness*?"

"Cut the fucking shit, London." I smirk loving how I can ruffle his feathers after all these years.

"Daddy, I would never cut any shit. I am a lady after all," I say in the most nasally stuck-up voice I can.

"Like fuck you are, you have the mouth of a sailor and the attitude of a feigning addict!" I splutter.

"The fuck? I'm so telling Grandpa you called me a crack whore."

"I never fucking said that!" he shouts.

"Did too," I bark back.

"Did not."

"Oh, I like this game! You did too."

He growls and I can't contain my laughter, I love fucking with my dad, it's one of my favorite hobbies.

"I swear to Christ almighty, London, you need to pull your head out of your fucking ass and realize this isn't a joke!" I tense at the reminder of the situation I am currently in. It was a fucking accident and now that one mistake is shaping up to be the worst fucking thing in my life. Before he can say more I switch the call to FaceTime and add Grandpa. My dad's angry face fills the screen and I smile brightly making sure to look like an innocent angelic being.

"Daddy!" I singsong and his eyes narrow.

"What the hell are you up to, you little shit?" Grandpa answers the call just as Dad calls me a little shit. The smile he was wearing vanishes as his eyes narrow and a cold look overtakes his face.

"Watch the fucking way you speak to my granddaughter, you little prick!" Grandpa seethes. Bishop Murdoch may be the cold heartless Mafia Don of New York to everyone else but to me, he is just Grandpa. If there is anyone in this world I can rely on to have my back, it's him. Over the years Dad and Grandpa have managed to form a mutual respect for the other and don't fight as much, except for when I call and snitch on my dad for being a dick, then he gets a new asshole from Grandpa.

Dad's eyes widen a fraction before he glares at me and grinds his teeth. "You added him to the fucking call?"

Smiling sweetly I nod as I say, "You hurt my feelings when you called me a crack whore." Grandpa's eyes darken as he scowls at my dad.

"I didn't call you that!" Dad defends but it's too late, Grandpa is pissed.

"You need me to come out there and remind you what a real ass whooping is, boy?" Aside from Dad having pale blue eyes and Grandpa having brown, they are carbon copies of each other. Dad's features darken.

"Bring it, old man, I'll break your fucking hip." Before this can go any further, I cut in and put an end to the bickering.

"Grandpa, Dad wants to lock me up here at school while he tries to play hero and meet with Costa. I don't want to be here." I can hear the whine in my own voice and I can't find it within myself to care. I hate this place, it's so dull and boring. I have no fucking friends–not that I need them but still, having someone to talk to every once in a while would be nice. My whole life I have known that because of who my parents and grandparents are that others would try to use me to get closer to them. I chose to separate myself from everyone so no one could get close enough to hurt me.

Grandpa sighs and runs a hand through his salt and pepper colored hair. "I know you don't want to be there, Sweetheart." Dad snorts and mutters about how he was never that nice or caring to him when he was younger but we ignore his moaning. "At this stage, until we can get a meeting set with Costa, Blackwood is the safest place for you."

"I'm safer at home with Dad, Uncle Chaos and Aunty Nell." An idea hits me just as Grandpa opens his mouth to reply so I cut in before he can. "I mean, if you think the Memento Mori isn't equipped to keep me safe, I could always come stay with you and Grandma?" Dad's brows leap to his hairline as he scowls at me.

"Take that back now, you little demon! I have managed to keep your ungrateful ass alive and out of harm despite your best efforts to try and kill me over the years!" I roll my eyes at my father's over dramatic spiel, he's so sensitive in his old age.

"Shut up, Royal!" Grandpa scolds before turning his gaze back to me. "I would start a fucking war for you, my beautiful granddaughter, you know that. I would love nothing more than to have you here with me and your grandmother, but given the fact you took the life of the white rabbit, that is something we cannot run from. The Greeks may be lenient with a lot, but when it comes to how their society is run, they will never bend the rules. The rabbit you took out was meant for the triplets, Costa's last hope of keeping the Argyros name alive and at the top."

Frowning down at my phone I ask. "But Dad said that his

oldest son was the youngest to ever kill the white rabbit, wouldn't he be the one taking the lead?"

Dad answers me. "Artemis was supposed to succeed his father and take over, but for reasons unknown to us, Artemis refused the crown and so did Costa's second born son so the mantle fell to the triplets. Thanks to your reckless driving, the triplets may now have to wait another five years before they have a shot at taking over."

"Why five years?" I ask.

"Because the Greeks believe that only the strongest can rule so every five years they set the heirs out to hunt the white rabbit. If they do not succeed, then their fathers are forced out of the family and shunned," Grandpa says.

I blow out a breath and shake my head. "Well, that sucks to be them."

"Costa Argyros, is the longest to ever head the Greeks, most only lasting roughly five years." I gape at my father.

"Seriously? How long has he been leading them?"

"Forty years," Grandpa answers solemnly. There is a glint in Grandpa's eyes that has a cold shiver of dread working its way down my spine.

"Dad, don't," my father warns but of course that only prompts me to drill my grandfather for more information.

"I need to know." The slight hitch in my voice has my father's features contorting, I know he wishes he could be here with me but what I don't understand is why? My dad isn't afraid of anything yet he sent me back here to hide.

"We believe he has led this long because he takes out his opposition by any means necessary and we believe he uses his sons to do it. Artemis was supposed to take the throne five years ago but he still hasn't. There are the other four–."

"Four?" I question my grandfather.

"Yea, Costa has five sons, Artemis, Apollo, Ares, Adonis and Cronos." I balk at the phone screen.

"He seriously named all his sons after Greek Gods?" My dad laughs while my grandfather scowls at the screen.

"I mean, your grandfather and his brothers are named after chess pieces so..." I can't help the laughter that bursts from me, Dad laughs with me while Grandpa just scowls at the screen and mutters about me being too much like my father.

"You both done yet?" Grandpa snaps. Dad and I manage to get ourselves under control and I nod. "You need to steer clear of the Argyros siblings while you are at Blackwood, London." My brows raise.

"They go here?"

Both of them frown at me. "You've never run into them at school?" Dad asks, I shake my head.

"No."

"Keep it that way," Dad growls.

I scoff. "Pretty hard to do since you told me that Artemis is going to be the new headmaster of my school!"

"If you didn't run the last fucking one off then we wouldn't have needed someone else to fill her shoes!" Dad shouts.

I roll my eyes. "It was a joke," I defend.

"You burnt *Pussy Ass Mofo* into the front lawn of the fucking school, London." I flinch and shoot them a sheepish smile.

"I mean... Can you prove it was moi?" I ask sweetly. Grandpa laughs while dad glares at me, I know I need to get off this call before he bursts a blood vessel or something, so I mutter a quick goodbye and end the call, tossing my phone onto my bed as I drop face-first onto it and growl into my comforter.

What the fuck am I supposed to do for a week?

As the thought crosses my mind, I hear the sound of someone outside my door. I push up and watch as a flyer is slipped beneath my door. I debate ignoring it but then it's not like I have anything else to do. I trudge over to the door and collect it from the floor and quickly read over it.

PARTY, PARTY, PARTY!
LET'S GET LIT AND TEAR THE ROOF OFF THIS BITCH,
SEE YOU ALL AT SHANKS AT 10PM, WEAR YOUR BEST
OR WEAR NOTHING AT ALL.

I screw my face up at the invitation to what is no doubt going to be an orgy of young teenage kids that are going to get wasted and fuck until they're chaffing between their thighs.

"Sounds like a good time," I say aloud as I smile to myself and dash into my closet to find an outfit for the night. I've never attended a party before so this will be a first for me. I needed a distraction and I guess the devil himself delivered, because normally all these fools avoid me and make sure to never mention shit like this in front of me.

Chapter Two

London

I round the corner and frown at the sight of the line outside of the club where the invite said to be. I may not have been invited to any parties before but I'm not a fucking hermit, I do know where all the local clubs are. I just choose not to frequent them and get fucked by pin dick wannabes who think their Daddy's money can compensate for their mediocre cocks. Most people would wait at the back of the line to be let in by the bouncers. But I'm not like most people. So I stroll to the front of the line, ignoring the sneers of all the bitches and catcalls from the thirsty guys. I pause for dramatic effect in front of both jar-head bouncers, allowing them to get their fill of me and all my exposed skin. I know I look hot and hey, if they want to stare at the goods my mama gave me I won't stop them.

"What's a pretty thing like you doing out here all alone,

darlin'?" the bouncer with the shaved head asks me. I dial up the sexiness and bat my lashes playing along.

"I was invited to a party..." I let my sentence trail off as I nibble on my bottom lip, ignoring the protest of the others waiting in the line as they shout for the bouncers to allow them in. Shaved head smirks and trails his eyes up and down my body before shooting me a sexy smile that says without words, *I want to fuck you!* I shoot him a demure smile that promises him I'll find him when the night is over—I have zero fucking plans of allowing this overweight piece of shit between my thighs. But I don't say that as he lifts the red velvet rope and flicks his head, motioning for me to pass. I know without a doubt he plans to cop a feel of my ass so I make sure to spin around as I pass him and shoot him a wink, which earns me a scowl that I shrug off.

Men like to think because women dress sexy and show a little skin that they are entitled to ogle us and take what isn't theirs. Newsflash, motherfuckers, if any one of these spineless bitches think they are touching me I will slit their fucking throats without batting a lash. The best part about being in Switzerland is that they class eighteen as the legal age unlike the US, so we are able to drink and enter clubs without a worry here. Dad was pissed when I sent him a selfie before I left the dorm, claiming that he would be on the first flight out to murder me so of course, I naturally screen-shotted his message and sent it to the group chat I have with my mom, Grandpa, Aunty Nell and Uncle Chaos. I know without a doubt the four of them are going to be tearing my dad a new asshole. I may not have friends, but I do have a father I can fuck with on the daily and that is way more fun than slumber parties.

I make my way over to the bar and push my way between the waiting patrons, not giving a shit about their shouts and protests—not my fault they are big jock type guys and I'm small enough to fit through the gap. I lean my arms on the bar and place my index and thumb in my mouth whistling. The three bartenders snap their heads in my direction, I smile and wag my brows. The one closest to me rolls his eyes and steps up to serve me.

"What'll it be?" He snaps. The guy is fucking hot, he is the most attractive man I have ever seen. His black hair and tan skin gleam even in the dim lighting of the club, his brown eyes bore into me. The little vest thing he wears looks taut and tight stretched across his muscled torso. I bite my lip drinking in the sight of him. God, he is so fucking gorgeous I have never felt this attracted to a person before. "You ordering or what?" he snaps, pulling me out of blatant ogling of him.

"Vodka and cranberry on the rocks," I say. I fish the money out of the bodice of my dress, not missing the way his eyes track my movements as he pours the drink without looking. What a skill, I think to myself as I hand him the cash and take the drink, shooting him a wink before turning away and making my way toward the center of the club. The dance floor is packed, people are practically plastered against each other. For a party this seems a bit intense but who am I to judge, at least it isn't dull. I watch as the girls allow random guys to come up behind them and grip their hips, grinding their cocks into their asses. They don't protest or shove them away, they just allow them to manhandle them and submit.

I shake my head, what absolute dumbasses.

I continue to sip my drink and people watch. It's nice to blend in and not be the center of attention for a change. I'm so used to everyone staring at me and snickering behind my back. Out of all the students here, my last name is the most well-known because of who my family is and how my father and

Grandfather run the US. They now control the whole country. They are still dealing in firearms and all that shit, allowing smaller families to work under them. But, of course they pay a tax for being allowed to still operate within the country.

"Hey there, pretty lady." I peer over my shoulder and fight the look of surprise from showing on my face. I keep my mask of indifference in place as I look between the triplets, Apollo, Adonis and Ares Argyros. The three of them look like carbon copies of the other. It's strange. I'm used to seeing twins because of my cousins and Uncle Rook and Uncle Knight as well as Uncle Chaos and Uncle Hav... I shake the thought away not wanting to dredge up the memory of him. "You look ravishing." I furrow my brow at the one in the middle, who the fuck says *ravishing*?

The three of them are dressed the same, black slacks and black button up shirts. I drop my gaze to their feet and fight the snort from breaking free, they even wear matching Tom Ford boots. I take in their appearance, brown hair, brown eyes. I know that sounds boring and plain but I can see nothing about these three is boring, their hair is styled to perfection and slicked back on their heads, and their eyes are alight with mischief and mirth. The one on the left lifts his hand and scratches at the day-old stubble on his chin and I notice the gold ring on his finger. I try to get a better look but the moment he sees what I'm staring at he drops his hand and stuffs it back in his pocket. I could tell from the first night I met these three that they would be trouble.

"What do the Three Stooges want?" I clip out as I take a sip of my drink, keeping my eyes on them over the brim of my glass.

The one on the right clutches his chest in mock hurt. "And here we thought you might be happy to see friendly faces."

"Handsome faces you mean," the one on the left adds, causing me to roll my eyes.

"Your faces look like smacked asses," I reply, the mischief evaporates from their eyes and is replaced by annoyance. The one in the middle steps forward, I can already tell he is the ring-leader of the three of them. He looks me up and down like he has every right to take in his fill of me, and my fist itches to rearrange his face.

"You looked better when you were pale and near tears after you killed our rabbit." I scoff, the only tears in my eyes were of happiness that he was actually dead and I didn't need to finish him off. My eyes narrow at the bastard as he tries to intimidate me by using his height to his advantage. He may be a foot taller than me, but that's nothing new to me. I've always been short and learned to use that to my advantage. I close the sliver of space between us and press my body flush against his, I see some of the bravado falter from his face at my bold move.

"He was never *our* rabbit, he was mine and from what I hear, your daddy is not too pleased that his three precious sons failed." The anger radiating off him is so pungent I can taste it on my tongue. The other two step forward to flank their brother. I pay them no mind, if they think they are an imposing force, then they have another thing coming. I have trained from the age of nine to fight. I can peel skin from the human body making sure to inflict as much pain as possible without killing them. I am trained in the art of knife throwing, shooting and hacking–I loath to admit my hacking skills are lacking but I've never been good with practical shit, I prefer to do the hands on stuff.

"You little bitch–," I cut lefty off.

"You think coming here and trying to corner me because I'm a little girl in a dress makes you superior?" I scoff and don't give them time to answer. "You little boys know nothing about me. If you wanted to have a dick measuring contest, you failed because out of the four of us, I have the biggest and the three of you are welcome to suck it anytime you like." I shoulder check the one on the right on my way past, I will not allow anyone to try to intimidate me. My father has always told me that I would be underestimated in this world because of my size and lack of cock.

I find a booth in a deserted corner of the club that gives me an unobscured view of the dance floor. It intrigues me to see people freely living life and allowing themselves the joys of intoxication. I have never been drunk, I can't allow myself to be incapacitated and have my senses dulled. Given who I am and who my family is, I am always on the defense when someone tries to get close to me or spark a conversation. No one in this world has pure intentions. After all, money is the greatest root of all evil and I come from a family that is richer than the Rockefellers.

I envy my Aunt Amelia. She is fierce, strong and refuses to submit to the demands of the family. She broke away and made a name and a life for herself. She hates that the world only knows her as Max Kingsley but at least she can be what she wants. Don't get me wrong, one day I do want the throne and will take over after my dad steps down, but in the meantime, I would just love to travel and see the world. Experience what it's like to not be London Murdoch. I love who I am and where I come from, don't get me wrong, but I'm stuck at this fucking school because of who I am!

"You're in my seat." I snap my gaze to the side to see the bartender from earlier standing there with an angry scowl on his face. I furrow my brow when I notice he's changed, he now wears a white button up and black slacks. My mouth waters at the sight of him, he's fucking gorgeous. "Move!" he grits out, the tone of his voice pisses me off. All thoughts about hating who I am and not being free dissipate. Because of who I am, I can sit here and plot his murder and know I can get away with it. So instead of moving and obeying his demands, I lean back into the booth and kick my feet on the bench seat, while resting my arms along the back as I stare up at him and smile.

"I kind of like this spot and think I'll remain where I am, but while you're standing there you may as well march that fine ass back to the bar and pour me another drink." If looks could melt the skin off your body, then I would be skinless. I dart my tongue out to moisten my lips in a nervous gesture, suddenly feeling the air around us cool when the look in his eyes darkens.

"You have two fucking seconds to get your dirty ass out of my booth before I throw you the fuck out. I am not a man to be tested." It's a strange sort of feeling, having someone speak to me like this. I'm used to being given snide looks and hearing whispers behind my back, but to have someone outright stand before me and speak to me in such a way like I am beneath them is mind blowing. My hesitation must piss him off further as he reaches forward and grips my ankles, yanking me to the edge of the booth. My legs are trapped between his large ones and my face in line with his crotch. I'm forced to lean back and crane my neck back to meet his sneering gaze.

"Who the hell are you?" I ask in astonishment. Never in my life have I ever been manhandled and this, so it is new for me. Call it what you will but this bartender has me intrigued.

He glares down his nose at me, his upper lip lifts in a sneer as his brown eyes spit fire and hatred. "I'm not someone to be trifled with, little girl." His *little girl* comment has my feathers ruffled and my anger peaking.

"And I'm not someone you want to make an enemy out of.

Haven't you ever heard that a woman's scorn is worse than the fires of hell?" As big as he is he moves swiftly without a sound or so much as a flicker of his eyes. His hand bands around my slender neck and forces me back so I'm lying flat on the seat with his hulking form pinning me in place. He presses in closer, so his nose is touching mine. I allow him to think he has the upper hand and truthfully, I need a minute to gather myself because his close proximity is doing things to my body I haven't had the pleasure of feeling before. His minty breath washes over my face when he exhales, his brown eyes look almost black up close. His black hair has flopped against his forehead and the urge to push it back from his face startles me.

"A woman has no place in my world. If you value your life at all, you will heed my warning and get the fuck out of my club." The music is loud and the bass is pumping, but he doesn't need to raise his voice for me to hear. I'm so enraptured with him that he is my sole focus and everything around me has become white noise. "A pretty little girl like you shouldn't be in a place like this." His warning is clear and sends a shiver down my spine. I knew this wasn't an average club when I clocked at least a dozen guys in suits with earpieces walking around as I entered.

"You think I'm pretty?" His eyes narrow.

"Don't test my patience any further. I'm not in the mood." I smirk and bat my lashes.

"See, the thing is I would believe you but then I can feel how hard you are." He grinds his teeth in aggression. I expect him to shift or deny my claim but instead he shocks the hell out of me when he grinds his hard cock against my pussy, drawing a sharp gasp from me. The satisfied smirk on his face pisses me off. I don't enjoy being on the receiving end of someone else's power, I am always the one in control so I turn the tables. I press the blade I had sheathed in my garter into his side, making his eyes widen a fraction and I smile. "You see, the moment you pinned me I drew my blade ready to end you if you did something I didn't like. You were too focused on asserting your dominance to notice I already had you where I wanted you."

"Where exactly do you want me?"

The corner of my mouth hikes up as I press the tip of the blade into his side, his face remaining stoic but the slight quiver of his lip tells me he's worried about what I might do—that is fucking exhilarating. "Beneath you?" A dark smirk graces that fucking gorgeous face, he places his hands flat above my head and leans in closer so his lips ghost over mine.

"If I wanted you, you would know." He sneers cockily.

"The feeling of your cock against my pussy paints a different picture."

"Americans, you always think you are superior to others, but the reality is that you would spread your legs for me if I told you to because you all want to see if the rumors are true."

I keep my brows from drawing in and keep my face blank. "And what rumors are those?" He moves so his lips brush the shell of my ear. I tense in anticipation but the moment he darts his tongue out and licks my lobe, I gasp, only for that to turn into a moan when he licks a trail down my neck and nips at the soft skin of my collarbone before working his way back up and pressing his lips against my ear.

"That Greek men can fuck better than any other race." At the mention of the Greeks I freeze beneath him.

"Who the fuck are you?" I grit out through clenched teeth as he rests his forehead against mine.

Chapter Three

Artemis

The shock is evident in her green eyes, she isn't what I expected her to be. I heard the rumors from my brothers about her beauty but they tend to exaggerate everything so I paid them no mind. It appears, they were right. She is fucking stunning and that's a problem. The moment I spotted her in my booth my cock leapt to attention. I've fucked plenty of beautiful women but never has my cock hardened for someone without their lips being wrapped around it.

"Who the fuck are you?" she grits out as I rest my forehead against her, the shock is replaced by anger. Rather than answering, I brush my lips against hers. I know without a doubt she is a spitfire and I would never win an argument against her, so I decide to break her by forcing her body to betray her basic instincts. Her gasp grants me the access I need to plunge my tongue inside her mouth, the taste of berries invading my senses and I fight back the groan that wants to break free. The blade she holds at my side begins to tremble as I override her system and derail her train of thought from just a kiss. She melts into the chair and the sound of metal clanging against the floor has me relaxing knowing she dropped her blade, her arms band around my neck and pull me in closer as her legs widen. The warm heat of her pussy is pressed against my cock. I grind into her, relishing in the sounds she makes. I swallow each moan hungry for the next. Jesus Christ, this girl has me dry humping her in the middle of my club. That realization of where we are and what is about to go down tonight has me snapping out of it and breaking the kiss.

I leap off her and stand at the edge of the booth panting, I stare down at her red face with swollen lips and a dazed look in her eyes. I can see her nipples through the fabric of her all-too-revealing dress. I know for a fact—with how high the slits are on either side—that she isn't wearing panties. Her ample tits look suffocated in the tiny cups, her chest rising and falling in quick succession as she tries to get enough air into her lungs. Her emerald eyes slowly begin to clear and once the fog is gone, she grips the blade from the floor and is on her feet glaring up at me.

"Don't you ever fucking touch me again!" she snarls. The way she looks at me like I am beneath her sets me ablaze. The wanton bitch was practically begging for my cock a second ago and now stands before me as if this shit was one sided.

"You were mediocre at best. Get the fuck out of my club now and don't come back!" This time, she doesn't argue, instead she steps around me and I smirk in triumph until I feel her slice through my shirt. I hiss as I feel the sharp edge of the blade glide across my skin. The bitch doesn't stop to check if she hit her mark, she keeps her back to me and her head held high as she makes her way toward the exit, leaving me standing here with a hole in my shirt and blood trickling down my side. That girl has no fucking idea who she just made an enemy of but she's about to learn real fucking fast who I am. I'll break her body first before I destroy her mind and send her back to her family as a shell of the person she once was. I press the tips of my fingers against the wound and hiss. Little bitch dug it in deep enough to make sure it stung, for some reason that has a smirk pulling at the corner of my mouth.

After cleaning my wound and changing my shirt, I decided to forego my usual place since London ruined that booth for me so I came into my office. I could strangle the fucking triplets for throwing a party at my club and inviting every student from Blackwood Academy here. This is a fucking disaster waiting to happen. I know the three of them needed to blow off some steam after failing to locate and eliminate the rabbit. If they had just got to him first and put a bullet in his head then we wouldn't be in this fucking mess!

"Got a minute?" Looking up from the stack of papers in front of me, I see Cronos standing in the doorway.

"Yeah. Shut the door behind you," I mutter as I push the stack of papers to the side and rest my forearms on the top of my desk as Cronos takes one of the seats in front of me. Most people need to look in a mirror to check their appearance but not me, I have a twin–kind of. I was born just before midnight and Cronos was born ten minutes after twelve so technically we are twins but born on different days.

"Costa called." Cronos never refers to our father as his *Dad*, there is a story there but neither of them have confided in us about it. All I know is that ever since Cronos didn't complete the trials he has become a dark entity, he's a wild card.

"What'd he have to say?"

"He's coming in tomorrow, he wants the five of us to meet

him at his house." I fight the urge to roll my eyes. When it was decided by the founding fathers, as we call them, that Blackwood Academy would be a thing, Costa bought a house here in Switzerland. You may think it's because he wanted to be closer to his sons but that's the lie he tells everyone. Costa has a house here so it's convenient for him to drop in whenever he wants. I was tasked with living here and watching over the triplets when they first started school here three years ago. Now, I have no choice but to step in as the headmaster thanks to London Murdoch chasing off the previous ones.

"Did he say why?" Cronos grits his teeth, his upper lip twitches as he tries not to snarl which puts me on edge.

"He wants me to redo the trials with the triplets." I keep my anger buried deep inside me as I take a couple of calming breaths.

"You do this, you know what that means, right?" Cronos nods and darts his gaze away from me.

"I won't hurt them, Artemis," he murmurs softly. It fucking destroys me to be so disconnected from my own twin. He built a wall around himself and closed everyone out. He works behind the bar here because he refuses to have anything to do with the family business. We aren't like the other families, we are the middleman if you will. We allow all the narcotics to go through our ports and turn a blind eye, we broker arms deals, and the skin trade is still active, thanks to my father. Bishop, Royal, Andreas and Knox detest this and have tried to shut it down but Ian, Karl and Costa have refused and fought them at every turn. Granted though, Costa doesn't exactly deal in the trade—he just captures the girls and gets them hooked on heroin before Karl and Ian come and collect them.

I don't enjoy that side of the business. Those girls are someone's daughter, sister, mother, friend, cousin. They are fucking people and yet they are traded like cattle at a slaughter house.

"We'll figure this out before it comes to that." He snaps his gaze back to me, his brown eyes are so dark they appear almost black.

"The girl needs to go in order for one of them to win."

"She won't be a problem. I'll break her before she can even pass the first trial," I say firmly.

"Is that before or after you fuck her?" he sneers, my eyes narrow at my twin.

"Say whatever the fuck it is that you are avoiding?" I grit out.

"You've had more ass than a fucking church pew, yet earlier I saw you pinning London Murdoch beneath you in the booth. Don't let your cock cloud your judgment because family will always come first and that girl isn't family." He doesn't wait for a reply as he climbs to his feet and storms out of my office, slamming my door behind himself hard enough to rattle the pictures on the walls. I sit here, staring at the closed door for so long my eyes begin to burn. I have no idea how all of this fell on me. I may be the oldest but not by much. Cronos was my wingman, my right hand, my go-to but ever since the trials, he's just... not himself. He's receded so deep inside himself that I'm not sure any of us would be able to reach him.

I pull into the long driveaway that leads to my father's house. He says it's our *home* but I'm not sure that man has any idea what that fucking word means. My brothers and I haven't had a home since our mother died. She grounded us and kept us together as a unit, but since she passed, we've all become people she wouldn't recognize—me especially.

Climbing out of my car I take a deep breath and scan the other cars in the driveway, noting that Cronos's Toyota Crown RS is missing from the lineup of vehicles. Pinching my lips to the side, I shake my head and make my way around the back, knowing Costa would have brunch served out on the back patio so we have a mountain view as we eat. He does subtle shit like this all time to show us how much money he possesses without actually having to say it. I round the corner and spy the triplets straight away, sitting at the large table that is piled with food–enough food to feed a fucking small army, just another thing Costa does to show his wealth.

"Brother." Adonis grins as he spots me first. Apollo and Ares both turn to me as I claim the spot next to Ares.

"Where's Cronos?" I ask the three of them, not bothering with pleasantries. Ares and Adonis share a look before turning their attention back to me.

"We thought he was coming with you," Ares says.

"You asking or you telling me, brother?" I growl. Apollo glares at me, out of the three of them he is the one with balls. He never shies away from a fight and that is his greatest strength but also his biggest weakness. He's a hothead.

"He said he was coming with you when I spoke to him last night," Apollo forces out through clenched teeth. Reclining in my chair, I pin him with a bored look. I can tell from the way his jaw is stiff and his eye keeps twitching that he's pissed off about something.

"What are you so mad about, little brother?" Ares and Adonis both slink back into their chairs and drop their gazes to their lap. Yeah, if that isn't a sign that their triplet is about to explode I don't know what else is.

"We saw you with *her*." I keep my face neutral and force my jaw to not lock as I hold his gaze.

"And?" Apollo grips the edge of the table and leans forward, I fight the smirk from breaking free at the challenge in his gaze. The five of us grew up using our fists to sort out our squabbles. Even now, we still fight to prove a point.

"You planning on helping us and *your* twin or you going to fuck the heiress and help her so Costa gets rid of us and you have no one to worry about coming after your crown?" As the last words leave his mouth I strike out without a sound. I ignore the shouts of my other brothers as I grip Apollo's throat and squeeze. The little shit doesn't fight me knowing I will win any fight between us.

I lean in, leaving a sliver of space between us. "I am going to fuck her." His eyes widen in surprise at my admission. "I'm going to make the bitch beg for me. I'll make sure she is so hooked on me that she has no idea that I am really destroying her from the inside out." I release him with a shove and lean back, running my gaze over each of them before finally settling on Apollo again. "London Murdoch will never win these trials, I won't allow it. Think what you want of me but know this, little brother, I would never let any cunt harm a hair on your head. I will make sure the three of you and Cronos come out of these trials the victors. We will watch the heiress burn and then we will finally be free of this bullshit." Adonis and Ares stare at me with wide eyes, this is the first time I have admitted that I want out of this life aloud. Apollo shakes his head and scoffs.

"He will never let you leave and if you do, we'll all pay the price for your betrayal." I clamp my mouth closed, unable to answer Apollo as Costa makes his grand entrance. My stomach churns at the sight of a girl beside him in a tiny black cocktail dress, her hair is messy and her makeup is smudged. Jesus

Christ, she can't be any older than the triplets. Costa whispers something in her ear and she turns her gaze to the four of us, her blue eyes widen.

"Your whore couldn't sneak out through the front door?" Adonis snarls. Costa pins him with a look that promises retribution.

"Go now, my dear, my sons need a lesson in manners," Costa says, keeping his gaze on Adonis. The girl turns to leave but not before Costa smacks her ass, making her yelp in surprise. I swallow the bile that threatens to spew from me and tear my gaze away.

"Sons, he says," Ares mutters. I glare at him and shake my head subtly, warning him to shut his mouth. He takes the hint and slouches back in his chair in a huff—we may fight and work on each other's last nerve but the triplets *and* Cronos know that I will always protect them from the wrath of the man that gave us life. Costa claims his seat at the head of the table, grabbing his napkin off the top of his plate. He shakes it out and drapes it over the top of his lap, his calm demeanor doesn't fool me. He's up to something.

"Where is my son?" The triplets look at their laps, leaving me to cover for Cronos.

I meet Costa's gaze unflinchingly, the longer I hold his stare the more the vein in his forehead begins to pop at my blatant show of disrespect. Before this becomes a bloodbath, I remember why I am playing nice and back in Switzerland so I avert my gaze as I answer, "I needed him to do a collection for me."

"I told him to be here," Costa shouts as he slams his palm down on the table. I fucking hate how the triplets subtly shift toward me in their seats. They act tough and talk a big game but the truth is, the three of them have been on the receiving end of Costa's anger one too many fucking times.

"And I told him I needed him to collect. I will not be seen as weak to the other Godfathers. They owed a debt and I wanted it collected so *I* sent my right hand man to do the job. Would you rather I call him and order him back for this little lunch and allow the Vasilous to think us incompetent?" Costa makes a show of gritting his teeth, his eyes burn with the need to maim but he knows he can't touch me because I'll fucking kill him if he ever tries again. I have spent my whole fucking life protecting my brothers from this waste of fucking space. They think I abandoned them after the trials but I could never.

"You are not the head of this family. I run things, little boy. Never fucking forget that... Do you understand?" My nostrils flare as I sit across from my father, wanting nothing more than to rip his fucking throat out and piss all over his dead body. Before I can put that plan into action, Cronos appears at the back doors, looking like the devil dressed in all black. He says nothing as he rounds the table and claims the chair beside me.

"Collected and dealt with." My brows furrow as I peer over at my twin. He flicks his gaze to Ares who places his phone on the top of the table. I nod subtly to Ares in thanks for texting Cronos, giving him a heads up about my excuse.

"You ever keep me waiting again, you will pay," Costa snaps. Cronos ignores him, pulling his hood over his head and slouching back into his chair, crossing his arms over his chest and looks to the mountains. I see it in his eyes, if given the chance Cronos would happily disappear into the mountains and never return. He only came today because he knew the triplets would pay the price for him skipping out. "Now, we have a problem I want dealt with."

"What problem?" Adonis asks our father.

"The problem of that Murdoch bitch being in the trials. Her father has reached out and wants a meet to discuss the terms and no doubt find a way for his daughter to be excused."

"Then why not allow him to barter her way out and put an end to this?" I say. Costa narrows his gaze at me.

"The whore must remain in the trials." I can't keep the shock from displaying across my face as the triplets begin to murmur among themselves.

"She can take my spot," Cronos says, keeping his stare focused on the mountains.

"You want to fucking die, boy?" Costa roars as he jumps to his feet, knocking his chair over in the process and drawing the attention of the guards that roam the property.

"You'd like that, wouldn't you?" Cronos bites back.

"What'd you just say?" Costa says in a voice far too calm for the look on his face.

"Enough! We need to focus on the girl and what we do about her," I interject, trying to redirect the conversation.

"She won't beat us," Apollo cockily says. Costa swings his gaze to him, the smile on his face disappears instantly. I tense in preparation, ready to take Costa down if he tries to hurt him.

"She managed to kill the rabbit before you three fucking disappointments could, didn't she?" The three of them all drop their gazes to their laps. I spot Cronos stiffening out of the corner of my eye.

"What do you have planned?" I ask the bastard. He swings his gaze to me and smiles. The sight has a shiver wanting to skate down my spine but I fight the feeling of doom from overtaking me. I know without a doubt he is going to use the opportunity the trials afford him in retribution for the Memento Mori making a fool out of him. They pushed for this school and in doing so it opened up the doors for the other Godfathers to send their children there for adequate training, training that could give them an advantage to overthrow one of us and end the reign of our family name.

"The Godfathers want her in the trials. The meeting with her father is set for the week school returns. The five of you will be there. We will decline his offer, he cannot interfere or help her in any way. The girl will be on her own and forced to either endure the trials or quit and forfeit her life."

"What happens if she fails?" Ares asks.

Costa's dark eyes alight with glee. "She will die and given the laws of our people, we are within our rights to end her life. Royal will come for us and so will Bishop and the rest of their family but they can't touch us."

"What?" The confusion in Adonis's voice is clear. Costa opens his mouth to answer but I beat him to it.

"Because if they touch us, then the rest of the founding families will intervene and fight alongside us because they broke the rules. The Murdoch mafia and Memento Mori can't seek revenge for the heiress, if she starts the trials of her own free will. Knox, Ian, Andreas and Karl will have no choice but to honor the agreement they all agreed to when peace was brokered by the founding fathers." I flick my gaze to Costa when I piece together the final piece of the puzzle and shake my head.

"You want her to fail because you know her father and grandfather will say fuck it to the agreement and come for us, resulting in the end of them."

He smiles wide and nods. "Clever boy."

"But why?" Ares rasps out,

"Because his greed knows no bounds. He wants their territory and them attacking us results in them having to hand over their holdings," Cronos says as he shakes his head in disgust. Costa doesn't reprimand him for his jibe.

The final piece clicks into place for me. I raise from my seat and eye my father in shock. "You planted the rabbit." He straightens and dusts non-existent lint from his shirt sleeve.

"No idea what you're talking about, boy," he says smugly.

"Jesus Christ, you set her up because you want her in the trials," I shout. His eyes narrow in warning but I'm past fucking caring now. "Your four sons are in these trials!" I shout.

"They won't have to complete them—"

"How the fuck can you be so sure?" I snap, cutting him off.

"Because the five of you are going to make sure that bitch doesn't pass the first trial. The Godfathers will end the trial after the war begins and then the five of you bastards get to live. We all win." I shake my head as anger courses through me.

"What if she surprises you and passes the fucking tests?" I grit out. A shadow falls over him as he glares down his big ass nose at me.

"The five of you waste of spaces haven't managed to pass, so what the fuck makes you think some whore can?"

I have a feeling London Murdoch is stronger than we all think. If she passes these trials my brothers die. If she doesn't, war breaks out and then we all die because there is no doubt in my mind that her family will come for me and my brothers.

Chapter Four

London

After my little night out and that run-in with the sexy asshole, I stayed holed up in my room. I'm bored out of my fucking mind and left with no choice but to actually amuse myself since my dad is giving me the cold shoulder for snitching on him about wanting to fly here and murder me. Apparently my aunt and uncle paid my dad a visit which ended in my dad getting in the ring with them and going a few rounds. Without speaking to him daily and being able to annoy the shit out of him, I'm a little lost, so I buried myself in work–research really. I have been looking into everything Greek. Costa Argyros' face is plastered all over the internet and so are all his businesses. There are no pictures of a wife or his children, it just states he has five sons and his wife passed away twelve years ago. My eyes begin to burn from staring at the screen for so long. I close the lid of my laptop and decide to take a break and shower before getting back into it.

I need more information on the five sons. I've met the triplets twice now and can tell they are little shits. They are trouble with a capital fucking T. I've tried to look into Artemis and Cronos but neither of them have a social media presence. I hate to admit it but I maybe, kind of, sort of didn't pay attention to what my dad was teaching me about hacking. I know if I called my Aunt or Uncle they would help. I also know I can ask Aunty Koby and Uncle Knight but then they would tell my dad and the last fucking thing I want to hear from him right now is, *I told you so.* You may think I'm being dramatic but I'm not. My father is not above rubbing my shortcomings in my face whenever he gets the chance.

Pushing those thoughts from my mind, I snag my towel and head for my bathroom. I tie my hair in a messy bun atop my head and step inside the stall. I make quick work of washing myself, wanting to get back to my research. Stepping out, I dry myself and pull on one of the oversized shirts I stole from the box in the attic that was filled with Uncle Havoc's things and shimmy into my cheeky panties before walking back into my room. The sight of a hooded figure on my bed has me stilling in the doorway. I dart my eyes across the room to my desk where I have a dagger stashed in the drawer, I also have one in my bedside drawer and one under my pillow. We aren't allowed guns or other weapons but I mean, a little knife never hurt anyone–what are they gonna do? Kick me out?

"You can try crossing the room to arm yourself but I'll stop you." The sound of his voice has my gaze zoning in on him.

I cock my hand on my hip and pin him with a bored look. "Drop the hood, Mr. Bartender." A low chuckle leaves him, the raspy sound has my lady bits clenching.

Stupid pussy, cut it out!

He pushes the hood back and the sight before me has me

wanting to thank the gods for creating such a fine ass human, but then I remember he's a cunt and all grateful thoughts flee my mind. I pin him with a glare. "How the fuck did you get in here?" All rooms are fitted with a retina scanner.

He shrugs. "I have my ways." He runs his gaze down my bare legs. I've never been a self-conscious type of gal but the intensity in his brown eyes has a shiver wanting to work its way down my spine. I'm astounded at my body's reaction to him. I've never been this attracted to anyone before, this is all new to me and I don't fucking like it!

"Well you can just find your way the fuck out of here and don't let the door hit ya where the good lord split ya," I say as I stride across the room toward my desk acting casual, when in truth I am just trying to get my blade. He must sense my intentions because in the next second he is on his feet and reaching for me. My instincts take over. I smack his hand away, then he strikes with the other. I duck and land a quick jab to his kidney before I go for the kill shot and grab his cock, clenching it. He throws his head back and roars. Before he can try anything I wrap my free hand around his throat and rush him across the room until his back is against the wall, the height difference grates on my nerves but I don't let it show. "Who the fuck are you?" My voice holds a cold edge. His eyes are alight with pain and that sight has me filling with warmth.

"I'll snap your fucking neck," he grits out through clenched teeth. His eyes are narrowed but the furrow in his brows and the crease in his forehead is a dead giveaway to the amount of pain he is in, even if he does try to mask it.

"You can try, you wouldn't be the first and I'm sure you won't be the last," I say in a deadly calm tone. "Why the fuck are you here?" His gaze darkens as he glares down at me. I tighten my hold on his cock, he hisses and I smile.

"Your trials start now," he forces out through clenched teeth, his words send shock rippling through me. He uses that to his advantage and breaks free of my hold, switching our positions so my back is against the wall, his hand around my throat and his thick thigh pressed between my legs. I go lax against the wall allowing him to think he has the upper hand, men always assume because I'm little and a woman that I'm weak, so I play that to my advantage. "You have ten minutes to be dressed and ready." His gaze slowly trails down my body and pauses at the sight of his leg pressed between mine, almost like he is just as shocked as I am that he made that move.

"My trials don't start till after the meeting with my father. You have a problem with that, you can take it up with him," I growl.

"You always hide behind your daddy's name and reputation?" Anger sparks to life inside me. I bite the inside of my cheek to keep from snapping back, knowing he is just trying to goad me.

"You don't know shit about me," I grit out through clenched teeth.

He bends until his lips skim the shell of my ear when he speaks. I'm powerless to stop my body responding when my thighs clench his leg. His throaty chuckle pisses me off but there is no point trying to deny my reaction to him.

"I know everything there is to know, London Murdoch. You will compete in the first trial tonight. Fail and you won't live long enough to make the meeting with your father, refuse and you will die." I turn the tables and lean forward, darting my tongue out, licking a trail from his neck to his ear relishing in the way he stiffens but he doesn't pull back.

"Baby boy, I'm going to rock your fucking world and show you why my father has no issue handing everything over to me.

I am the darkness your mother warned you to stay the fuck away from. I will ruin you and anyone who tries to stand in my way. I'm a Murdoch, we never fail." He pulls back leaving a sliver of space between our faces, his brown eyes bore into mine but I shy away because now he has stoked the burning embers of the fire that constantly rages inside me. I am going to rock his fucking world and make him and anyone else in these trials beg for fucking mercy. I may wish for a different life and some form of normality but that isn't who I am. I am my father's daughter and I will do my family name fucking proud by showing these Greek fuckers that I can beat them at their own game.

"You think because of who your daddy and granddaddy are that their names will protect you through these trials?" He doesn't give me a chance to answer. "You are weak. You think your smart mouth and mediocre fighting skills will garner you the win? You're wrong, little girl. You will perish like all the others before you because you are not worthy, you are nothing but the name you carry and..." he leans in until his lips ghost over mine, "... said name was given to you, not by birth or merit but because you were nothing but a street rat and called to the motherly instinct of a woman who can't even bear her own children."

A red haze of anger like I have never felt before overcomes me. I black out. I hear yelling and see my arms moving and striking at him as he tries to deflect my blows but I'm too quick. My size is my advantage and I use it, it's like I'm having an out of body experience. I see myself attacking him without mercy and suddenly the fog clears and I'm straddling his lap with the blade from my desk in my hand and pressed against his face. I feel pain radiating through my body from the hits he landed but the anger is still riding me hard has me numb to it once again as I stare down into his shocked eyes. I have no idea how I managed to get the blade Aunty Nell gave me but the split above his brow and the blood trickling from his lip brings me great satisfaction.

I press the blade against his throat relishing in the hiss that escapes him when I draw blood. "You. Know. Nothing. About. Me!"

"I know everything I need to know to make sure you never win. You can't and won't."

"Watch me prove you the fuck wrong," I snap back.

"Get dressed, London, you have a meeting to get to."

I narrow my eyes. "I told you, I'm not doing the trial—"

"You don't have a fucking choice! Get changed now or I will drag your ass out of here in what you are wearing now and believe me, you don't want the Godfathers seeing you dressed like this. They won't think twice about strapping you down to a table and taking turns." Disgust rolls through me.

"You people are fucking savages!" I sneer.

"Maybe. Now, get the fuck off me and get dressed. You have two minutes." I search his gaze for a second trying to decipher if he is full of shit but when I see nothing but seriousness, I relent and push off him. I stalk toward my bed and snag my phone as I make my way to my dresser dialing my dad. He answers on the third ring.

"I don't have time for your shit—"

I cut him off as I pull out a pair of jeans and a black *Kiss* shirt. "The Greeks are here, the trials begin tonight." I switch the phone to speaker and toss it on my bed as I peel my sleep shirt off. I can feel his gaze burning into my naked back but I ignore it as I snag the bra I discarded earlier from the bottom of my bed and put it on.

"No, they fucking don't. I have a meeting with Costa—"

I cut him off again. "Dad." That one word has him closing his mouth and listening, I never talk to him like this so he knows I'm not fucking around. "They're here now and taking me to the first one tonight." I pull my jeans on and quickly slip my shirt on before rearranging my hair into a high ponytail.

"Listen to me, don't argue, London, just listen, okay?" The worry in his tone has the hairs on the back of my neck standing, I know this is fucking hard for him not being here and being able to protect me but he taught me everything I know, I can hold my own.

"Okay."

"I know someone is there with you, I can hear it in your tone." I don't deny his claim. "If the trials are starting before the meeting, it means the Greeks are playing dirty, they don't want to strike a deal and want you in this game."

I sigh and nod even though he can't see me. "I know."

"I'll be on the first flight there, but I won't make it in time." I can hear the panic and anger in his voice but his rage isn't directed at me, it's directed at the fact he isn't here to protect his daughter.

"I can do this, Dad," I whisper.

"Time to go." Comes from behind, before I can finish my dad speaks with a cold tone that has a chill working its way down my spine.

"You listen to me, you little motherfucker. Anything happens to my daughter in this trial and I will slaughter you and your family. I'll take every single one of you Greek cunts out and not give a fuck about starting a war."

"Noted," the bastard clips out.

"Dad?"

"Don't think, don't feel. You treat this like another one of the training sessions with us. You go in and strike first, strike

43

hard and claim the victory. You are my daughter and I won't let any fucking thing happen to you, do you understand? I'm coming, baby girl." The lump that forms in my throat has me slamming my eyes closed. My dad knows I'm scared and this is his way of telling me that I am strong enough without undermining me in front of this fucker.

"I'll make you proud," I murmur.

"You've made me proud from the moment you came into my life." I end the call and turn to the son of the bitch who stands across from me with his arms crossed over his chest. That was one of the first heart to hearts my father and I have ever had and I hate the fact this bastard was a witness to it.

"You won't make it out alive," he says in a firm tone.

I smile at the fucker. "Keep underestimating me, little boy, I love proving fuckers like you wrong."

The dark chuckle that escapes him has me tensing. "I can't wait to watch your bravado fail you. You have no idea what you are in for and I am going to love watching you break." I say nothing as he turns and pulls his hood over his head and leads the way out of my room. I debate saying fuck it all and making a run for it but my momma didn't raise no quitter, so I follow after him. The halls are barren and eerily quiet. My senses go on high alert, so I stuff my phone into the back pocket of my jeans so my hands are free to fight. The burn in my ribs begins to make itself apparent and my shoulder aches but I refuse to acknowledge it.

I slam to a halt when the triplets dart out from around a corner. The sexy bartender turns and smirks at me over his shoulder, sending dread pooling into my stomach. "Your first mistake was thinking you know who I am." I frown but that moment of distraction costs me, I feel a sharp prick in the side of my neck and spin around gasping at the sight of... the bartender? Holy fuck, there are two of him.

"I'm sorry," the new bartender whispers. I feel the frown building on my face but everything feels sluggish as I swing my arm out, I won't go down without a fight.

Chapter Five

Artemis

Before she can hit the floor, Cronos darts his arms out and catches her around the waist, she's dead weight in his hold. "Carry her ass to the car, we are on a time limit to get her there," I clip out.

"How the fuck did you get her to follow you?" Cronos snaps, glaring at me.

Shrugging my shoulders as I turn and walk away, I call back, " I told her the trials began tonight." I ignore them cursing behind me as I make my way out the front. I made sure that the other students would be occupied tonight so no one would be able to witness what we are doing. My club is hosting an all-white party and it doesn't take a genius to know that all of these idiots would jump at the chance at another party before school resumes. If lying to her and forcing her to participate in this little staged trial I have set for her tonight gets her to drop the fuck out, then so be it. I will not risk this bitch winning the trial and costing my brothers their lives.

I lean against my car and wait for Cronos and the triplets to emerge. I know they don't agree with my decision but as the oldest, they have no choice but to follow my orders. If Cronos wasn't so out of control and hiding within himself, then his opinion would hold more sway. As they push through the front doors of Blackwood the sight of London passed out in my twin's arms has me feeling unsettled, the feeling being foreign and unwelcome. I brush that shit off and hold the back door open for him. He places her in the car and steps back, staring down at her with a frown on his face. Not liking the intensity of his gaze on her, I slam the door and turn to the triplets.

"Follow me. We end this tonight and make sure she taps the fuck out." The three of them exchange a look. I grind my teeth when Adonis begins to shake his head and Ares nods, they do this all the time like they can read each other's minds.

"How long are we leaving her?" Apollo asks.

"As long as it takes for her to break. We have three days before school starts back and I want her gone before then so you four can focus on the trials," I answer as I turn my back and climb inside my car. Cronos jumps in beside me. I turn and quirk a brow at him. "Since when do you ride with me?" Cronos always makes it a point to drive by himself so he isn't trapped inside a car with one of us in case we question him.

"Just drive, I don't have time for your shit," he growls, facing forward, focusing his gaze out the windshield. The triplets tail me out of the school. I plan to head toward Mount Matterhorn, it borders on the Italian border but it's a risk I'm willing to take. Even if she does manage to cross the border, it's not like her father or grandfather have any pull in Italy. They may be the mafia but they are the American mafia, they seem to think they have a say over the Colombians and the Russians but it's a loose hold. Andreas runs the Bratva and even he has pulled away from the rule of the Murdochs. The Colombians aren't happy with the change of power to Erika Murdoch even though her husband claims to run it, they won't keep their hold on her home country for long. Technically, it's London's home country as well but the girl was raised as an American and it shows in the way her mouth constantly runs and how she dresses. "You can't kill her," Cronos bites out, keeping his gaze focused out his window.

"She is a means to an end. I won't run the risk of her surviving the trials—"

"She's already beating the triplets as it is." My grip on the steering wheel tightens at the reminder.

"She doesn't know that!" I grit out through clenched teeth.

"Once her father meets with Costa, she will know. This may be a test of your own but if she does manage to survive this, she would have completed a third trial." I snap my gaze to his and frown.

"What the fuck are you saying?" I'm fed up with his cryptic bullshit.

"*Escape the unknown unscathed*. That's a trial, Artemis, we are taking her to the fucking unknown. If she passes your little test, then you just gave her another advantage over the triplets."

"And what about you? You plan on finishing the trials this time around, brother?" The moment the words spew from my mouth, regret churns inside me when he clamps his mouth closed and shuts down. "Nos, I didn't–"

"Yeah, you did," he bites back. "My life was over years ago, he made sure of that and so did you." I jerk back like he hit me. I knew I fucked up during our trials but I didn't mean for it to happen and it will forever haunt me. My weakness cost my brother his soul. I did this to my twin. I forced him to become the shell of the person he is now. We spend the rest of the drive in silence, lost in our own thoughts. For three years Cronos has barely been able to stand the sight of me. I know he had all the mirrors in his cabin at the back of the school grounds removed. He hates the sight of himself and that's because of me, he was forced to work at the school as punishment by Costa. The thing is, I think he actually likes working at the school and club.

I'm pulled from my thoughts when my phone rings. I check the caller ID on the dash and growl before hitting answer. Our father's voice filters through the sound system of the car.

"What the fuck have you done?" Costa shouts so fucking loud I have to turn the volume down.

"You said to do what we needed to make sure the bitch doesn't compete. I'm doing that!" I snarl.

"Watch that fucking tone, boy, you don't want your precious brothers paying the price for your insolence, do you?" I grind my teeth so fucking hard my jaw begins to ache. "I thought so. Now, where the fuck is the girl? Her father called and had a lot to say about the trials beginning early."

"In the back seat, passed out," I grit out.

"You either turn the fuck around and put the whore back *or* you make sure she never returns. There is no third fucking option. Am I clear?"

"Crystal," I snap before ending the call. I can't wait for the day that Costa is no longer Godfather. We may refer to the other founders of Godfathers too, but the reality is that there can only be one and Costa is fucking it. Since the day we came of age, we have been forced to do whatever the sick bastard ordered so he could remain in power, but this year, that ends. We don't have a choice. If we fail the five of us die, this is our only hope. London Murdoch must perish in order for us to live.

"I won't kill her," Cronos says in a tone devoid of all emotion.

"Then you may as well pull that piece from your side and kill our brothers and us. Either she stops breathing or we all do. Is that what you want?"

We arrive just under an hour later and get to work quickly. I instruct the triplets to scope out the area and make sure there is no one around as I drag her limp body from the back seat and sling her over my shoulder. Cronos leads the way along the trail with the duffle bag in his hand. Ten minutes later my shoulder begins to ache and I have no choice but to change her position and carry her bridal style. The little shit is stronger than I thought she'd be, Cronos had to inject her again when she began to stir twenty minutes ago. Her intoxicating scent assaults me, she smells like rain and...sex. What the fuck? How the hell can someone reek of sex unless... was she fucking someone earlier? No, she just got out of the shower when I used the master key to enter her room, perks of being the headmaster.

"How deep are we going?" Adonis asks as he and the other two catch up to us.

"I want her away from the trails and deep in the brush," I say.

"Dude, the trail stopped like a couple miles back. No one

uses this entry because of how dense the woods are and the mountain is too hard to climb up on this side," Apollo voices. I roll my eyes.

"No shit, why the fuck do you think I picked this side?" I clip out, ignoring their muttered insults. I quicken my pace and stay close to my twin's back, as he pushes branches out of the way, careful not to break any or disturb much in the hopes she won't be able to track her way out of here. I'm not stupid enough to think that she isn't trained for situations like this but I can bet she has never been trained to escape something like this whilst freezing and naked.

We continue to trek through the wilderness like we are pros when in truth, none of us have ever been camping or spent a night in the wild. Cronos pushes through a thick patch of shrubs and comes to a stop in the middle of a small clearing, dropping the duffle bag before turning back to me, pinning me with a cold stare.

"Don't fucking start. This is the humane way to do it since you won't let us strangle the bitch," I sneer. The triplets laugh as they fan out around the small space. Unlike Cronos, those three enjoy the goriness this life we lead affords them.

"Who gets to strip her?" Adonis asks gleefully.

"I volunteer as tribute!" Ares shouts with a wide grin on his face.

"Fuck you two. I'll take one for the team and do it," Apollo says as he pushes his way between the other two dickheads. I pin each of them with a look that has the smiles dropping from each of their faces, these three need a lesson on fucking boundaries.

"The three of you will keep your fucking hands to yourself. No one is touching her—"

"Aside from you?" Adonis smugly cuts in, saying.

"Fuck off, shit heads, and get everything in place," I snap, without direction these three get into more trouble than I can handle cleaning up. I can already tell Cronos's patience is thinning by the second and if the triplets aren't careful, they will face his wrath. The triplets grumble but do as they're told. Cronos stands there brooding silently but we're all used to it and just ignore him. I place London down gently in the middle on a patch of grass. I can smell it in the air that snow is close to falling. As I reach for the button on her jeans Cronos snaps his arm out gripping my wrist and halting my movements. I turn and scowl up at him.

"Leave her in her clothes," he forces out through clenched teeth.

"You dumbass, the only way to break a girl like her is to tear away her armor and force all her scars to the surface. In order for this to work we need to bare her to the world so she has no choice but to face her demons. That is the only way you break someone like her." I rip my arm free and return to my task. Cronos knows better than anyone that I would never take advantage of her like this, I wouldn't do that to any woman. I peel the jeans down her legs and bite down on my lip to focus on the pain I'm inflicting on myself rather than stare at the material that covers her pussy from me. I throw my leg over her and straddle her lap as I peel the hoodie off her, her shirt is next to go, leaving her in her bra and panties. The girl's body is a work of fucking art, making my cock twitch in my pants.

"What's that?" Cronos asks. I look to where he is pointing and frown. The only lighting is from the moon, so I pull my phone from my pocket and turn the torch on.

My brows raise at the sight. "A tattoo," I breathe out. It's not just any tattoo, it is in my language–Greek.

Η ελευθερία είναι δική μου.

"Freedom is mine to take," I translate aloud. Cronos frowns and shakes his head.

"Why the fuck would she have a tattoo in Greek?" he asks.

Shaking my head I answer, "No idea, the girl is a fucking puzzle."

"More like a present that I am jealous you got to unwrap." I snap my head up and glare at Ares, who stands with Adonis and Apollo grinning.

"Shut the hell up, you idiot," I snarl. Just as I'm about to slip off her, her eyes snap open and before I can do a fucking thing she strikes me with an open palm to the nose and shoves me off her. "Get her!" I shout as she jumps to her feet and makes a run for it. The triplets chase after her while Cronos stands there smirking. "Why the fuck are you smirking?" I yell.

"You underestimated her because she has a pussy you want to sink your cock into. Rookie error, brother," he says in a mocking tone as he turns his back and walks away, leaving me here on the ground with blood running down my face. I wipe it away with the sleeve of my hoodie and leap to my feet. This fucking girl is going down. I take a step in the direction that the others went but pause. Turning back to the duffle bag, I crouch down and yank the zipper open and pull out the little case that holds the sedatives we used to knock her out. Opening the small case I cursed aloud. Cronos only used half the second dose, he never planned to let her stay out here!

Fuck!

Dropping the case, I race after the others. I can hear the distant shouts of my brothers. It's so fucking dark without Cronos leading the way with his torch, I would use my own but if she is hiding then I don't want to give up my location. I still in the middle of a bunch of trees and strain my hearing, the triplets shouts grow further away, good, those three couldn't even hunt the fucking rabbit let alone someone as skilled as London.

"Come on, baby, I only want to play." I roll my eyes at Adonis, he is a fucking sick little shit.

"Come on, London baby, I won't ruin you for every other man," Ares shouts. I shake my head in disgust. I've done a poor fucking job of raising those three if this is how they fucking act. Those fuckers will be punished for this shit, they won't be making any taunts like this again. I slowly creep forward, drawing on my own training, keeping my feet light and making sure not to make a single peep or breath too hard.

Cronos is right, I did underestimate her but it isn't because I want to fuck her. It wasn't exactly her I had underestimated, it was her skillset. Clearly I made a huge error in thinking that she was some bimbo from the US that lived a lavish life. I checked her school records and found nothing but complaints from her teachers, none of them mentioned how well she did or didn't do in her classes. She has never been in combat training with Cronos, it's a class for seniors only so I won't be able to get a good read on her skills until then.

My phone begins to vibrate in my pocket. I fish it out and hit answer when I see Ares's name. Just as I bring it to my ear I feel the needle press against my neck and her at my back. I still in anticipation.

"Tell them to head back to the school," she whispers low enough that Ares won't be able to hear her through the phone. When I take too long, she presses the needle harder against my neck until it breaks the surface.

"Yeah?" I say playing it cool.

"We can't find her, there's no tracks to follow," Ares says.

"Take Adonis and Apollo back to the school and wait there in case she somehow manages to get back there."

"Dude, there is no way that bitch–" She presses the needle in deeper, so I cut my brother off before he can piss her off more.

"Do as you're told. Cronos and I will keep searching for her." I end the call without waiting for a reply.

"Hand me the phone," she orders. I pass it to her over my shoulder playing along with her game for the time being.

"What's your plan, London, drug me and leave me out here?" I ask smugly. She kicks the backs on my legs. I grunt when I land on the hard earth. She moves so she now stands before me. She's so tiny that my face is in line with her stomach, I make sure to take my time as I slowly lift my gaze up her body. I meet her stare with a cocky smile.

"See something you like?" she snarks.

I nibble on the corner of my lip, putting on a show for her before I tear her the fuck down. "All I see is a washed up little girl trying to play in the big boys world that she doesn't belong in." Rather crumble or stumble back at my harsh words she just smiles and clicks her tongue.

"Even without a cock swinging between my legs, I will always have bigger balls than you, pretty boy." Before I can utter a reply, she injects the sedative into me. I reach out and grip the backs of her thighs pulling her down, she lands on her back with a grunt, I use the last bit of strength I have to pounce on top of her, my movements sluggish. She glares up at me but doesn't fight to be free, she knows I'll be out in seconds.

"I felt your pussy rubbing against my cock in the club. Trust me, little girl, I am the only one with balls around here and when this shit wears off, I plan to empty them inside that sweet little cunt of yours."

Chapter Six

London

The moment the sedative takes over, he collapses on top of me and I grunt from the force of the air being knocked out of me. I twist and use all my strength to push his heavy ass off me. I lay there for a second trying to get my breathing under control but the second a gust of wind whips past me, I am on my feet and racing back the way I came. I need to get back to my clothes, it may not be snowing but it's fucking cold and the air is fucking frigid. The only reason I am still able to feel my limbs is because I have been moving, but the moment I slow down I know the cold will take hold and weigh me down. I have a high chance of freezing to death out here if I don't get my shit back. I manage to break through the clearing and sigh at the sight of the duffle bag. I rummage through the contents and growl when I don't find my clothes. With no time to spare, I shove everything back in the bag and dart back toward the bastard I knocked out.

Those dumbass triplets ran straight past me. I didn't head

far from where they undressed me, just sprinted around the tree and waited. The moment they left the clearing, I rushed back and tried to find a weapon but only found a case of needles. I swear I spotted my clothes next to the bag but I guess I was wrong. I rush back toward the asshole and peel his hoodie off him before yanking it over my head. His scent surrounds me and it takes a lot of willpower on my part not to sniff the damn thing. My legs are beginning to grow numb, so I turn, ready to leave the bastard behind until a thought hits me.

Who the fuck is he?

I know I could tie his ass to the tree and torture the information I need out of him but I have no idea where the other four are and I'm fucking freezing my tits off, so I do what any respectable woman would do and strip him down to his boxers like he did me and leave his ass there. Thanks to the low lighting and thick shrubs it takes me a lot longer than I would have liked to find my way out of this godforsaken place. As I break through the final line of trees, I peer back over my shoulder to make sure no one is following, but the sound of clapping has me halting and snapping my gaze in front of me. My eyes narrow at the sight of the captor I know I left naked on the ground in the woods, but unlike Nude Jude I left behind this one seems haunted. The closer I get to him the more I can recognize the tormented look in his eyes, it calls to a part of me that I keep buried and never allow myself to think or feel. I closed that door to those emotions years ago when it nearly consumed and destroyed everything that I am.

"Bravo, you managed to escape the shithead triplets and by the looks of things, you even managed to flee the big bad wolf."

I eye him suspiciously ignoring the burn in my feet and legs from being so freaking cold. "What makes you think I didn't kill the fucking wolf?"

A slow smile stretches across his face, I loathe to admit it but he looks fucking sexy. "Now, you don't want to be making those doe eyes at me, darlin', I'm not the good guy."

I scoff. "What the fuck makes you think that I care about who the hell you are?"

That same smile slides back into place as he pushes off the car and steps into me until we are chest to chest, well, my chin to his chest. I give him credit, he is a bold motherfucker when he grips my waist and bends so his lips ghost over the shell of my ear.

"The fact you haven't disarmed me when I know you clocked my sidearm the moment you cleared the tree line tells me you care, darlin'." I grit my teeth, tampering the annoyance rising inside me. "You have the keys in the pocket of my brothers jeans you currently hold. Get out of here before he wakes and kills you."

I pull free of his hold and stare up at him. "Why aren't you trying to subdue me?"

A glazed-out look overtakes his features as he releases me and steps back running a hand through his hair. "I don't touch women. Now get out of here, darlin', that sedative will be wearing off by now." I grab the keys before tossing the pile of clothes in my arms to him. His gaze immediately drops to my legs, the hoodie comes to my knees, the intensity of his gaze has me feeling naked like he can see through to my soul or some shit. It's unnerving to have someone stare at you but not really see you. I walk past him but pause when I grip the door handle in my hand and look over my shoulder. I frown when I see his gaze is already on me.

"Who the hell is that bastard?"

He smirks and shakes his head lightly. "I think you just pissed off your new headmaster, darlin'."

I stand here for a good minute just staring at him with an open mouth, there is no fucking way I just made out with my new headmaster. Renewed determination flows through me. I smirk darkly and nod my head.

"Challenge accepted. He'll be gone in a week, two tops."

He shakes his head. "Artemis loves a fight, he won't fold like the others, darlin'." The humor in his tone tells me he is loving this. I don't have siblings so this is new for me. I would have thought he would have warned me off trying to fuck with his brother, not give me a heads up.

"And I'm not a quitter so your brother is going to have to do better than drugging me and trying to ditch me in the woods." Cronos smiles wide and the tiny sparkle in his eye holds my attention. "I think we are going to be friends."

The sparkle disappears and a horrified look takes its place. "I don't have friends," he clips out in an even tone.

"Well, now you do."

He rapidly shakes his head. "No."

"Oh, I love this game. I play it with my dad all the time."

He frowns. "What game?"

"The *yes* and *no* game. You will learn really fast that I always win, so go fetch your brother, bestie, I'll see you real soon." I end the conversation by climbing into the car, wasting no time peeling out of there. I have to program the car's GPS to direct me back to Blackwood. If this is their warm up to the trials I need to face, then they will be in for a rude shock. They are going to meet the real London who gives zero fucks and will destroy anything in her path.

It's over an hour's drive. I would call my dad and tell him I'm okay but those fuckers took my phone! Guess I'll just have to facetime him from my Mac when I get back to my room. A little stress and worry never hurt anyone, plus my dad is young and surely can't die of a heart attack at his age.

Pulling through the gates of Blackwood, I stare up at the gothic looking castle. To the outside world it doesn't appear as a school, but those with high ranking know this place is nothing but a jail for kids. We are trained in the art of politics, negotiation, hand to hand combat, leadership and so much other crap. I don't see how sending kids to this place will broker peace among the different families. They say we can't tell others who we are and where we come from, but when you come from well-known families like mine, my last name says it all. The huge fountain in front of the entryway has an idea sparking inside my head. I smile to myself as I slam my foot down on the gas. The impact has me whipping forward but I'm prepared and brace myself so I don't smack my head against the steering wheel. The car begins to beep erratically as all the sensors go off. I unclip my seat and attempt to open the door but it's stuck leaving me no choice but to climb out the window. I manage to not fall in as I balance on the edge of the fountain, jump down and take a few steps back smiling at the sight.

"Put that in your pipe and smoke it, you fucker," I say. The fountain is fucked, water gushes out onto the manicured lawn and his car is definitely totaled. I skip back inside the school, whistling as I make my way back to my room. I pass two students who eye me warily, can't blame the bitches though. I must look like shit in nothing but a hoodie that isn't mine. I don't give a flying fuck what people think about me. I am who I am and if they don't like it, they can suck my metaphorical dick.

When I reach my room I make sure to lock the deadbolt on the door and shove my desk chair under the handle for extra security. I debate calling my dad for a split second before thinking better of it and taking a shower first. Once I'm cleaned up and look decent, I grab my Mac and settle myself in the center of my bed before calling my dad. It rings a few times before his panicked face fills the screen.

"Thank fuck," he breathes out.

"You didn't really think those assholes would get the upper hand on me, did ya?" A low chuckle escapes him but it holds no humor, just relief.

"I've never been more grateful for you being a vindictive little shit." I smirk and wag my brows. "Chaos, call off the men and bring Sin back." I tense at the mention of my uncle. I may be in a group chat with him but he never replies or speaks to me.

"The demon still alive?" I hear Uncle Chaos ask.

"Yeah, she's good," Dad answers. "Here, your mother wants to speak to you," he says a second before the phone is passed and my mom's face fills the screen. Just the sight of her has tension fleeing me. Erika Murdoch is a badass but never with me. My mom is the most kind-spirited woman you will ever meet. Me being away is fucking hard for her. She tried to help me find a way out of this stupid school.

"Thank God, you're okay," she says.

"I'm fine, Mom, I swear." I try to placate her but I can see it in her eyes that she isn't buying what I'm selling.

"They weren't supposed to start until they met with your father. There will be repercussions for this, baby, I promise you." The conviction in her tone tells me that my mom is fucking raging.

"I know. I don't think this was a trial, Mom. I think the brothers set me up to try and get me to quit." She snorts and shakes her head.

"Clearly they don't know my daughter if they think she would quit."

"Damn right, I'll show those Greek fucks what happens when they get on my bad side." Mom flinches.

"Baby, one of those boys is the new headmaster—"

I cut her off. "I know. He's the one who stripped me and tried to leave me in the woods." The words have barely left my mouth when the phone is snatched from my mom and my dad's angry face fills the screen.

"The cunt did what to you?" The deathly calm tone of his voice is the way to tell that he is thirsting for blood.

"Dad, I handled it. His car is parked in the fountain out front and I made sure to drug him and return the favor. He's currently naked in the woods with no way back to the school." Dad's brows raise. "I don't think our new headmaster will last, Daddy," I say sweetly and bat my lashes. For the first time he doesn't shout and rage at me, he just laughs.

"Atta girl, get the fucker to quit and I promise you there will be no repercussions from me this time." I beam at the screen.

"Really?"

"Yes, I never wanted Artemis Argyros to lead the school."

"Say you swear you won't be mad and I'll have him out within the next week of school returning." He sighs and nods. I squeal in delight as all the possibilities of what I can do to him run through my mind.

"Do not burn the fucking school down, London, I mean it." I roll my eyes.

"I already told you! I didn't mean to burn the east wing, it was an accident. You need to let that shit go, man." His eyes narrow.

"Two kids were injured in that fire!" he shouts and I wave him off.

"Those bitches had it coming. They shouldn't have tried to sabotage me—"

"They only sat in a seat!" he barks.

"Everyone in that class knew that was *my* seat. They didn't want to move, so I told them I would burn them in it and they laughed. Not my fault they didn't heed my warning." He stabs a hand through his hair and growls. He is so highly strung out, honestly he needs to relax more, the guy is way too serious all the time.

"Just don't burn the fucking school down. I'll be there in three days to meet with Costa. I believe his sons will be there—"

"Good, so where should I meet you?"

"You are not coming!" I glare at the screen.

"Why the hell not?" I snap.

He pins me with a deadpan look. "Because your big ass mouth will just make everything worse. Go to bed." He ends the call and I sit here seething with anger. If he thinks for a second that I will be left out of this meeting, he has another thing coming, I won't allow them to make decisions about *my* life without me there. Too tired and feeling slightly queasy from the side effects of the drugs they used, I know I won't be able to sleep, so I start digging into the Greeks and doing as much recon as I can.

Up early and ready to go for a jog, I head downstairs and outside, only to pause at the sight of students with their phones out. I frown as I push my way through the crowd, these bastards should be sleeping off their hangover not out here watching... Oh shit, I roll my lips over my teeth to keep from smiling at the sight of a tow truck dragging Artemis's car out of the fountain. When I feel the weight of someone's gaze on me, I look to the other side of the fountain to find the man himself standing there glaring at me. I shoot him a wink and purse my lips, blowing him an air kiss before spinning on my heel and shoving through the crowd to head into the woods where the best trail is.

I'm pissed off I don't have my phone so I can't listen to music while I run. I ordered one last night and it should be here later today but I fucking detest learning how to use a new device. I may only be eighteen but that doesn't mean I love the idea of being stuck on a phone all day texting. There is more important shit to be doing, like planning my revenge against my new headmaster. I just need to figure out what his weaknesses are and exploit them.

I know I can't do anything too drastic because it will fall back on me and my family. I thought about breaking into his room and dumping a shitload of fleas on his bed, but that seems so immature. I need something that will break his ego and tear him down from his mightier than thou complex. As I round the bend the sound of footfalls pounding the ground behind me have me spinning around and crouching into a fighting stance, I hear another set coming from the other side of me and shift but then I hear another set and smirk. I stand and cross my arms over my chest as I wait for the three dipshits to make their presence known. I've been coming to Blackwood since I was sixteen and it amazes me how I have never run into these three dumbasses before now.

Not a minute later, the triple A Three Stooges come at me from three different directions. I expected them to come and spew threats, not fight. Immediately I am at a disadvantage because there are three of them and one of me. Unlike the movies they don't come at me one at a time, the three of them strike as a unit. I manage to block a few hits but they also land a couple to my sides, where my kidneys are but I won't allow them to get in any more than that. I pull the dagger I had sheathed in the back of my Lorna Jane running pants and dart forward, slicing Adonis–I think it's him—across the chest. He roars in pain and the other two falter in their attacks. I use that to my advantage and get the next one along the leg and the other across his arm. The three of them stand there holding their wounds as I smile.

"You fucking phsyco bitch, no weapons allowed!" Ares shouts. Out of the three he is the easiest to distinguish from the others as he has a slightly crooked nose, clearly he broke it before.

"Fuck you, bitch boy, you attacked me," I snap.

"You deserved it after what you did to our brother." Apollo sneers, standing next to Adonis, clutching his arm. Those two are harder to tell apart but the only clear sign is that Adonis's eyes are just slightly lighter than the other two.

I twirl the blade in my hand, loving how they now eye me skeptically. "You bastards drugged me, stripped me and planned to leave me in the woods. I think it was only fair that I return the favor and bestow the same courtesy upon your brother that he had planned to do to me." They growl but say nothing as I continue. "The next time the five of you come for me, I will be prepared, that was your one and only shot to take me down. You are going to learn really fucking fast why I don't need my last name to inspire fear in my peers." I turn on my heel and head back the way I came, pissed off that I couldn't even enjoy a simple run without those cock suckers coming at me. I know weapons are forbidden inside the school but if I didn't have the blade Aunt Sin gave me, that shit would have gone way differently.

As I enter the school, I slow my steps at the sight of the students lurking in the entryway looking tense and uneasy. The hackles on the back of my neck raise. Darting my gaze around the room I try to find what has captured their attention and when my gaze finally lands on the source, I grit my teeth. Artemis stands there with his twin at his side looking smug with an evil glint in his eyes.

"Miss Murdoch, my office now," he grits out in a stern voice.

I quirk a brow and scrunch my face pretending to ponder his request. This arrogant fuck thinks he can bark orders at me, not today, bitch. "Hmmmm, last time we were alone together you had your tongue down my throat, then the next time I ended up naked and drugged in the woods, so I think I'll pass." Gasps ring out around and murmurs begin to surround us. Artemis's left eye twitches and his jaw locks, my response has him shocked. Good, because who he met in that club isn't the woman standing before him. I shoot the bastard a wink before stalking out of the room.

Chapter Seven

Artemis

I clench my fists at my sides, grinding my teeth so fucking hard they begin to ache as I watch the bitch walk away from me in her skin-tight leggings and sports bra with her tattoo on full display. I'm going to wrap my hands around her fucking throat and watch the life drain out of her. I stalk out of the crowded entryway and head for my new office. Cronos follows me inside. I hate this fucking place as it reminds me of something from a fantasy movie or some shit. Bookshelves line the walls and it even has one of those ladder things that trails along the length of them like in that god-awful Disney movie *Beauty and the Beast*. An open fireplace and wingback chairs, a large oakwood desk, filing cabinets and so much other bullshit that isn't needed take up the space. The one thing I do like though is the floor to ceiling window behind the desk, it gives me a clear unobscured view of the lands.

"She is going to fight you at every turn," Cronos says from

behind me. I keep my gaze focused out the window and twirl my ring as I answer him.

"Costa heard that I failed last night. I have to meet him soon. Keep the triplets here with you and make sure you don't let them out of your sight," I ordered.

"You idiot, you can't go alone—" I spin around and pin him with a look of warning.

"If any of you come with me, he will force me to watch as he dishes out his punishment. I will go alone and you will obey my orders and keep our brothers here with you where they will be safe. Don't fucking push me, Cronos, this girl needs to tap out before the real trials begin."

"Why are you so worried?" he asks as he stares at me, trying to see beneath the mask I wear. He will never be able to see what I'm hiding. I have perfected this mask since we were kids in order to conceal everything I feel from our father. "You think she could beat us," he mutters.

I conceal the shock from showing on my face, opening my mouth ready to rebuke his claim but the door bursts open and the triplets stumble in, bloodied and looking ready to commit mass homicide.

"What the fuck happened to you three?" I snap. Cronos rushes to close the door as I stare down at my little brothers.

"London-fucking-Murdoch tried to kill us," Adonis shouts, my brows jump to my hairline.

"Come again?" I grit out as anger begins to resurface inside me.

"So she randomly decided to come after you three?" Cronos asks them. The three of them begin shouting and calling Cronos a prick for doubting them. The fact they are all on the same side is a dead giveaway that they were the ones who are in the wrong.

"Shut the fuck up!" I roar. The three of them clamp their mouths closed and face me. "What the fuck did you do?" Ares opens his mouth but I raise my hand silencing him. "Don't bullshit me. The three of you never agree on anything, there is always one man out when you're telling the truth, so come fucking clean now before I have to meet Costa." At the mention of our father the three of them pale and stiffen, the fight in them from a minute ago evaporates. It pisses me off that the mention of his name inspires this much fear in all of them. I always tried to protect them as best as I could from his wrath. I know they don't see it, but I do all of this for them. They think I am selfish and just want the power of Costa's position as the head affords me but that isn't the case. I just want him gone so we can be free. Unfortunately for me, once he falls someone must claim his place as the head and I can't allow that to fall to another family. It's in our laws that all males from the head of the fallen leader will perish with their father.

"We tried to take her out on the trail but—" Cronos cuts Ares off.

"She beat your asses and sent you back here crying?" Apollo glares at Cronos.

"That is not what happened!" Ares shouts.

"Then break it down for me here because I am inclined to agree with Cronos, it looks like the bitch got the jump on you three and not the other way around." The three of them bristle. I narrow my eyes and pin them with an impatient look. Adonis tells us what happened and how they planned to beat her. I grip the edge of my desk in anger, spying Cronos out of the corner of my eyes, turning red with rage.

"You planned to beat a fucking woman?" he roars.

"I liked you better when you just brooded silently in the

corner," Ares quips. When Cronos takes a step toward him, I rush around the desk and block his path knowing that if he gets his hands on the mouthy little shit he is going to be in a world of pain.

"Calm the fuck down," I say. Cronos presses into me seething.

"You want her out, do it right and not gang up on her. She is a fucking female!" he shouts in my face.

"She isn't her, Cronos!" The moment the words leave my mouth, I regret them instantly, Cronos shuts down and the angry look in his eyes fades to nothing. He steps back and drops his gaze to the floor.

"How could she be her?" he whispers as he slowly lifts his guilt ridden gaze to mine. That look flays me open and I hate myself a little bit more for not being able to help her. "She's dead, but you already know that." I hide the flinch from showing at his words and watch him storm out of my office, slamming the door so hard it rattles the pictures on the walls.

"Fuck," I grit out as I run a hand through my hair and tug on the strands.

"What the hell was that?" Adonis asks, I ignore him as I head back to my new desk and drop down into the seat.

"Artemis, what did he mean?" Ares pushes but I wave him off.

"The three of you are to stay away from the girl. I'll handle her from now on–"

Apollo cuts me off. "We can make her quit!" he defends.

"No, you can't. You idiots proved that today. Stay the fuck away from London Murdoch. That's an order." Their jaws lock at my order. "Stay the fuck out of trouble, I mean it. Her family is coming for a meeting with Costa and we are all to be present."

"When is the meeting?" Ares asks.

"Next week when school starts back, we'll meet with them and discuss the trials and what is to become of her."

"Art, he won't let her bow out of the trials, he wants her dead so her family will start a war," Apollo voices.

"I know, which is why I need to come up with a new plan," I answer.

"What happens if we don't... Win the trials?" Ares asks, the lilt in his voice gives way to the fact he is worried.

"Even with London in the trials, Costa has pit the three of you against Cronos, one Argyros will be the victor."

"But what about the other three Argyros, what happens to them?" Adonis asks.

"Nothing will happen to them, I won't let it. I have a plan. I just need the three of you to trust me to get us out of this mess."

"Why aren't you doing the trials?" Ares queries.

"Don't worry about that, just stay out of trouble," I say dismissing them. The moment the door closes behind them I slouch into my chair and run a hand down my face.

I sit across from Costa in the empty club, the only people here are the staff out back prepping for the opening tonight. I made sure they weren't out front to witness what is about to happen. I chose this location because I knew it would be empty and it beat meeting him at his house where he would have the upper hand. Costa has no idea that my brothers and I have investments and own more clubs around the world. It's the easiest way to clean money without having the feds on our asses. I've been able to dummy the books so he wouldn't notice small amounts of money disappearing each quarter.

"What happened, boy?" he snaps as he spins his glass of whiskey on the top of the table. I dart my gaze around and force myself to remain calm at the sight of six guards scattered around us. I know without a doubt I'm not making it out of here unscathed.

"She escaped. I fucked up the amount of the dosage and she woke up taking us all by surprise." I keep the blame on myself so he can focus all his rage on me and not my brothers.

"From what I hear, she stole your car and parked it in the fountain of the school?" I flinch, the glint in his eye has me tensing.

"Yes," I clip out.

"You failed." I take a deep breath and nod preparing myself for what comes next. "I told you not to let me down." Without having to be told, I slip from the booth keeping my gaze on his as I grip my shirt and yank it over my head, tossing it onto the top of the table. I undo my belt and wrap it around my fist. Cracking my neck side to side, I give him a curt nod. He smirks and nods his head indicating for his men to get this show on the road. The six of them rush me. I crack the first one across the jaw, knocking him to the ground. The next one comes in swinging, I duck and land two jabs to his stomach before darting back only to have an arm wrap around my neck, I elbow the fucker in the stomach, loosening his hold enough for me to escape only for two more cocksuckers to rush me from either side.

I know fighting back only makes it worse but I'm no fucking pussy and I'll never take a beating willingly. I will always fight back until the day my heart stops beating. I feel elbows slamming into my back and roar out in pain as I lurch forward only to be met with a knee to face. I drop to the ground but I don't stop fighting. I throw out punch after punch and kick out, trying to take as many of them down as I can. When the pain becomes too much, I'm forced to tuck into a fetal position on the floor and weather their blows.

It makes me sick to my stomach knowing that my own father ordered this. I retreat inside my mind to escape the pain radiating inside me. By the time they finish beating the shit out of me, I'm on the verge of passing the fuck out. Two of the fuckers grab my arms and haul me to my feet. I'm too weak to hold my own head up but I can see the tops of Costa's loafers, his hollow laughter has me cringing. He grips my hair and yanks my head up so I can meet his gaze. I can barely see the hatred that shines in the depths of his gaze, from all the blood flowing into my eyes from the numerous gashes on my head and face.

"She had to give me sons. Why couldn't you just have a cunt?" I don't answer, I don't even think I could if I wanted to thanks to the pain radiating in my jaw. When one of his men steps up to him and hands him a large hunting knife, everything inside me turns to ice as I try to brace for what's to come. No matter how much I have tried to prepare myself for this it never dulls the pain. "Front or back?" he asks, smiling like a psychotic fuck.

"F-f." I stop and clear my throat before trying again. "Front," I say as I hold his gaze not masking the hatred, I want him to see it in my eyes.

"You would think after all these years, you would have allowed your pathetic brothers to take some of the punishment for you. Those triplets need to be taught a lesson—"

"You stay the fuck away from them!" I snap. His eyes darken and his nostrils flare at my outburst. He strikes out, slicing me from my chest to my navel. I scream out in pain. Another strangled cry comes from me when he does it again but this time deeper making sure to inflict as much pain as possible. Sweat covers my entire body and nausea churns inside me but I swallow it down.

"You got two today for your lack of control. I raised you better than that." I grit my teeth and focus on breathing through the pain. "Get yourself cleaned the fuck up, we meet her family in three days and I expect you to look presentable." He flicks his gaze to the guys holding me and nods. The fuckers release me and I crumble to my knees like a sack of shit. Their laughter burns inside me long after they flee, leaving me on the floor of my club. It takes me a long ass time to gather the strength I need to pull myself to my feet, using the table to stabilize me until I am steady. I hiss in pain, snag my shirt and stumble toward the exit.

I need to get back to Blackwood so Cronos can stitch my wounds, that bastard made sure to cut me deep enough so that I would need the help of my brother. He wants Cronos to know what happened tonight. I don't fucking relish the thought of him seeing me like this, but I don't have any other choice. My vision begins to blur as I drive through the darkened streets, my head pounding and pain thrumming throughout my entire body. I manage to park my new car in my spot at the back of the school. When I try to get out, I collapse to my knees on the gravel. My breathing is ragged and labored, I feel bile rushing up my throat but swallow it back down.

"What the fuck happened to you?" It takes all my strength to clutch the door and use it as a crutch to pull me to my feet, my head spinning as I stare down at London. From the looks of the outfit she's wearing, she's been jogging. When black spots dance in the corner of my eyes I know I have a minute max before I pass out.

"Find Cronos," I manage to say before my body gives out and I'm falling forward again. I expect to face plant on the ground, what I don't expect is for London-fucking-Murdoch to dart forward and catch me. I grunt when her chest pushes against mine. She maneuvers herself against my side, wrapping her arm around my waist and helping me inside through the staff only entry. I don't question her as she practically drags my ass through the hall and takes a sharp right to my office. She kicks the door open and leads me over to one of the wingback chairs in front of the fire that is still smoldering. She drops me into the chair and I hiss in pain, her face scrunches as she looks over me but says nothing.

"Good luck," she says before turning, ready to flee the room but my words stop her.

"I need my brother." Rather than turn around she peers at me over her shoulder.

"And I need a mind blowing orgasm but we can't all get what we want now can we, *headmaster*?" I narrow my eyes as best as I can through the pain. I can feel my blood soaking through my shirt, if I don't stop the bleeding soon I'll lose too much blood and need a fucking ambulance ride to the hospital.

"Find my brother," I snarl.

"Why the fuck would I do that after what you did to me?" she rebukes.

"Do it." She quirks a brow and slowly turns to face me, placing her hands on her hips. Even through the pain I can't help look at the view before me. She may be in my way and a nuisance but even I can appreciate how fucking hot she is.

"What do I get out of it?"

"I told the triplets to leave you be."

She scoffs. "I can handle those idiots."

"What the fuck do you want then?" I snap.

Her features harden. "I want you to tell me about the trials."

Now, I scoff and shake my head. "No deal."

She shrugs. "Okay, have fun finding your brother," she says as she turns to flee. I can barely keep my head up let alone go in search of Cronos. If I am the one telling her about the trials, then maybe I can swing it so it'll work it in my brother's favor.

"Fine." She pauses but turns.

"Fine, what?"

I take a breath and wince in pain. "I'll tell you about the trials, now find my brother," I grit out through clenched teeth. She turns around and smiles brightly, the sight of her trying to appear cheerful has the opposite effect, she looks fucking deranged.

"Your brother and the three dumbasses left an hour ago." I stiffen.

"Where the fuck did they go?" I demand. Her eyes narrow to slits and her upper lip twitches in outrage.

"I didn't care to fucking ask," she snarls.

"Our deal is off, if they aren't here then I don't get what I need," I spit out.

"What the hell do you need?" she snaps.

"Nothing from you."

"Suit yourself then asshole, I hope you die in that seat." With no other choice but to risk my pride I stop her from fleeing out the open door for a second time.

"Can you stitch me up?" Asking her for help hurts more than the beating and Costa slicing me open. She smiles wide and bats her lashes at me as she slams the door closed.

"Now, why didn't you just say that? Of course, I would be

more than happy to drag a needle through your skin and stitch you up, after all, I couldn't have our new headmaster dying before the semester even begins." Dread washes over me, this bitch is fucking nuts and I have just asked her to help patch up my wounds. I'm starting to regret asking her when she skips— yes, she fucking skips across my office and hums the tune to "London Bridge Is Falling Down".

Chapter Eight

London

After adding another log to the fire and snagging the lamp from the corner of his desk, I helped the bastard lay flat on the bear skin rug in front of the fireplace. I set the lamp up beside him before climbing to my feet and dashing down the hall to the nurses office where I gather everything I'll need to stitch him and patch him up. When I enter his office again I freeze at the sight of him sitting up shirtless, frowning as I take in the wounds on his chest. He's covered in blood but one of them is so deep it's clear whoever did that wanted to inflict as much pain as possible. It's sloppy fucking work if you ask me and a disgrace to the art of torturing a man!

At the sound of my approach he lifts tired pain-filled eyes to me and lays flat on his back. He tries to hide the agony he is in behind a mask but I see it in his eyes. He's pale and sweating, bruises mar his body and he's got a good one beginning to sprout along his jaw. He watches me intently as I set the supplies down beside him before rushing out again to grab a bucket and some water so I can clean his wounds, when I return his eyes are closed and he appears to be sleeping but I know better.

There is no way he would trust me enough to pass out.

I'm proven right when I kneel down beside him and his eyes snap open. I ignore him as I set about my task of cleaning the cuts. He grunts and hisses but doesn't protest. I cover his wounds in Iodine before I thread the needle, I look down at him to find his gaze already on me.

"This changes nothing," he says.

Rolling my eyes I return to my task finally getting the thread through the needle as I answer, "Of course, dear. Tomorrow we can go back to planning to kill each other and then all will be right in the world." The frustrated look on his face makes me laugh. The only reason I am helping this fucker instead of celebrating his death is because I want to know about the trials, well that and the fact if anyone is going to be killing him, it will be me!

"Do you know what you're doing?" The way he is eyeing the needle as I pour the Iodine over it has me smiling.

"Don't look so shocked, I hear where you come from, women know nothing aside from domestic duties. Lucky for you I'm not one of those women."

"You kill me, the rules of sanctum are enacted and you will forfeit the trials and die." I pause and give him my full attention.

"The fuck is that supposed to mean, pretty boy?" He takes on a serious edge as he stares up at me.

"You really have no fucking clue what is about to happen, do you?" Rather than answer his question I set about doing the first stitch, he grunts but there is nothing I can do about it, no morphine or any type of drugs like that are kept on school grounds. When I reach the fourth stitch he finally gives up gnawing on his bottom lip and cries out, a warmth washes over me at the sound. "Can you at least try to act like you're not enjoying this?" he breathes out in pain, his body is beginning to tremble and if he isn't careful he'll probably go into shock and begin seizing.

"Now, why on earth would I do such a thing like that?" I say in my best southern drawl.

"You seriously are fucking crazy!" I make sure to dig the needle in a tiny–fine, a lot deeper relishing in the scream that rips from him. "Fuck!"

"Stop being a baby, it's not that bad," I admonish. He opens his mouth to shout at me but then his eyes roll back into his head and he passes the fuck out. Now, I do debate waiting till he wakes up again to finish the job just so he can feel every-thing I am doing to him but then, my thirst for knowledge of the trials has me rushing through the stitches and trying to finish the job before he wakes. I'm just tying off the last stitch when he finally begins to stir, I wipe the sweat from my brow with the back of my hand before grabbing the gauze and tape to cover the large cut, I only needed to stitch one of them. As I'm applying the gauze, I notice other scars, some are faint but others are raised and look red an angry.

What the fuck happened to him?

"Finished checking me out?" His voice is thick with pain but I don't call him on it, instead I grab his shoulders and help him to sit up. I frown at the sight of more scars covering his back, unlike the front these are... thick and raised, some looking really old while others look recent. I don't realize I have reached out and begun tracing them until he stiffens and jerks forward, forcing me to drop my hand. Neither of us says a word as I climb to my feet ready to get the fuck out of here. "Meet me here at six tomorrow morning and I'll tell you about the first trial before school starts."

"How do I know you won't bullshit me?" He snorts then cringes in pain.

"You're a real fucking lady, aren't you?"

I shrug. "I was raised to be true to who I am, can you say the same thing about yourself?" I don't know why the fuck I said that but something about Artemis and the way he carries himself has me believing that he is hiding who he truly is.

"Some of us don't have that luxury." I don't offer to help him as he slowly climbs to his feet. When he finally stands before me, I have to crane my neck to meet his gaze, the bastard loves this advantage he has over me. "Be warned, London, there is a trial that you will not want to face. No matter how tough you think you are, it will break you." I snort and shake my head as I place my hands on my hips.

"Why, because I'm a girl?" I mock in a high pitched tone.

"No, because you have a soul and this trial will rob you of that." I search his gaze trying to find a sign of deceit but see none.

"Whatever you say, pretty boy, see you in the A.M.," I call out as I stalk out of his office, making sure to swing my hips a little extra. I stop in the doorway and peer over my shoulder at him, then scoff when I find his gaze glued to my ass. "Fucking males always eye fucking us women."

He chuckles lightly and slowly lifts his head to meet my gaze. "I may hate you but I'm still a man and any man with eyes would be watching that ass and picturing it bouncing up and down on his cock."

"Hmmm."

"That's all you've got to say?" he asks.

I purse my lips and nod. "Yeah, I mean it seems only fair you get to picture me fucking you since I've been picturing riding your face since I met you at the club." I turn away quickly so he can't see me smile. The shocked look on his face and the fact he started choking on his own spit means I hit my mark.

Point to me and zero to the Greek God.

After showering and changing into another one of the shirts I stole from my uncle's box—I don't even think Uncle Chaos knew that box was up there and it's not like I'm going to tell him, he barely tolerates the sight of me let alone having a conversation—I slip beneath the covers and stare up at the ceiling. I don't sleep much, every time I close my eyes all I see is his blood soaking through my shirt and the bullet wound in the side of his neck. My mom worried about me for months after the *incident* as I call it but I played it off, I didn't want her to keep worrying about my nightmares. She thinks they stopped years ago. Truth is, they never did. The older I got the worse it became because now I understand everything about what happened that day. I read all the news reports and scoured through the documents my dad had on his desk.

I killed my uncle.

Before I can spiral any further down the rabbit hole I grab my new phone from the bedside table and dial my aunt, praying she is awake. She answers after the fifth ring and just the sound of her voice soothes the darkness inside me.

"Hey, karma, what's up?" I smile.

"Hold up, I'm gonna make this FaceTime and add Aunt Meelz." Aunt Sin says nothing as I add in my other aunt and switch to video call. Her beautiful face fills the screen and I'm hit with homesickness at the sight of her. Aunt Meelz joins the call before I can say anything else, her cheerful smile contagious and I can't help but smile back at her.

"Hey, gorgeous," she says to me. "Chanel," Aunt Meelz clips out.

"Amelia, never a pleasure to see you." I bite my lip to keep from laughing. My aunts glare at each other through the phone screen. I know they don't have the best relationship but they always put that shit aside when it concerns me and I love them for it.

"Do you always have to be a cunt?" Aunt Meelz snaps.

"It's my default setting whenever I see your face," Aunt Sin claps back. Before they can continue to bicker, I cut in and put an end to it.

"I used the training you taught me, Aunt Meelz." She shoots me a megawatt smile, pride shines in her eyes.

"You saved someone?" she asks.

"I kind of had to stitch my headmaster," I say. Aunt Meelz looks shocked while Aunt Sin smiles.

"You cleaned up after yourself, well done, karma." I shake my head.

"Nah, I didn't inflict his wounds, Aunt Sin." I fill them both in on what happened and about the deal I struck with Artemis.

"You can't trust him. He is one of them, London," Aunt Meelz warns.

"It disgusts me to admit it but Amelia is right. He is the son of Costa and could be leading you astray." I listen to my aunts and their warnings about how to proceed with this. Aunt Meelz thinks I should steer clear of him and wait for Grandpa and Dad to have their meeting but Aunt Sin, of course, tells me to take the five of them out before they can come for me. I nix her idea and tell them I will keep them updated with how my meeting with Artemis goes in the morning. Before I end the call, Aunt Sin tells me that she and the others are flying out tomorrow night for the meet with Costa and she will make sure I am present even if my dad hates the idea.

Slipping on a pair of black jeans and my favorite Doc Martens paired with a faded band tee and a crop leather jacket, I pile my hair into a ponytail and deem myself ready to meet with Artemis. I make my way to his office twenty minutes early. My mom always said if you're on time then you're late so I am always early to everything. I don't bother knocking as I push his office door open. I look around the crowded space and frown. I have always hated the clutter in this space, believe me I have spent more times in here than I would have liked so I am well equipped to know where everything is. I make my way over to his desk and claim his chair. Swiveling around, I snap my arms out and grip the edge of his desk when a gold ring catches my attention.

"Motherfucker," I breathe out as I pick it up and inspect the thing. It's the same as the one I saw the triplets wearing and much like theirs, this one is missing a stone as well. It's solid gold, the lion roaring and there are claws that should hold a diamond or something at the edges of its mouth. Is this a family thing or some shit?

"What the fuck are you doing?" I jerk in fright and snap my head up to glare at Artemis as he limps toward me and snatches the ring from my hold. I scoff and recline back in his chair, running my gaze over him. He doesn't dress like a headmaster should. He wears a fitted black shirt, jeans and... Holy shit. He's wearing Chuck Taylors.

"Dude, you seriously need to think about your wardrobe choice if you want everyone to take you seriously around here." He places the ring back on his index finger before pinning me with a scathing look.

"Get your ass out of my seat."

I ignore his demand and kick my legs up on the edge of his desk, crossing them at the ankles and folding my arms over my chest. "Let's be real here. I know for a fact you can't do shit given your current..." I tap my finger against my chin pretending to think of the right word, "... predicament. So, let's not measure cocks because I guarantee you, mine is bigger." His face scrunches in disgust.

"You need a fucking muzzle."

"You need to get laid so you're not so uptight."

"You offering?" he claps back.

"You prepared to get on your knees?" I counter.

He shakes his head and stabs a hand through his thick brown hair. "You are fucking vulgar!"

I shrug. "Didn't stop you from checking out my ass last night."

"Jesus, just get the fuck out of my seat so I can tell you about the trials, then you can fuck off to class."

"Well, why didn't you just say that to begin with?" I question in my best airhead voice before standing and patting the chair. He narrows his eyes but says nothing as he rounds his desk and warily drops into his seat. I pat the top of his head before rounding the desk and claiming one of the seats opposite him, I cross my legs and place my hands atop of them. "Hit me with it, pretty boy."

"Are you always this fucking infuriating?" he grits out through clenched teeth.

"Do you always stumble back here cut up and beaten?" I counter. His brown eyes darken as he glares at me, the bruise on his face nasty looking, but the majority of them are covered by his clothes. I hate to admit it but I spent more time than I would have liked last night wondering about what the hell happened to him.

"You'll keep your mouth fucking shut about that."

I pout. "But Cronos and I are besties and we don't keep secrets from each other." I expected to see shock on his face, not fear.

"You stay the fuck away from my brother. You want to play your games, then you play them with me, not him!" I keep my face blank but inside I'm giddy, so his twin is his weakness. Good to know.

I wave him off. "Fret not, pretty boy, your brother is in the best hands with me and I promise not to let them wander south unless he asks me to." Instantly his features morph to rage.

"Stay the fuck away from him, London!" he shouts.

"Jesus, no need to shout. I promise I won't fuck him into a coma."

"You want to fuck, you come to me."

I don't falter in my reply. "But I don't like you."

"You don't even know my brother to like him."

"I know him well enough to want to scream his name and not yours."

"Is that what this is about?" He doesn't give me a chance to answer. "You want a nice hard cock inside your pussy? Say the words, baby, and I'll have you screaming *my* name and not my brother's." I pretend to ponder his request for a second before I gag.

"Sorry, the thought of your baby dick inside me has me feeling nauseous." He's practically vibrating with rage and I love it. I've learned that men are more forthcoming with information when they are either horny as fuck or angry as hell which is the only reason I am entertaining this conversation. He opens his mouth to no doubt scream at me but I beat him to it. "Now, tell me about the trials."

Chapter Nine

Artemis

This fucking girl is the most infuriating fucking person I have ever met in my life!

How she can sit there and look like a lady but dress and speak like a dude is fucking insane. She's fucking stunning and the fact her beauty is natural and not because of makeup only makes her more appealing. But the moment she opens that godforsaken mouth, she drops from a ten to a one point five.

"You already passed the first trial," I grit out and recline as much as I can without pulling at my stitches. It's taking a shit load of effort to conceal the pain I'm in.

"How?" Oh, so hearing she passed a trial shocks her but not me offering to slam my cock inside her pussy.

"You stole the kill of the rabbit."

She glowers at me. "I didn't steal shit. Not my fault your brothers are incompetent and couldn't manage to kill him themselves. Who was he anyway?" She tries to pass off her question like she doesn't care but her eyes betray her. I don't think she has any idea that her eyes change shades.

"He was an *arouraíos*–a rat. We don't kill our snitches like you Americans, we capture them and set them free for the hunt."

I can see the cogs turning in her brain as she tries to piece this all together. "You use them for sport?"

"No. We use them for the purpose of the hunt. One is marked as the rabbit and any who wish to trial are to hunt them down. The first to kill the rabbit wins."

"Okay, so I am the one who killed the rabbit. How are your brothers in the trial with me when they didn't win the hunt?" I fight the urge to grind my teeth, she is more perceptive than I gave her credit for.

"That is something you don't need to worry about." She opens her mouth to argue but I push on. "There are five trials in total. Kill. Take. Escape. Describe. Steal."

"What the hell does that mean?" I debate not telling her, but if she is about to participate in these then she has a right to know about the final trial.

"The final trial is the hardest. You may think you are strong and can take on the world but believe me, this trial will break you. I don't say this as a threat, I say it as a warning, London." At the sound of her name she sits up straighter and stares at me intently. "That trial is not for the faint of heart. If it doesn't break you physically, it will *destroy* you mentally and emotionally."

"Why do I feel like you aren't bullshitting me?"

"Because I'm not. There is a reason no one has been able to overthrow my father and it's because of that final trial. The current leader chooses who you meet in that room and believe me, he will not make it easy on you. If anything, he will make it twice as fucking hard."

"He's the one who gave you all those scars, isn't he?" she whispers, all trace of her usual sass gone and in its place is nothing but sincerity.

"We aren't friends, London. Don't mistake my warning for anything other than what it is."

She snorts. "So, we're not friends but we can fuck?"

I quirk a brow. "If you're offering I won't say no."

She fake gags again. "I'd rather finger fuck my own pussy, thank you very much." I sit here and stare at her as she stands and leaves my office. She pauses in the doorway and looks back at me over her shoulder. "Here's some non-friendly advice for ya. Next time he tries to slice you up, kill him."

My first day as headmaster and already I have had to deal with five students who have either been fighting, stealing or planning a mass murder. This school is filled with fucking psychos. I only took this job because I wasn't given a choice. I know the other families didn't care that I took the job, well, except for Bishop and Royal Murdoch. They both protested and fought the decision but they were out voted. It's the final period and I know Cronos is teaching combat out the back on the quad so I make my way out there.

I stay hidden, lean against the building and watch as the students exit the building to meet with their instructor. London has no idea her new combat teacher is her *bestie*. I don't see her through the crowd but I hear her squeal of delight at the sight of my twin. The other students part making sure to stay out of her way as she races toward my brother and throws herself at him, wrapping her arms around his neck. Cronos stands there stiff and stunned for a second before he gently grips her exposed waist and sets her down. I grind my teeth at the sight of her gym clothes—sports bra and tight black leggings— with her hair in a ponytail. She looks good.

I won't lie to myself, the sight of her has my cock hardening in my pants. I meant what I said this morning about fucking her. I would be all too willing to have her screaming my name, ripping my stitches to fuck her would be worth it. London moves back to join her peers but she keeps distance between her and them. That's when I notice it, the divide. None of the other students seem warm or friendly toward her. Is she a loner?

"You're here to learn to survive and if the need should arise, you are here to take a life with your bare hands," Cronos says to the class.

"You can demonstrate it on me," a girl calls out, earning giggles and whistles from her peers. Cronos frowns but my gaze is laser focused on London as she spins around and glares at the girl who called out.

"Touch him or make a pass at him again and I'll snap your fucking neck, Sadie." The laughter and murmurs cease at the sound of London's voice. All of these students fear her. She has garnered their respect through fear and that is no easy fucking feat considering the guys in her class are six foot and the size of a linebacker.

"It was a joke," the girl defends.

"No, a joke is having to stand here and look at you." I

watch the students around the girl shake with silent laughter. London turns back to Cronos and nods. "Carry on, bestie." At her statement about Cronos being her bestie, the class all gasps, while my brother just shakes his head and smiles.

He fucking smiled!

How is it that this girl can bring a smile to his face after only knowing her for mere days, yet me and the triplets have to fight with everything we have to even get him to crack a smirk. That's when it hits me. The only way to bring down a girl like London is to get inside her. I'm not like my father but some things are true, a man can fuck and feel nothing but a woman can't. If I can manage to get her to spread her legs for me then I can get inside her head and Cronos is going to help me do it.

I stay here for an hour watching Cronos. When a demonstration needs to be done, London doesn't even ask or wait for him to say anything, she just walks out into the center and spars with my brother. Yes, I knew she was trained by her family but knowing and seeing are two different things. She strikes with poise and purpose, every move calculated and thorough. Her stance is perfection and she never once drops her guard even as Cronos continues to come at her. She waits for her opening. When my brother drops his guard, she strikes out, lands two quick jabs to his jaw and nose before she takes two steps back and then runs at him, climbing his body until she is sitting on his shoulders. She locks her legs around his neck and drops back, using his own size against him, and flips him onto the ground where she tightens her hold on his neck.

I push off the wall and watch in astonishment, never have I ever seen my brother be subdued in a choke hold by anyone, much less a female. His face begins to turn a shade of red and purple. London sees the color in his face and reluctantly releases her hold on him and rolls away. Climbing to her feet, she doesn't stick around, marching toward the building, ignoring the cheering of her peers. I race back inside and head toward the locker room from the other side of the school. I have no fucks to give so I don't check if the locker room is empty before I walk in.

I lock the door behind myself and move through the rows of lockers before I come to a stop at the sight of London sitting on the bench seat in front of her open locker with her head down. Frowning at the sight of her looking so distraught, I move closer. At the sound of my approach, she leaps to her feet and glares at me.

"What the fuck are you doing here, Artemis?" I smirk.

"Well, I can see you have no trouble telling me and my brother apart."

She scoffs as she turns her back to me and grabs her towel and some other shit from her locker. "Your brother is wearing shorts and a singlet and is currently teaching a class," she dead-pans before shouldering past me. I grunt but say nothing as I follow after her. I pause in the entryway of the showers. There are no doors or curtains, it's just one giant stall with a dozen shower heads. London drops her things onto one of the bench seats, then turns her head to me. "You gonna watch like a perv?"

"I thought I might check out the pussy I'm getting on my knees for."

She scoffs. "Whatever you say, pretty boy. You aren't the first and you won't be the last to make a pass at me. Nudity doesn't bother me like other girls, so get your fill and then store it away in your mind for your spank bank." I'm about to reply but clamp my mouth closed as she yanks her sports bra off. She keeps her gaze on me the entire time, challenging me but I can't stop my gaze lowering to take in the sight of her tits—fuck they are perfect and full. Big enough to fit in my hands as I push them together and thrust my cock between them. I return my gaze to hers, meeting her challenge with one of my own.

Drop those pants.

She can see it in my eyes and doesn't back down. She pushes her leggings down her long toned legs and kicks them to the side. I get a second to drink in the sight of her pink pussy before she turns and marches toward the shower, giving me the perfect view of her luscious ass—fuck me sideways, she puts the *bubble* in bubble butt. She turns the shower on and doesn't wait for it to heat up before she steps beneath the spray. I debate leaving her be and finding her later but she turns to face me and meets me with a challenge in her green eyes.

"You gonna stand there and watch or test out how durable your stitches are?" The confidence she exudes is like none other I have ever seen before. London isn't shy and coy like most girls. She doesn't mince her words or try to pretend to be someone she isn't. She loves who she is and the fact she isn't ashamed to say what she means or wants is... attractive as fuck.

"You gonna go cry to your daddy after?" I taunt.

She rolls her eyes. "Who I decide to fuck is none of my dad's concern." Taking her at her word, I close the space between us, not giving a fuck that my clothes are wet and I'm pressed against her hot, naked little body. I grip the back of her neck and force her onto her tiptoes, loving the lustful look in her eyes as I ghost my lips over hers. I feel the shiver racing down her spine and relish in it.

"Beg."

Her eyes widen. "You have the wrong girl if you think for a second I am going to beg you to fuck me."

"Tell me you need me and I'll fuck you right here, right now." I'm fucking with her head and if she wasn't so turned on, she would realize that but her mind isn't in control, her pussy is.

"Fuck me," she breathes out. I want to push her and demand her on her knees but all I need is to just get inside her once and then she will be coming back for more, I guarantee it.

"Take my cock out," I order. With sure movements she reaches between our bodies and unclasps my belt then pops the button on my jeans before yanking the zipper down. Her gaze is locked on mine as she reaches inside my boxers and grabs my cock. Her eyes widen when she tries to wrap her fingers around me. "Surprised?" I taunt.

"Not gonna lie, I thought you were an arrogant prick all the time because you lacked somewhere else, so yeah I am surprised." My grip on her neck tightens. The crazy bitch just smirks and cuts off the reply on the tip of my tongue when she pumps my cock, drawing a strangled groan from me. I'm in no mood to play games, it's been too long since I've been inside a woman.

"Turn around and brace your hands on the wall." To my surprise she does as she's told. I run my hands over her ass and enjoy the way she begins to tremble beneath my touch.

"Just to be clear, this is the only time you will be fucking me."

"We'll see about that." Her eyes narrow.

"Next time, I'll be the one doing the fucking." I chuckle because what else can I say, I would expect nothing less from this girl. I grip my cock in my hand and pump it twice before gliding the head through her slick folds.

"Fuck," I growl, feeling her wetness coating my dick. I line up with her entrance and slam inside her, then freeze when a scream of pain tears from within her. Horror washes over me when realization crashes into me. Both of us remain silent, her pussy pulsing around me, making it fucking near impossible to remain still inside her. "London—"

Chapter Ten

London

I cut him off before he can continue. "Don't fucking say it," I grit out through clenched teeth as I breath through the pain. I wanted this. I've always wanted to experience this but I've never found anyone remotely attractive or trustworthy enough. Make no mistake, I know Artemis Argyros isn't trustworthy but I also know on a deeper level he isn't someone who will go around the school and brag about fucking London Murdoch.

"You're a virgin?" He had to go and fucking say it. I turn and glare at him over my shoulder.

"Not anymore." His eyes are wide, horror lurking in the depths of his brown eyes. His grip on my waist loosens, I can tell he is about to flee so I bite down on my lip and push through the pain as I rock back against him, forcing him to tighten his hold on me.

"London–" I cut him off by rocking back against him

again. He opens his mouth again but I continue to rock against him until his restraint snaps and his hold on me turns punishing. He pulls almost all the way out of me before slamming back into me. I cry out, but this time from pleasure. As he continues to rock inside me the pain quickly bleeds way to a strange feeling that has my toes curling and my head swimming. "Fuck, you're so tight," he growls as he continues to fuck me.

I can feel my orgasm cresting but it's out of reach, I need more. "Fuck me harder, pretty boy," I cry out when he hits that spot deep inside me.

"Beg me," he grits out.

"Never," I snap. The fucker slows his pace. I open my mouth to curse him out but he picks up his speed, pushing me right to the edge only to stop before I can latch onto my orgasm. He does this to me twice more and I am woman enough to admit I am on the verge of fucking tears. I want—no, I need this fucking orgasm more than I need my next breath so I suck up my fucking pride and do something I have never done before... beg. "Please, fuck me. This is me begging you to make me fucking come!" I scream. I nearly drop to the floor in a heap when he pulls out of me, his grip on me stops me from falling. He spins me around and grips the backs of my thighs lifting me.

"Lock your legs around my waist." I do as he demands, also wrapping my arms around his neck, bracing myself for him to slam back inside me. He shifts until his cock is lined up with my entrance. I tense in preparation. "Kiss me."

"What?" I bark.

"Kiss me, it will distract you and help you relax." I search his gaze and find nothing but sincerity in his eyes. I close the space between us and mesh my lips to his. When his tongue invades my mouth, I moan and melt into him. He uses that moment to gently ease back inside me. It stings and burns but it's nothing compared to the first time he slammed inside me. His hands grip the globes of my ass as he rocks into me at a leisurely pace. I break the kiss and throw my head back as a moan rips out of me. He nips at the side of my neck and groans as I push down onto him meeting him thrust for thrust. I feel like I'm possessed, I'm not in control of my own body. My hands claw down his chest as I ride him, chasing my release. He grunts and hisses but doesn't stop me.

"Oh my God," I cry out when I feel something inside me brewing, it's such an intense feeling that it terrifies me.

"Let go and come all over my cock, *Omorfia*." His words are my undoing. I meet his heated gaze as he slams into me once more before the strongest orgasm I have ever experienced in my life rips through me.

"Artemis!" I scream his name as I come all over his cock. My vision turns hazy and I'm nothing but dead weight in his hold as I flop forward and bury my face in the crook of his neck. He thrusts inside me twice more before he comes with my name on lips. He stumbles forward until my back is flush against the tiled wall, bracing his hands against the wall and remaining still as we try to regulate our breathing.

After a moment he asks. "You okay?" I pull back from my hiding spot and stare down at him. He flicks his gaze between mine and whatever he sees has him gently pulling out of me. I flinch and try to mask it but it's too late, his perspective ass saw. "It's gonna sting for a while," he says in a guilt-ridden tone that surprises me.

"You a pro at stealing virginities or something?" I joke but he isn't biting. He shakes his head and takes a step back, only to wince. That's when I remember his stitches. I dart forward and lift his shirt, ignoring his protests and whistle between my teeth. "You tore a couple."

"I didn't do shit, that was all you," he snaps back. I roll my eyes and step back under the spray to wash off.

"Pussy," I mutter.

"Dick." I can't help the laughter that bubbles out of me. Said laughter dies in my throat when I feel his cum dripping out of me. I spin around and face him. He frowns.

"You came inside me!" It takes a moment for my words to sink in before his expression matches mine.

"You're on birth control, right?" His pleading tone would be funny at any other time aside from now.

"Seriously? How many fucking hymens do you think I have for guys to break?" He scrunches his face in confusion, I throw my hands in the air exasperated with this dumbass. "I was a virgin five minutes ago. I never had a need to be on birth control, dumbass."

"Don't get angry with me, you begged me to fuck you!" Anger burns inside me. I turn the shower off and stomp my feet as I shoulder past him, snag my towel off the seat and wrap it around myself. Before more can be said Cronos clears his throat drawing our attention to him.

"What?" Artemis barks.

Cronos glares at his twin. "The girls heard screaming. I told them to wait outside while I came and checked it out."

Shame washes over me but I don't let it show. "Your brother tore his stitches," I sneer. I shoot Artemis a scathing look that promises pain before I make my way back to my locker. I pause in front of Cronos and smile up at him. "Your turn to stitch the bitch up." He frowns in confusion but I don't stick around to explain it to him. What the fuck just happened? He's a big boy and I'm sure he can figure it out on his own.

After ditching Artemis and Cronos in the locker room, I make my way back to my bedroom. My mind is reeling and I know I fucked up big time. I lost control for the first time ever and didn't think before acting. My body took on a mind of its own and I was nothing but a passenger to its needs. I dig my phone out of my pocket and dial Aunt Amelia. After a couple rings her angelic face fills the screen. I know some of my family wonder how her and I are so close but they would never understand. She is the only one who can understand me and the struggles I face.

"Hey, what's wrong?" she says, the concern in her tone makes me feel like an ass but it's not like I can call my mom and tell her about this. She would tell Dad and then all hell would break lose.

"I slept with my headmaster," I blurt out. It's comical to watch as my words slowly sink in and her brows raise to her hairline, her mouth hanging open in shock.

"I have no words." I laugh because I feel the exact same way. She waits until my hysterical laughter dies down before she asks. "Are you okay?"

I flop on my bed and groan. "Yeah, I'm okay but I do have a problem."

"What is it? Did he force himself on you? I'll kill—" I cut her off before she can get too far into planning murder.

"No, I wanted it to happen but we weren't exactly safe."

"Oh. So no condom?" I shake my head. "At the risk of sounding like your mother, how old is this headmaster?" I gnaw on my bottom lip, debating lying to her but she pins me with her best stern look. "Spit it out."

"Fine. According to the new school file that was sent out he's twenty-four." Curses fly out of her mouth and I have to bite my lip to keep from smiling. Aunt Meelz isn't one to cuss a lot so when she does it's always funny.

"He's nearly the same freaking age as your father!"

"Eww." I shout in disgust. "Dad's old!"

"I'm older than your father!" she snaps.

"Yeah, but you're cool and he's... not." That gets her to laugh and breaks some of the tension.

"Okay. back on task, what do you need from me?"

"I need birth control."

"London, if I do that I will have to log it into the system and it will trigger your parents insurance."

"Fuck."

"Can you ask your school nurse? They are under no obligation to log that type of thing into the system." I roll onto my back and sigh.

"The school nurse quit, they are trying to find a replacement for her now," I whine. She sighs and smiles sadly.

"London, I can keep this off the books for this time only but next time you need to tell your parents or speak to the nurse when the school finds one."

I beam at her. "Have I told you how fucking stunning you are?" She rolls her eyes.

"Save the sucking up for your father, I gotta get back to work."

"Love you."

"Love you too." She ends the call and now I'm forced to wallow in the silence with only my thoughts to keep me company. I don't hate being alone when I have something to do but in moments like this with nothing to do, my mind always drifts back to that day. I try to prepare myself for the memories to flash through my mind of all the blood except it's not those memories that play on a reel, this time when I close my eyes all I see is memories of me and Artemis in the shower. A smile tugs at the corners of my mouth at the state of his chest from my nails, I can still feel the ghost of him inside me, it's like a dull ache but fuck it feels delicious. A groan tumbles free when a knock sounds at the door. I roll over and glare at the door before getting up and yanking the door open, ready to tell whoever it is to fuck off.

"Cronos?" I mutter at the sight of him standing there with his hands in his pockets looking uncomfortable as fuck.

"Hey, I just wanted to... I just thought that maybe..." He clamps his mouth closed and shakes his head. I smile at the big fucker.

"Awww, did you come to check up on me?" He purses his lips and narrows his eyes, then turns ready to flee, but I dart my hand out and grip his forearm stopping him. I can feel the eyes of the other students on us so I turn and look both ways before saying, "Next one to look this way is going to get their fucking eyes burnt the fuck out. Try me, I dare ya." The sounds of hurried footfalls brings a smile to my face as I pull Cronos inside my room and close the door behind him. He stands before me tense and looking awkward as hell. Honestly I'm not mad about him being here, he is my bestie and best friends hang out, right?

"I just wanted to see if you were okay," he says barely above a whisper. I move to stand before him, searching his gaze, trying to figure out what his story is and why he is so unlike his siblings.

"You're genuinely worried about me, aren't you?" He nods. "Why?" He turns his head away from me, his face is contorted in pain and for the first time ever I don't push. I leave him to decide if he wants to share his secrets with me. Normally I would pester someone until they spilled the beans but there is something about Cronos that just... soothes something inside me.

"There was a time I wouldn't have given a shit and high fived my brother for bagging the heir to the US mafia." I clench my fists at my side and bite the inside of my cheek to keep from snapping at him or worse, breaking his fucking nose. "Things changed and now..." he slowly turns his head to face me, the sorrowful look in his brown eyes has pain radiating inside my chest for my bestie, "I care more about keeping you safe."

"I can look after myself, Cronos," I say adamantly.

"I know you can, darlin', but you shouldn't have to protect yourself from life and living. This world we are born into isn't for the faint of heart. I see through the macho bitch act you put on."

I scoff. "This isn't an act, it's who I am."

His features soften, "I know you wish that were true but it isn't. Be careful, darlin', everyone here is out for themselves and that is my brother included."

"What are you trying to tell me?" I push in a firm tone.

"Artemis never does something without a plan in place. He has the most to lose out of all of us when these trials begin. If you ever find yourself in the presence of my father alone, run. I know you think you are strong but he is evil, London, and will not think twice about hurting you."

"I'll kill him before he can touch me," I snarl.

His eyes soften as he reaches out and cups my cheek. I jolt in surprise but he doesn't drop his hold. "She thought the same thing, now she is six feet deep with worms and maggots eating her corpse."

Chapter Eleven

Artemis

After getting my ass chewed out by my brother before he stormed out of the locker room, to no doubt go chase after his new *bestie*, I retreated to my room to change before heading back to my office to bury myself in work to keep my mind from drifting back to London and how fucking amazing she felt wrapped around me. I tore at least four stitches so I just place a patch over each of them for now, Cronos can stitch them after he calms the fuck down.

My phone ringing pulls me from my thoughts. I plan to ignore it until I see it's Blake calling. I hit answer and place it on speaker. "Blake," I say in lieu of greeting.

"Artemis, did you forget how to use your phone?" I smirk.

"A phone works two ways, Blake," I counter.

"Yeah, well, I've been busy sue me! So, what's been happening with this girl and the trials?" Blake is the only person in the world outside of my brothers that I give a fuck about and trust. Blake and I have been friends since senior year in high school and went to college together.

"The girl is a fucking nightmare and crazy as hell. The trials won't begin until this week after we meet with her family to discuss what is going to happen."

"Why is her family getting involved?"

"Did I forget to mention she isn't just the first female to enter the trials but she is American?" Blake whistles.

"Fucking hell, this is going to hinder your plans to get your brothers out from under that bastard." I sigh and lean back in my chair.

"She isn't a problem. After this meet the trials will begin and I'll make sure she doesn't pass the first one."

"What if she does?"

"She won't," I grit out.

"*But*, what if she does, Art?"

I scrub a hand down my face and close my eyes. "Then I have no choice but to do what needs to be done."

"You would kill her?"

"If it means my brothers living, I would kill anyone."

"Then why do you sound so unsure?" If there is anyone aside from Cronos that can see and hear through my bullshit, it's Blake.

"I gotta go, I'll check in later," I say, dismissing the question and ending the call. As if the world hates me more than usual my phone begins to ring. Checking the caller ID, I see it's Annalie, she teachers politics here.

I hit answer and bring it to my ear. "Annalie, what can I do for you?"

"Mr. Argyros, I know this is your first week and you may not know a lot about the students here–"

"Anna, I am very busy. Can you please get to the point?"

"There is a student in my class who continues to cause a... ruckus and today was no different. She brought a set of hair clippers into the classroom and shaved the back of Thomas Lincoln's head. When the boy began shouting she then broke his nose and snapped a picture of the damage she caused, then sent the picture to his father."

I lull my head back and stare up at the ceiling. Thomas Lincoln is the son of one of the politicians in the UK. His father is a very powerful man and this could cause a shitload of problems for me and the fucking school.

"Which student was it?"

"London Murdoch."

"Fuck!" I clip out before ending the call and dialing my assistant, Tiffany.

"Mr. Argyros, how can I help you?" she says.

"Get me the contact details for Donald Lincoln."

"Ah, sir, I left you notes on your calendar. He has tried to call you several times today."

"Jesus, next time something like this happens fucking find me!" I growl before ending the call with her and checking my calendar to find the contact information for Donald Lincoln. I call the bastard. Unlike most politicians, Donald isn't able to be bought. As far as he knows, this school is just for children born from high-ranking families.

Donald answers on the third ring. "Who the hell is this?" His tone is filled with anger.

"This is Artemis Argyros, headmaster of Blackwood Academy," I answer.

"I have been trying to reach you all damn day!" I grind my teeth reminding myself to remain calm, I can't exactly threaten the fucker or I risk exposing the other students at this school.

"I've been out of my office–"

"I don't give a shit. I want that little bitch who harmed my son expelled!" Anger rises to the surface inside me as I scroll through Thomas's file. Every student here has a file listing everything they have done and do here. In case a situation like this arises we have material to blackmail their parents into shutting their mouths. Little Thomas is a fucking pig.

"She will not be expelled."

"Do you have any idea who the fuck I am?" My restraint snaps.

"Do you have any idea who the fuck I am and who the girl was that did this to your son?"

"You listen to me, you little punk—"

"You listen to me, Donald. You will let this go or I will expose your sons fetish for drugging girls and raping them." I'm met with silence so I push on. "Yes, Donald, I am very much aware to the reasons why you shipped your snot nosed brat to *my* school. It's the least he deserved after what he did. You drop this now or I kick your son out of my school." I end the call fuming, it's day one of this fucking job and I can already see London is going to be a fucking pain in my ass! I shoot Tiffany a text telling her to get London and send her ass to my office. I don't give a fuck if it's after hours or not, this girl will learn I don't fuck around.

I've waited seventy five goddamn minutes, over a fucking hour, for her to grace me with her presence and now I've gone from slightly irritated to fucking murderous. I stalk out of my office and head straight for London's room. Students stare but say nothing as I pass by them. I know they are shocked that someone my age is their new headmaster but I won't be here for long. As soon as these trials are complete, I'm gone. When I reach London's room, I pound my fist against the wooden door doing nothing to taper the anger inside me.

"Fuck off!" Her shout just fuels the fucking fire burning inside me.

"Open the fucking door now, London!" I shout back, not giving a fuck that the students in the hall can hear. A second later she opens the door a tiny bit and I barge the rest of the way in ready to fucking lay into her but pause at the sight of Cronos sitting in her office chair. "What the fuck are you doing here?" I snap at him.

"Minding my own damn business. Maybe you should try it sometime, now get the fuck out." Ignoring London, I step toward my brother but halt when the bitch cuts in front of me and shoves me against my chest, a hiss of pain escaping me but I ignore the sting as I scowl at her.

"You were supposed to meet me an hour ago," I force out through clenched teeth.

She places her hands on her hips and rolls her eyes. "Yeah, see we need to get some things straight here, pretty boy. I don't conform to the rules of this fucking prison and I give zero fucks about what you want." I close the space between us, brushing my chest against hers. I don't miss my brother climbing to his feet from the corner of my eye ready to protect this bitch if needed.

"You will conform to my fucking rules. You are no better than anyone else here. You continue to cause problems for me and I will make you fucking rue the day you were born," I sneer.

She smiles and bats her lashes. "If that's what you wanted then all you had to do was fuck me again." My eyes twitch in anger, this bitch is baiting me and I refuse to give into her. She leans closer and fake whispers, "I've been regretting my life choices all afternoon since I left you. Golly gosh, I didn't think it was possible to hate myself but fucking you showed me I can."

I snap my arm out, gripping a handful of her hair, pulling her to her tiptoes. She doesn't fight me, instead the crazy cunt just smiles.

"Artemis, let her go now!" I ignore my twin's warning as I lean down and get right in her face.

"The only time I'll ever sink my cock into that retched cunt again is when I kill you."

"Oh, so you're into necrophilia? Explains a lot since you were a useless fuck." Okay, that one hit my fucking ego.

"Keep lying to yourself, *Omorfia,* that pussy was milking my cock as you came so fucking hard you couldn't even stand." Her green eyes spark with heat. This fucking girl is insane, her form of foreplay is fighting. She runs her hands up my chest causing me to stiffen beneath her touch until she wraps her arms around my neck. I smirk triumphantly, I knew the reminder of her coming on my cock would subdue her rebellious attitude, she just needs a firm hand to mold her.

She leans in closer brushing her lips against mine as she whispers, "You think you wrecked me?" I shift my hold to grip her waist, loving the lustful look that sparks in her eyes.

"I know I did."

"And yet here you are in my room, holding me and trying to bend me to your will. Let's be real here, pretty boy. You're the one chasing me because *I* wrecked you with my retched ass pussy." I shove her away from me, clenching my fists at my sides as she stands there laughing.

"You're a fucking bitch," I roar.

She fake pouts. "Yet you still want to fuck me... again."

"You're fucking dreaming." She drops her gaze to my cock and quirks a brow before meeting my stare again.

"So, are you hard for me or your brother? If it's for Nos, then I'm down to watch." Disgust ripples through me.

"You're fucking sick!" I snap my gaze to my brother who stands there stoically. "You let her give you a fucking nickname?"

He shrugs. "It sounds better coming from her than you." When the sound of her laughter rings out around the room, I see red.

"You're suspended from every class and will continue your learning in my office." Her eyes widen in anger.

"Fuck you," she shouts. "You can't do that!"

"Yes the fuck, I can. You try to defy me and your bestie over here will be on yard duty. Defy me a second time and I'll be forced to fire my own brother until you learn you are not in charge around here, I am."

"I'll slit your fucking throat. You have no idea who you are fucking with," she warns.

"No, you have no idea who the fuck you just made an enemy of. I am not soft or sweet like my brothers. I do not bend to anyone's will and will never bow to you. Be at my office by the start of school tomorrow or *Nos* will pay the price for your disobedience. Your father will thank me for breaking his cunt of a kid." The mention of her father has her face blanking of any emotions. I keep the confusion from showing on my face.

"My father isn't the one who will be thanking you, he will be the one standing behind me as I end your life. You will die by my hand, Artemis, make no mistake. I'm not like your past bitches."

"Don't I fucking know it," I sneer.

"You fucking me will never have me fawning over you or falling in love, love is for the weak and pathetic."

I snort. "So you must think Cronos is weak as fuck then?" The second the words leave my mouth I have instant regret. I snap my gaze to my brother and watch as he lowers his head before stalking out of her room slamming the door closed. "Fuck!" I roar. This bitch makes me unhinged and has me wanting to do anything to get under her fucking skin. I just hurt my brother in an attempt to get at her.

"You gonna go after him or should I?" All the anger flees me as I shake my head, she scoffs. "You stand there acting like a fucking king, yet you're too much of a fucking pussy to go and right your wrongs."

"You don't know me!" I sneer.

"I don't need to. I'll do as you say only because I won't allow your brother to pay the price for me."

"Why the fuck do you care about what happens to him?" I blurt out.

"Someone like you would never understand," she accuses as she shoulders past me and leaves. I stand here alone and hating myself a bit more inside. These trials have me acting like a bastard and I hate that. The worry of what has to happen is weighing me down and I can't keep lashing out at my brothers, we are all each other has. I won't let London come between us. Her being with me daily means I can keep an eye on her and make sure she stays the fuck away from Cronos. He can't deal with another loss, he barely survived the last one.

Chapter Twelve

London

I spent the whole fucking day cooped up in Artemis's office without saying a word. The bastard dumped a bunch of dusty ass books on the desk he had moved in there for me and told me to write him a fucking essay on Greek mythology. I swear to God I snapped at least four pencils. Today, I now sit here with another lot of books filled with history of the Greeks that he tells me to write another essay about. I refuse to speak to the unbearable bastard. He sits behind his desk like he is some fucking God. The plans I have for this fucker would make the devil blush.

I read the fucking books like a good girl. At the start, I do it to spite him and to keep my mind off the meeting tonight but after an hour or so I realize these books aren't on the actual history of the Greeks themselves, these books are filled with the history of the *Godfathers Of The Night*. The pages hold knowledge that I know no one in my family is aware of. I flip through the pages trying to find any information about the trials but when I'm halfway through I see pages have been torn out and just know this was Artemis's doing. I slam the thing closed and climb to my feet. He's too engrossed in his computer to notice I have crossed the room so I slam the book on his desk.

"Fuck!" he shouts as he jolts in fright before pinning me with a scathing look. "What the fuck is wrong with you?"

"You are! Why the fuck would you give me a history book on the history of your family but remove the pages containing the information about the trials?" I accuse.

He frowns. "What the fuck are you talking about?" I open the book to where the pages containing the information about the trials should be and show him. His brows furrow as he stares at the book before flipping his shocked gaze back to me. "London, where the fuck did you get that book?"

Now, I frown. "You left them on my desk."

He shakes his head as he stands and makes his way toward where my desk is in the corner of his office and flips through the other three books there. I make my way over and peek over his shoulder, clearly he didn't mean for me to get these books.

"What the fuck," he breathes out to himself.

"You didn't give me these books, did you?" He slowly straightens to his full height and turns to face me. It's then that I notice how close we are standing, there is only a sliver of space between our bodies. My dirty little whore of a vagina decides to pulse.

Down you dirty pussy!

"No one should have these books. They are never allowed outside of the sanctuary of the cove."

"What's the cove?" I see the turmoil in his gaze, he's debating if he should tell me or not so I push on. "Artemis, who the fuck am I going to tell? The only friend I have is your brother." He purses his lips.

"You fail to recall the amount of times you have reminded me that your father and grandfather are the Dons of rival families."

I shrug my shoulders. "Didn't stop you from fucking me," I counter. It shocks the fuck out of me when he smirks and nods.

"Fair point." I find myself fighting back my own smile. What the fuck is going on, I never smile or feel... giddy. "The cove is the place where all meetings are held back home in Mykonos beneath the windmill. These books should be locked away there. How they got here is a fucking mystery." I hear the truth in his words.

"Who the hell would want me to know the history of your organization?" We remain silent for a moment thinking until a knowing look enters his eyes and he scoffs whilst running a hand through his hair. I study him, trying to decipher what is running through his mind. He perches his ass on the edge of my desk, bringing him closer to my height. I take my time to drink in the sight of him. The bruise on his face is fading and he seems to walk a little easier now and not wince when he stands or sits so I guess he is healing well. Aunt Amelia would be proud of the job I did on him, she taught me everything I know about first aid.

"I think your *bestie* is trying to help you." The husky lilt of his voice has heat pulsing inside my belly.

"Nos gave me the books?" He purses his lips and nods.

"That would be my guess. I think my brother wants you to win these trials."

I search his gaze, trying to gauge his feelings but can't. I step between his outstretched legs relishing in the surprised look in his eyes at my bold move.

"He wants me to have a chance, but you don't. Why?"

He gaze bores into mine as he answers. "You win, we die. It's as simple as that." His answer stuns me. Before I can formulate a response, he darts his arm out, grips the back of my neck and hauls me in closer so he can kiss me. My usual response would be to break the bastards nose who got handsy with me, but something about the way Artemis pushes me and refuses to backdown or give into me turns me the fuck on. Ever since I let him inside me I haven't been able to stop thinking about it and the way he made me feel. He breaks the kiss. We stand here breathless and panting as we stare at each other. "You want to fuck, you find me, not my brother," he says.

Normally I would scoff and tear anyone down who demands anything of me but instead I find myself saying, "I don't look at your brother like that."

He smiles. "You know we're identical twins, right?"

I roll my eyes and try to push him away but he grabs my waist pulling me in closer until my chest is flush against his. "You look nothing alike."

He frowns. "How so?" The general curiosity in his voice is the only reason I answer.

"Cronos has shadows in his eyes, he has an edge of darkness that clings to him."

"What about me?"

I smirk. "Simple, you reek of assholeness and exude stick-up-your-ass type of vibes." To my surprise, he throws his head back laughing. I cock my head to the side, confused by how much I like the sound.

"You are so full of shit," he says through his laughter.

"Maybe, but it's still true." He leans in as if to kiss me again but stops when there is a knock at his door. The person doesn't wait to enter and just barges in. The shocked look on his assistant's face at finding the headmaster and a student in such a position is evident but she says nothing as I step back and Artemis stands putting space between us.

"What is it?" he asks her in an annoyed tone.

She clears her throat and masks the shock look on her face as best she can. I can see the judgment in her shit colored eyes and it pisses me off.

"Can you hurry the fuck up and answer the question so I can get back to blowing the headmaster under his desk?" Her jaw unhinges and Artemis chokes on nothing. I can feel his disapproving look on me, but I ignore him as I stare Tiff down.

The bitch clearly has the hots for him and is just pissed it wasn't her between his legs. Her crush is made more obvious when she smiles like a crazed fucker as she speaks. "Your father is at the gates demanding entrance." She wants to shock me and see me flounder from her news but that won't happen. I stand here looking bored as fuck as I reply.

"Can you go tell my daddy I'll be there as soon as I finish fucking my new daddy." Artemis chokes again for the second time in a minute, while Tiff turns bright red and growls before stomping out of the office like a spoiled brat slamming the door behind her. "Well, that wasn't very professional of her," I deadpan as I turn to face Artemis who is glaring at me.

"Your new daddy, really?" I smirk.

"Come on, that was fucking golden."

"You're a pain in my fucking ass!" he snarls as he heads for the door. I dart in front of him, forcing him to a halt.

"One, fuck you, two, kiss my fucking ass, and three, where the fuck are you going?"

He looks less than amused and that just makes me smile,

knowing I'm getting on his nerves. "Unless you really do want to be sucking my dick under my desk while your father sits opposite me, get out of my fucking way." I don't move because the mental picture he just painted is playing on a reel inside my head. "Jesus Christ, you really are out of your fucking mind," he snaps before brushing past me.

"I wasn't going to do it!" I defend as he opens the door and peers over his shoulder at me.

"You are a shitty fucking liar." I laugh as I chase after him. We exit the building side by side but Artemis snaps his arm out in front of me forcing me to a stop and earning a glare. "What the fuck do you think you're doing?"

"Ah, going to see my dad. Now unless you want to lose that fucking arm, you'll drop it and step the fuck aside." I don't wait for a response as I shove his arm away and make my way toward the gates. I spot Cronos out of the corner of my eye making his way toward us, this should go down well. Me turning up with the Argyros twins is going to piss my dad off, fucking winning. As we near the gate I spot the blacked out Range Rover but it isn't the sight of the car that has me smiling, it's the sight of my dad holding the security guard against the iron gates by his throat.

"Open the fucking gates now before I snap your neck!" Dad roars, bringing a smile to my face.

"And you say I have anger issues." At the sound of my voice, Dad drops the guard and shifts so he can see me through the bars of the gate. He smiles at the sight of me until he darts his gaze over my shoulder and spots the twins behind me. Anger sparks to life in his blue eyes. I come to a stop a foot away from the gate and smirk at my old man.

He keeps his gaze on the twins who stop behind as he speaks. "Real fucking funny, London, get rid of them now."

"Dad, they're not my toys," I say in my best Mom-like voice. He lazily brings his gaze to me and quirks a brow.

"Bullshit."

I drop my mouth open in mock shock. "Dad, I swear I did not force them through violence to be here. I promise I haven't hurt them." Both boys behind me scoff but I ignore them. "Okay, maybe I hurt one of them but I didn't force the other, I swear." I can see the disbelief in his gaze but say nothing. I know he's proud of me for gaining an in with the twins.

"We need to talk... alone... send your little boy toys away." I spin around to shoo the boys away but Artemis is already glaring at me.

"I fucking dare you to try it, London." I roll my lips over my teeth to keep from smiling. He can see the challenge in my eyes and opens his mouth to argue but Dad's outburst draws our attention back to him.

"You want me to break your fucking neck?" I cringe. Dad looks fucking furious and it's then that I realize he just heard how Artemis spoke to me. He is supposed to be the headmaster and not some guy who is comfortable enough to speak to me like that. My attention is once again snagged when the passenger door opens followed by the back door and Aunt Sin and Uncle Chaos climb out, making their way over to flank my father on either side.

Here they are, the feared *Memento Mori*. Unlike most families who have one don, my father doesn't. My aunt and uncle allow him to take the lead on things but the truth is, the three of them are all Don's, they are equal.

"*I* dare you to speak to her like that again and I'll send your father your fucking tongue for shits and giggles." I beam at my aunt, she is fucking bad ass! I want to be her when I grow up.

"Open the gates," comes from Uncle Chaos. I don't meet

his gaze, inside finding my shoes more interesting. Our relationship is rocky at best, I mean if you can call coexisting a relationship.

"You are not permitted to enter school grounds as per *your* rules," Artemis says in a tone reeking of authority as he comes to stand beside me. I don't miss the way my dad is watching his every move and he just made a bold fucking one by standing next to me, like we are a united front.

"London, get your shit, you're coming with us," Dad demands.

"I get to leave here?"

"She isn't going anywhere," Artemis and I both answer at the same time. I spin to face the fucker who thinks he can speak for me, ignoring everyone as I focus on him.

"Ah, excuse me?" He lazily lulls his head to the side to stare down his fucking nose at me.

"You aren't leaving," he says as if he can control what the fuck I do.

"You don't get to tell me what the fuck I can and can't do, asshole," I snap.

He turns to face me fully, his eyes burn with rage and I rise to the challenge. "Leave and you will regret it." I ignore the threats of my family as I speak directly to this bastard.

"Try and stop me and you will see the wrath every motherfucker here fears." I keep my focus on him as I ask my dad, "Am I leaving for good?"

"No," he clips out. I keep my annoyance from showing that I'm stuck here from showing.

"See you tonight pretty boy." I shoot him a wink before I turn toward my dad and grip the bars of the gate ready to climb the fucker, but an arm bands around my waist and I'm hurled back. I throw my head back and relish in the hiss that comes from the ballsy bastard knowing I hurt him. I draw my arm back ready to elbow him right in his stitches but freeze at the sound of three guns cocking.

"I got a clear shot," Aunt Sin says.

"I got the other in my scope," Uncle Chaos adds as Cronos comes to stand beside his brother.

"You willing to start a war you can't win, boy?" Dad says in a tone filled with unfiltered hatred.

"You willing to watch your entire family die if you pull that trigger?" Artemis counters. Now that was too fucking far, I elbow the bastard and yank out of his hold before landing a hit to his stomach and take pleasure in the sight of him doubling over before making a break for it. I scale the gate in seconds and land next to my aunt.

"London!" he roars. I ignore him as I head to the car knowing my dad and the others will follow. "See you soon, Omorfia." I shoot him the middle finger over my shoulder as I climb in the back. I peer between the seats, unable to hear whatever my dad is saying to the twins but I know whatever it is, it's not good judging by the look on Cronos's face.

Chapter Thirteen

Artemis

She is going to fucking regret this!

"You think you have a hold over her?" Royal taunts. I push to my feet and remain silent. The fucker smiles but it's a cunning type of smile. "You think you can use her to get to me and my father, think again. My daughter will chew you the fuck up and spit you out before you even know what the fuck happened."

"Hmm, your daughter is pretty good at swallowing, not spitting." The sharp intake of breath from my side is all I need to know that Cronos is fucking fuming I let that slip. I ignore the promises of Royal and his cousins threatening my life as I turn and stalk toward the garage with my brother hot on my heels. I'm so full of shit and didn't mean what I said but I couldn't just stand there and take his bullshit. I can feel the rage wafting off Cronos but he says nothing, there are too many students around and he won't allow anyone to see us fight, we must always show a united front out in the public eye or risk the wrath of Costa. The moment we enter the garage I head for my new car, needing to get the fuck out of here but he grips my arm and spins me around. I expected that but what I didn't expect was for him to throw a punch that sends me stumbling back into my car.

"You son of a bitch!" He shouts.

I wipe the blood from the corner of my mouth and push off the car. "Don't call our mother a bitch."

"You think this is a fucking joke? They could end us."

Now, my anger bursts through me at his double standards. "You tried to end us by giving her the fucking books!" I scream in his face. He doesn't seem surprised and that is all I needed to prove that my suspicion was right. "If she recites the history at the cove, she could win. You want our brothers to fucking die?"

"Fuck you! You don't give a shit about us, you just want his fucking spot."

"You have no fucking idea—"

"Then tell me!"

Before I can stop myself, the truth burst from my lips. "He plans to kill the four of you before the end of the trials!"

Cronos's eyes widen and guilt churns inside me. "He never wanted us to win the trials, did he?"

I shake my head. "If you win, he loses his spot."

"Why didn't you complete the trials?"

I open my mouth and close it twice before I finally speak. "I couldn't do that to you—"

"Bullshit!" He roars before he begins to pace, pausing every couple seconds to glare at me. "If taking over meant ending him, then you would have done it, no matter how much it would have hurt me you would have done it to save the triplets." I drop my gaze to the floor unable to answer, if he knew why I let her die he would blame himself. "Artemis?" At the broken sound of his voice I slowly lift my gaze to his and when I see the shattered look in his eyes, it flays me open.

He knows.

"I couldn't... I had to make a choice, I'm so fucking sorry–" He raises his hand, cutting me off, pain is pulsing inside me.

"Aida was killed because Costa planned to kill the triplets if you beat the trial, wasn't she?"

"Before the final trial he told me if I succeeded in saving one brother I would lose three. I didn't know what he meant until we entered that room and I saw Aida. He had three men at the house ready to take out the triplets if I completed the trial." Pain is evident on his face but the sight that kills me inside is the sight of the unshed tears in his eyes. "I never meant to hurt you—"

"The scars on your body, they aren't from underground fights, are they?" I drop my gaze to the floor again. I've always told Cronos that I fight to relieve myself of some of the anger not wanting him to know the extent of our fathers sickness. Don't get me wrong, he has beaten all of us but not to the extent he does me. "Answer me."

I snap my gaze back to his locking down all my emotions. "I'm the selfish brother who only cares about himself and stealing the power of our father. It's better you keep that view of me, it will fuel your need to win these trials."

"Horse shit! Don't fucking lie to me, he did that shit to you, didn't he?"

"Stop fucking asking questions you don't want to know the answers to!" I roar. "You blame me for Aida's death and I'm sorry for that, but I can't change it. I can change the outcome of this trial."

"What did you do?" I say nothing as I climb in my car and get the fuck out of there.

Breaking her will save them. I keep repeating that mantra in my head all day. As I enter the restaurant that is empty except for the families at the back, the sound of my approach has all their gazes lift to me. Bishop, Royal, King, Chaos, Chanel, Vincent, Knight, Gage, Rook and the bane of my existence London sits opposite Costa and my brother's.

"Nice of you to join us, Son," Costa says in a tone that passes as fatherly but I hear the undercurrent of his threat. I claim the empty seat across from London who sits between her father and grandfather, looking like the cold hearted badass that she is. "This is my eldest son and heir, Artemis." I say nothing as I keep my gaze on her. She stares right back giving nothing away.

"Unless your heir wants me to kill him now, he'll stop staring at my granddaughter," Bishop grits out, the fucker is intimidating. I've never met any of them in the flesh before, only heard stories and seen pictures but those don't do them justice.

Costa laughs. "The girl is beautiful, can you blame him?" My upper lip twitches in anger at him speaking about her like that. The slight frown on her face tells me she can sense my anger.

London snaps her gaze to my father. "The girl has a name, use it." The cold tone of her voice has pride sparking inside me but I snuff that shit out, this girl is nothing to me but a pawn to be turned.

I can feel Costa simmering beside me but he masks it with a fake laugh. "Forgive me, London." Hearing her name from his lips has me clenching my fists.

"What's it going to take to get her out of the trials?" Royal asks, I can feel him glaring at me, but I keep my gaze on his daughter. Before Costa can reply, Ian, Knox, Andreas and Karl enter the restaurant drawing all our attention to the head of the table. I spy the Murdochs out of the corner of my eye to see them with a surprised look on their faces.

"Why are you all here?" King says, two guards bring over chairs for the newcomers who don't answer until they claim their seats and Knox is the one who answers.

"Given the circumstances of this situation we thought it better we be present to mediate this situation." He shifts his gaze from King to Chanel. "Given some of you seem to fire first and ask questions later." Chanel smirks but says nothing, I've heard rumors about her and her ruthlessness.

"Unless you want that rumor to become a reality, I suggest we get back to discussing my niece no longer being in these trials." London bites down on her lip to keep from smiling at her Aunt's taunt.

"There is no way out," Costa states.

"The fuck do you mean?" Royal snaps.

"She killed the rabbit, she must take part in the trials, it's our law—"

London cuts Costa off. "The bastard ran in front of *my* car, it wasn't intentional like you're making it out to be." She keeps her hateful glare pointed at my father. I see Costa's jaw ticking at her blatant disrespect and it fucking gives me satisfaction seeing her push him.

"It's the law, you will participate in these trials regardless of what you or your family wishes."

"Name your price," Bishop counters, earning a scoff from my father.

"There is no price," Costa rebukes.

"So, you want me to do these fucking trials against four of your sons?"

Costa smirks at London. "Yes."

The evil glint in her eyes has me tensing. "Hm, well if I have to battle against four Argyros, I think it only fair that I get a little help of my own."

"It doesn't work like that," Costa counters.

"I don't give a shit. You plan to watch me fail so you can insight the wrath of my family." At her declaration my eyes widen, how the fuck did she put that together on her own? "You will not use my demise as a way to wage a war against my family."

Costa keeps his tone calm as he replies, "There will be no war, you compete the same as my sons."

"With four to one odds, I'm sure I'll win." The sarcasm in her voice is noted by all but no one comments. I cut a glance to Cronos to see him dropping his chin to his chest to conceal his smile.

"We want in on the trials—" Costa cuts Royal off before he can finish.

"No. The laws of our family state there are no outsiders allowed and we will not change those for you. Your daughter will take part in this on her own, if you interfere, she forfeits her place."

"Fuck you. You think I will sit back and allow my daughter to be killed if she fails? You are out of your fucking mind, Argyros. You say there will be no war but mark my words and hear me very fucking clearly, if anything happens to my daughter I will mark and hunt you." Royal flicks his gaze to me as he finishes. "And each of your sons until your entire bloodline is eradicated from this fucking world."

"Royal, calm down," Knox says but the crown prince keeps his heated glare on me.

"You doubt her abilities to excel in a challenge that is designed for male heirs and yet you plan to make her the queen of yours and your father's empires, seems contradicting to me," I say.

"He doubts nothing." I cut my gaze to London, fire burns in her green eyes. "He knows what I am capable of. I've been trained by the best and I'm far from stupid, contrary to what your father thinks. I know why he is pushing this and so do you. I love being underestimated, it makes proving all you fuckers wrong that much sweeter." She pushes back from the table and stands turning to face Costa. "Make the odds three to one with Cronos sitting out and I swear to you I will rock the foundation you think you own. Your people believe I am less because I have a pussy." All the men in her family groan and mutter beneath their breath but don't move to stop her. "Newsflash, asshole, I am heiress to the fucking US and I didn't claim that title from birth, I fucking earned it." Both her father and grandfather's eyes shine with pride. My gaze is glued to her as she storms out of the restaurant.

"Do you accept her offer?" Karl asks.

Costa turns to Cronos and eyes him for a second before answering, "Yes, the girl can have her wish but the stance on my people has not changed. Her family will not be present and cannot help her with these trials."

"But you can help your sons?" Chaos snaps, speaking for the first time.

"My sons were raised with the knowledge of these trials, it is not my problem the girl killed the rabbit and cemented her place in this." I can hear the anger in Costa's tone.

"Anything happens to that girl, I'll say fuck it to this peace treaty between the families and kill you all," Chaos vows before shoving away from the table and storming out with his own father chasing after him. Costa turns to the heads of the other families.

"I cannot change the nature of these trials, do I have your backing that if the girl should fall while competing that you will stand by me if the *Memento Mori* and Murdoch mafia seek vengeance for her death?" The four men look torn but the nature of the agreement they all settled upon forces them to agree with my father.

"Before this comes to a close, I want you to know one thing." Costa drags his gaze to Chanel, the disgust in his eyes is clear, he hates that two women were present here at this meeting. "Keep doubting her, keep planning to go to war with my family because I promise you this," she tears her gaze from him to look at me with a cunning smile on her face, "the only one getting *fucked*..." my eyes widen at her innuendo, "here is you. She is already three steps ahead and planning her rise. *Never* underestimate her because it will be your greatest mistake."

"You put too much faith in the girl," Costa grits out.

"F.E.A.R can have two meanings, forget everything and run or face everything and rise," Bishop says. I frown and watch as they all climb to their feet, but before they can leave I ask,

"What does that mean?" Bishop smirks.

"Which one do you think my granddaughter will choose?" He doesn't wait for a reply as he leads his family out. When we are alone with the four heads of the family, Costa says,

"They will attack if she dies."

"If her death is from the trials we will stand by you," Costa smiles at Knox's reply.

"But, if we find out you had anything to do with the cause of her death to insight the wrath of her family, we will not intervene when they come for you," Andreas says in a cold tone.

For the first time, I see how much power her family truly wields.

Chapter Fourteen

London

I stand outside the school gates with my dad and grandpa, neither of us have said a word since we left the meeting. I know they are worried, but they shouldn't be, I know what I'm doing and I can hold my own against these boys. I had to make sure Cronos wasn't a part of the trials, I can deal with hurting those three little fucks but not him.

"London—"

"Dad, don't." He clamps his mouth closed and bows his head.

"He is right to worry," Grandpa says as he places a hand atop my shoulder. He always has this effect on me where a simple touch or a look calms me which is why I find myself softening. "What you face is something we have no idea about. I have no information about the trials, nor does your father."

I smirk at my grandfather. "You both don't, but I do,

Grandpa." They both exchange a look before turning back to me.

"How?" Dad asks.

I pin him with a disapproving look. "Mom would be so ashamed of you right now." Grandpa snickers while my dad tries to mask his annoyance but fails when his face turns red.

"Don't be a dick, tell me how you know," he snaps.

"I made a deal with the headmaster. I stitched him up and he told me about the trials." Both of them frown and share another look.

"What do you mean stitched him up, sweetheart?" Dad snorts at my pet name from Grandpa. He says Grandpa is going senile and that's the only reason he thinks I'm sweet.

"He came back here, cut up and beaten. I helped him so he helped me, end of story," I answer.

"Bullshit, since when do you ever let someone walk away without a broken nose or split lip for speaking to you the way he did today?" Of course Dad had to pick up on that, didn't he!

"I'm trying to establish an alliance here and the only way to do that is through them. If I have to bite my tongue to do it and keep my hands to myself, so be it." I can tell Dad isn't buying the bullshit I'm selling, but I'll never admit to the fact that I've slept with the enemy, he would kill Artemis and start a fucking war. Then he would kill me, only to bring me back to life to clean up the fucking mess!

"You can try and spin this story any way you want but I know you're lying." I keep my expression neutral and try to look bored with this line of questioning from my dad. "What the fuck does he have over you?"

"Nothing!" I shout, getting fucking pissed off that he isn't letting this go.

"Fine, if you won't tell me I will find someone who will." I snort.

"Good luck with that one, old man." His eyes spark with outrage at my nickname for him but he says nothing as Grandpa shakes with silent laughter.

"Oh, sweet girl, you are the best karma I could have ever wished for. That ungrateful fuck has met his match in you and I am so grateful for that." I shoot Grandpa a wink before wrapping my arms around him. He rests his head atop my own and sighs before saying low enough for only me to hear. "That boy never took his eyes off you, there is something happening and it is more than what you are saying." I remain still and fight to not tense, if I do he will know I'm screwing the headmaster. Grandpa releases me and places a kiss to the top of my head before getting in the car, leaving me and my dad alone. The tension between us is strong, he knows I'm hiding shit and it pisses him off when I leave him in the dark, but this is something I can't confide in my dad about.

"You know I will figure out what you are hiding." It's not a statement, just a fact.

"Dad, I'm eighteen–"

He scoffs, cutting me off. "I said the same thing to my own father. Want to know something I have never told another living soul, not even Chaos or Sin?" My eyes widen and I lean in closer.

"Yes!" The excitement in my tone is clear.

He flicks his gaze back to the car where Grandpa sits for a second before turning back to me. "I thought I never needed my father, I had something to prove and wanted to show the world that I could outdo Bishop Murdoch." He smiles sadly and shakes his head. "London, I was wrong." My brows leap to my hairline, hearing him admit he is wrong is as rare as a solar eclipse. "I didn't need to outdo my dad. I didn't need to prove anything to him or anyone else because he always knew I was good enough. I just had to believe that myself."

"What are you trying to say?" I ask hesitantly. He places both his hands atop my shoulders and bends until we are eye level.

"You never have to worry about proving yourself. I *know* you are good enough and can lead our family but you just need to learn to think like a leader and not a soldier." He snorts as if I'm missing a private joke or something, but I don't call him on it. "If this fucker tries anything and I mean *anything*, you take Artemis Argyros down and I swear on my love for your mother the entirety of the *Memento Mori* and the Murdoch Mafia will stand behind you."

"Dad–"

"You are our queen, our future and I will never let anyone hurt my only child. Make no mistake, London, I know people question you because of your blood but hear me now. I knew I had a lot of catching up to do when your mother brought you home. You don't have my eyes or smile." An ache begins to form in my chest as he brings my greatest insecurity to life. "But what you do have, is my heart." I feel my bottom lip tremble slightly and I bite down to keep from showing any emotion. "I love Erika more than anything in this fucking world, but I love you more. You are mine."

I bury my face in his chest and lock my arms around him, he holds me close and places a kiss to the top of my head. "I love you, Dad," I mumble.

"I love you more. No DNA test will ever tell me you aren't mine, never doubt my love for you, London, because I would give everything I worked my entire life for up for you in the blink of an eye. Fuck Costa, I will be with you through these trials, let me help you."

I pull back and stare into his eyes, the plea I see in the depths of his gaze steals my breath. He's letting me see everything he is feeling and that is something he has never done before.

"Okay." He beams down at me but this whole emotional shit is fucking with me so I have to bring us back to normal ground. "So I shouldn't sleep with him to get what I want?" He leaps back as if I burned him and scowls down at me.

"Why do you have to ruin every fucking good moment?" Laughter bursts out of me. "Touch the cunt and see what I do to him," he snaps.

"But, he could become addicted if you get my drift."

Horror splays across his face. "Jesus Christ, the moment you finish here I'm sending your ass to a convent, you're becoming a fucking nun!" He turns away, heading for the car but I call out.

"I've always dreamed of doing a priest and bringing him to the dark side!"

"You'd never get to the pearly gates, God doesn't accept demons into his kingdom," he calls back before climbing inside the car.

Feeling drained and ready for a good night's rest now that I've showered, I make my way back into my room only to be greeted by the sight of Cronos and Artemis standing in it. I ignore Artemis's gaze on my towel-covered body and make my way to my dresser, giving them my back. Just to piss him off, I drop the towel when I find a shirt.

"Shut your fucking eyes!" he shouts. I fight the smile from breaking free as I yank the shirt on. I can feel him standing behind me but don't acknowledge his presence. As I fish out a pair of panties and bend over to pull them on, he presses in closer so I can feel his cock against my ass, which I may add is hard. Once I pull my panties on I step away from him not sparing him a look as I face my bestie and smile.

"You're playing with fire, darlin'." I shoot him a wink and shrug my shoulders as I head for my bed, dismissing them—well, trying to at least. Slipping beneath the covers I roll onto my side facing Cronos and giving Artemis my back. The growl that comes from behind me has me smirking when I pat the vacant spot beside me, inviting Cronos over.

"You really want to get fucking burned don't you?" The anger in Artemis's tone is clear, but does he not realize, I don't respond well to dick bags.

"Cronos, come cuddle with me and read me a bedtime story while I dream about fucking your brother." Nos chokes on laughter as Artemis begins spewing explicits behind me.

"Cronos, get the fuck out," Artemis orders.

"No, stay," I clip out.

"Go."

"Stay." I roll over and smile wide at Artemis who looks like he is going to blow a blood vessel in his forehead. "I told you, I love this game. I play it with my dad all the time!"

The look he shoots me would have anyone bowing their heads and offering their submission but I'm not anyone so, I hold his stare. "Cronos, get the fuck out now." When his brother doesn't move after a minute he flicks his gaze to him. "I won't hurt her." I ponder his words for a moment, that is such a fucking odd thing to say but it seems to appease Nos.

"Call me if you need me, Lon." I nod but say nothing as I keep my eyes on his twin. The second the door clicks shut the room plunges into subzero temperatures.

"*Lon*?" I roll my eyes.

"Problem?" Rather than answer my question he closes the space between us. I lay here motionless just watching as he climbs on the bed and straddles my lap. Neither of us utters a word as we glare at the other. This is a power play and if he thinks he is going to beat me at the game I was born to win, then he has another thing coming.

"You are the most infuriating woman I have ever fucking met."

"Ditto, asshole."

"You think because you saved the life of my brother that you are some sort of saint?" I say nothing because the truth is, I don't care about the triplets enough to have bargained for their lives. "You saved one brother from the trials but you condemned three more to them. Do you know what he will do to them?" The anguish in his tone gives me pause. "You just issued their death warrants," he mutters.

"What the hell are you trying to say?"

He shakes his head and rolls off me, claiming the vacant side of the side of *my* bed like he fucking owns it. He just lays there staring up at the ceiling like the weight of the world is on his shoulders.

"Costa will kill them if you win. Even if they win, they are dead." I roll onto my side and prop myself up on my elbow as I stare down at him. He flicks his gaze to me and it chuffs on my nerves to admit I can see nothing but the truth in his brown eyes.

"I can't lose these trials," I answer honestly.

The sad smile that graces his face has a strange feeling swirling inside me, it almost feels like guilt.

"I know."

"Then why are you here, Artemis? I'm not going to go easy on your brothers because we slept together. If you think coming here and trying to beg—"

"I don't beg but if I recall correctly, you do." I try to play off his teasing but I can't. I can feel heat pooling in my belly and need racing through my entire being as I stare down at him. I've grown up around a lot of men but none of them has ever inspired this type of reaction from me. I even liked some of them, they were nice. Artemis, I don't like him and want to watch him burn at the stake like the witch he is but my body has other ideas. His assholeness calls to something deep inside me. It's wrong and off limits but fuck, feeling him inside me was one of the most exhilarating feelings I have ever felt in my life. I surrendered control to him at that moment. I *never* give up control to anyone, ever.

"I think I need you to refresh my memory." My words have his pupils dilating and filling with heat.

"Are you still sore?" His concern shocks me, he's made it clear he despises me as much as I do him.

"No." He eyes me warily as he reaches up and cups my cheek, searching my gaze for any sign of deceit. Using his hold on me, he pulls me toward him, giving me every chance to turn away and stop this from going further, but I don't. The moment our lips mesh together, fire explodes inside me. I swirl my tongue against his and relish in the groan that spills from him. I deepen the kiss, not knowing what's the right thing to do. I allow my body to guide me. I throw my leg over him and straddle his lap, resting my hands against his chest.

A hiss escapes him and he breaks the kiss. "Fuck."

I lean back and withdraw my touch. "What happened?" I rush to ask.

"Nothing, just tender still."

"Shit, I forgot." I attempt to climb off him but he grabs my waist and holds me in place.

"We aren't stopping this," he grinds out as he pushes me down on his hard length, drawing a gasp from me. Before I can utter a word and prepare myself, he has us flipped over and me flat on my back with him looming above me. I glare at him while he smiles. "A wee bit distracted by dick, were we?"

I scoff. "You wish, I knew you were going to do that," I lie.

"Hmm," he says, mocking me. Before I can protest, his lips are on mine, robbing me of air. Unlike last time this is different, I can't explain but this just feels... more. He continues to kiss me as he grips the hem of my shirt and draws it up, exposing me to him. I lift up and break the kiss helping him rid me of the shirt. He drinks in the sight of me beneath him in nothing but my panties. The hungry look in his eyes has me feeling... beautiful. That is not a feeling I have ever had. Everyone looks at me with respect, love or fear but they have never looked at me like I am treasured before. Leaning down, he captures one of my nipples into his mouth and a sharp cry tears from me. When he swirls his tongue, my back arches off the bed.

He switches sides and draws the same reaction from me. My body is in control right now and my mind is in the back seat. He licks a trail down my stomach and doesn't stop at my panties, pushing them to the side. His gaze flicks up to mine and without warning he buries that masterful fucking tongue inside me. Like a wanton bitch in heat I grind my pussy against his face. I have no idea what the fuck is happening right now but the feelings he is dragging out of me is downright fucking euphoric.

"Artemis?" It comes out more like a question I can't help it, I've never felt this type of need building inside me before. Sure, I've played around with myself and all that, but I've never had someone's face buried between my legs. My thighs are crushing his head but he doesn't seem to give a fuck.

"Let go, London," he growls against me before he sucks my clit into his mouth. It takes every ounce of strength I have inside me to obey his demand and let go.

I see fucking stars!

Chapter Fifteen

Artemis

She screams so fucking loud that I know without a doubt the other students on this wing would have heard her coming. Tremors rip through her like a tidal wave. My cock is demanding to be buried inside her right this second but I can't, I need to bring her down gently. The tremors slowly begin to ease as I lap her pussy, loving the fucking taste. I've never been one to enjoy the prospect of going down on a woman, but after just one taste of London, I can tell this is going to become an addiction for me. I shift and rest back on my haunches as I stare down at her, her cheeks flushed, her eyes glassy.

"That was..." I smirk loving that she is speechless.

"Just the beginning. Think you can take me?" As I knew it would, my challenge has the fog of her orgasm clearing and her focus sharpening.

"With ease." I snort, even stark naked beneath me this girl still enjoys busting my balls. I unsnap the button on my pants but she reaches out and grabs my wrist, halting my movements. Looking at her I can see a question lurking in her eyes, but I refuse to give in and ask her what's wrong so I wait. "I've never..." She clamps her mouth closed and clears her throat trying to work up the courage to ask me. I know what she wants and she thinks I will give in and save her, but seeing her so uneasy and out of her element is fucking empowering, knowing I am the one holding all the cards. "I want to try something." She doesn't wait for me to answer, she reaches for my zipper and pushes my pants down. Her hands tremble slightly as she grips the waistband of my boxers. I know what she wants to do and I also know she isn't ready for it.

"London." At the sound of my voice she jolts and cuts her gaze to me. "I get what you are trying to do but right now you aren't ready to submit to me."

"What?"

I strike forward and shove her flat on her back so I loom above her. "When I shove my cock down your throat it means you will be surrendering control to me. You aren't ready to do that right now." The relief that shines in her eyes is clear, she will never admit it but I know she is thankful I gave her a fucking out when I shouldn't have. What I should have done is asserted my dominance over her and forced her to her knees but... I couldn't do that to her.

"I'll never give up control to you," she says quietly.

"You already did the moment you let me fuck you." I don't give her a chance to answer as I smash my lips against hers, silencing any protest she may have had. She hooks her leg around my waist, drawing me in closer. I grind against her pussy, loving the soft whimper that comes from her. Unable to bear this teasing any longer, I reach between our bodies and free my cock. I shift back on my haunches, lifting her legs to rest on my shoulders as I line my cock up with her entrance. "This is going to hurt." She bites down on her lip and nods. I push inside her slowly trying to ease as much of the discomfort as I can, but I'm not small so either way this is going to hurt her. Her pussy is fucking strangling the life out of my cock. I feel a cold sweat break out across my brow as I finally sheath myself fully inside her.

"I need a second," she grits out. I can't tell what hurts her more, the fact she has to admit she is in pain or the fact I have forced my way inside her again. Remaining still inside her as she adjusts to my size is fucking killing me. Feeling her cunt clenching and unclenching has me wanting to cum already.

"I need to move," I grit out.

"Do it." I want to weep with gratefulness at her acceptance. Drawing almost all the way out before slamming back inside, she arches off the bed and screams out. I repeat the same move twice before I keep an even tempo, making sure to push as deep as I can—I want her to taste me on her fucking tonsils and remember exactly who the fuck makes her feel this good. She may be the enemy but this girl is mine to fuck. If my brother thinks she is open to other suitors, he has another fucking thing coming. "Oh, fuck, Artemis, I'm gonna come." Pride swells inside me at how responsive she is. I don't alter my thrusts or speed but my gaze is laser focused on her face, needing to see her as she comes.

I've seen plenty of women come before but none have ever looked as good as London does. Seeing this girl surrender to me and trust me enough with her body, knowing I will give her exactly what she needs, is better than winning a fucking war. Hearing my name on her lips as she shatters beneath me is the sweetest sound in the fucking world. I grit my teeth as I continue to thrust inside her, chasing my own release. At the last second I pull out of her and grip my cock in my hand, her gaze glued to my movements. She darts her tongue out to wet her lips at the sight of me jerking my cock. I roar out my release as jets of cum spurt all over London's naked body. Her eyes widen at the sight of my cum covering her stomach, tits and pussy. Before she can cuss me out, I reach down and smear my cum all over her, making sure to swipe up enough on my finger before bringing it to her lips.

"Taste me, Omorfia." She keeps her eyes on me as she tentatively opens her mouth. I push my cum covered finger inside. She wraps her lips around it and when she swirls her tongue around the digit I groan.

"Hmmm," she mewls at the taste of me as I slowly pull my finger out and run the tip along her lips. "I want you to come in my mouth next time." If she were anyone else, her declaration would shock me.

"Next time, huh?" I tease.

She narrows her eyes. "Contrary to what you think, I don't plan to let the fucking team hit it. I have an itch and you can scratch it, so yes, there will be a next time and a time after that and after that."

Why the fuck does hearing that piss me off?

"I'm not your whore, I fuck when I want, not when you say," I snap before climbing off the bed, fastening my pants and pulling my shirt on.

"Oh, did I hurt your ego?" The bitch rolls over and props her head on her hand, smiling at me.

"Nah, in order for you to hurt that, I would have to give a fuck about you and clearly I don't since I just came all over you like a cheap slut." I ignore her cursing and the promise of pain as I slam her bedroom door closed behind me and stalk toward my office, needing a fucking drink and a chance to calm the fuck down after that shit.

When I enter my office the sight of my four brothers seated adds gasoline to an already burning bridge. I just wanted one fucking minute to myself and now that isn't going to happen.

"You've got to be fucking kidding me!" Ares growls as I make my way to the liquor cart, keeping my back to them.

"Are you seriously fucking her?" I turn around and lean against the cart as I pin Apollo with a warning glare.

"He sure is." All five of us turn and face the door where London stands, looking like Lucifer's bride. She tears her glare from my brothers to face me. The angry glint in her eyes would have most men begging for forgiveness but not me, I don't owe her shit. "You think you get to just blow your fucking load and then storm out on me?"

I fight the smirk from breaking free, I got under her skin. "I had an itch and you scratched it."

Her jaw unhinges for a second before her mask of seduction slips into place. I tense in anticipation as she saunters into the room, ignoring Cronos who tries to stop her from coming to me. She doesn't stop until she stands between my legs and has her hands flat against my chest. She bats her lashes as she leans in closer and peppers open mouthed kisses to the side of my neck. My gaze darts to my brothers who all stand there with wide eyes. Cronos looks worried, not for himself but for me. When her lips brush against the shell of my ear I stiffen further.

"Get ready, pretty boy," she whispers.

My nostrils flare and my eyes lock onto Cronos's who is shaking his head like a pissed off father. "For what?" I reply in a tight tone.

She moves until her lips ghost over mine, her eyes shine with happiness—that look has ice running thorough my veins.

She places a chaste kiss to my lips before she says, "For me to fucking ruin you and your family. You just made me angry and everyone knows when I'm mad, people get hurt, so I would train those dumb fucks fast before the first trial because I am not above harming them to get back at you." Without thinking I drop the glass and clamp my hand around her throat.

"Fuck!" I shout when the bitch counters my move and grabs my dick in a vice like hold. Sweat immediately forms on my brow and my breaths come in short rapid pants. My brothers step forward to help, but I shake my head, not trusting her to not take out their defense of me on my cock.

"You ever try to lay your hands on me like that again and I will fucking rip your baby dick off and make the three pigs you call brothers eat it. I'm the big bad wolf here, Arty darling. Learn your place because it isn't above me, it's beneath me." She tightens her hold drawing another shout of pain from me before she shoves me back and storms toward the door. "Bestie, I need you to come with me." she calls out as she exits the room. Cronos smirks at me before chasing after that fucking psycho bitch!

"Did she just summon Cronos?"

"Dude, she brought Artemis to his knees!"

"I think I'm in love."

I grind my teeth and breath through the pain as I push to my feet and stumble behind my desk, dropping in my chair and shoot each of the triplets a scathing look that has the smiles on their faces disappearing.

"You three are exempt from classes. You will train with Cronos from sunup to sundown and I will attend the trainings when I can," I say.

"Why?" Ares asks.

"Because London fucking Murdoch is gunning for each of

you. Clearly she is holding a grudge after the three of you idiots tried to ambush her in the woods."

They each exchange a look before nodding their agreement. "Maybe if you fucked better and actually gave her an orgasm she wouldn't be this mad," Adonis says, the other two fuckers laugh alongside their fucking triplet as I sit here stewing in my rage.

"Get the fuck out now. You'll pay for that comment tomorrow."

Ares snorts. "Cronos isn't going to work us hard," he says smugly.

I push to my feet and smile wide. "You will be wishing I was laid up in bed giving her orgasm after orgasm tomorrow."

"Eww, no I wouldn't," Apollo snaps in disgust.

"Oh, but you will because I will be taking your training tomorrow, not Cronos." The three of them pale and begin to shout apologies and promises of not meaning what they said. I ignore the assholes as I leave the room, ready to call it a fucking night. Spending an hour with London drained me, no pun intended there.

"Again you lazy sacks of shit!" I shout, the triplets groan as they push to their feet looking like they are about to pass out. Ares has already thrown up. Adonis cried but refuses to admit it was tears rolling down his cheeks, he says it was sweat. Apollo has threatened to call the council because headmasters can't treat students like this. All that earned them was another round of laps and fifty burpees.

"We need a break!" Ares shouts as he hunches over. Adonis

sways on his feet. Apollo is trying not to show pain or exhaustion but the way his eyes keep twitching and his legs keep trembling shows me he is going to crumble soon.

"A break?" I say calmly, the three of them face me looking uneasy at how calm I am.

"Yes, we need five minutes. We've been out here for hours!" Apollo says. I purse my lips and nod. I peel my shirt over my head and ignore the way their eyes drop to my new scars, guilt is written across all their faces. They suspect how I get them but I never confirm it, I never will either.

"Two minutes, then you three are coming at me."

"Artemis, we have been doing this all day, man. School is finished and you've proven your point. We were assholes and we are sorry for mocking you about tapping the heiress," Ares tries to appeal to me as their brother and not as their trainer.

"You three need to learn discipline and you won't learn that without going through this so stop your bitching and take your two minutes." They moan and mutter beneath their breath about me being an asshole but I pay them no mind as my attention is snagged by the figure across the quad leaning against the building with her arms crossed over her chest and my twin at her back. The sight of them so close and looking comfortable with each other grates on my fucking nerves. I push that feeling away and force my mind to clear and prepare for the triplets. I know London is in a foul mood, I left her in my office to go over all the Greek history books Cronos stole for her. He still refuses to tell me how he got it.

Three hours later when the sun had set, I finally let the triplets go. They looked like shit and dead on their feet. I hope this is a lesson they will remember because they are going to need to up their game if they wish to outsmart the girl who has been watching us spar for the afternoon. I snatch my hoodie off the ground and ignore her presence as I head inside to welcome the new nurse. I can feel her following me but don't react to her presence, knowing it will piss her off more. As I enter the school, I smile to myself when I hear her growl behind me, I can already tell that London Murdoch isn't used to not getting her way or being told *no*. She is clearly used to getting what she wants, when she wants.

I round the corner and pass my office heading for the nurses office. I push through the door and make a show of stepping to the side so London doesn't crash into my back. "You pompous prick, you knew I was—" I cut off her bullshit angry rant.

"Shut your mouth." Her eyes blaze with indignation. "I'm the headmaster of this school and you behave accordingly or serve the remainder of the year in after school detention." A frown mars her face, confused as fuck as to what I'm saying until a throat clears. She swings around to the face the source and her face slackens.

"Aun–."

The nurse cuts off whatever London was about to say and reaches her hand out to her to shake it. "I'm Max Kingsley, the new nurse at Blackwood Academy, nice to meet you..."

Chapter Sixteen

London

I quickly snap my mouth closed and clear my throat before placing my hand in hers. "London, I'm London Murdoch." Her green eyes shine with mirth as she pushes her lips to the side and nods before releasing me and turning to Artemis. Her features harden as she stares down the headmaster.

She holds her hand out to him and forces a smile to her face. "Max Kingsley," she states in a no nonsense tone. It doesn't escape Artemis's attention how she went from kind and sweet when speaking to me and cold and downright scary with him.

"Artemis Argyros, headmaster," he states like an arrogant bastard. "I hope you find everything to your liking." He drops her hand and takes a step back, keeping both of us in his sight.

"Yes, everything seems to be in order," Max clips out. Silence encases the room, making the awkward tension almost visible between the three of us. Me? I refuse to break the silence because watching Artemis look so out of place and uneasy is fucking beautiful to see. After having to endure the sight of him shirtless and beating the shit out of his dumbass brothers all afternoon I am slightly on... edge. As much as I hate the bastard, I need him to do that thing he does with his tongue again because I know for a fact, finger fucking my own pussy just isn't going to cut it after knowing what sinful things he can do with his mouth.

"Right, well I have a job for you now if you don't mind?" Max nods and waits for him to continue. A frown forms on my face as he turns his attention to me and smiles as he speaks. "London has been participating in some extracurricular activities in her spare time and needs some birth control."

Mother fucking cock sucking son of a cunt!

I stand here gaping at the asswipe as he smiles triumphantly. Max responds without missing a beat. "Of course, I'll have to run some test to make sure she hasn't contracted any sexually transmitted diseases first." He snaps his head toward her so fast, he stumbles. The horrified look on his face has me fighting back laughter.

"What?" he screeches.

"I mean, I think that might be for the best because the guy I have been sleeping with does look like the type to have gonorrhea." Artemis splutters and clenches his fists at his sides. He opens his mouth to argue but I smile brightly at him and push on. "Thank you so much for bringing me here, *Headmaster*, you must have a lot of work to do and Nurse Kingsley needs me to drop my pants and get my pussy out. Can't have the headmaster of this fine establishment seeing me naked now, can we?" If this was a cartoon movie, steam would be billowing out of his ears. He's red-faced and grinding his teeth so fucking hard I think he may actually crack them.

"I want you in my office as soon as you are done," he forces out through clenched teeth and then stomps his grumpy ass out of here like a toddler. He even makes it a point to slam the door closed behind him. Within a second of the door closing Max and I keel over and burst into laughter. The moment our laughter cuts off I rush forward and wrap my arms around her, holding her tight. She pushes me back and cups my cheeks in her hands.

"Are you okay? Are you mad? I swear if I had a choice I would have given you the heads up!" I bat her hands away and latch onto her again. She chuckles and returns my embrace. "I missed you too."

"I could never be pissed at you," I say.

She releases and takes a step back smiling. "God, I missed you so freaking much."

"Why are you here?" The smile slowly fades from her face and a look of regret clouds her features.

"I'm here to help you train and be by your side through the trials."

"He forced you here, didn't he?" The clipped tone of my voice has her sighing.

"He's your father, he loves you and is just worried—"

"Aunt Meelz, I can look after myself!" I defend. She purses her lips and quirks a brow, giving me her best stern look.

"Coming from the girl who rang me to tell me she is sleeping with her headmaster who was just in here demanding birth control for *my* niece."

I cringe. "He didn't say that." I shoot her a toothy grin, she scoffs and shoots me a knowing look.

"I doubt he would be sleeping with anyone else."

Now I scoff. "How would you know that?"

"You would murder the other woman he is screwing," she deadpans.

"You know me too well," I say sweetly.

She snorts. "Well, since I am now the nurse, I can prescribe you birth control without your father finding out–"

"Thank you!"

"Don't thank me yet." I deflate. "I won't say anything to him, nor will Chanel but Royal always has a way of finding things out."

"He does not."

"London, he will find out and when he does, I hope you are prepared to bury your new boyfriend."

I cringe and stumble back a step. "Never say that. He is so not my boyfriend and never will be."

She pushes her lips to the side and pins me with her best you're full of shit look. "He may not be your boyfriend but you clearly have feelings for him."

"Do not!"

"I am not playing that game with you." I laugh and shoot her a wink. "Just be careful okay."

"Your concern is noted but I don't need it, he means nothing to me."

"Yeah, denial clearly runs deep in this family," she mumbles as she turns away and heads for her computer in the corner. Forty minutes later I am leaving her office with the promise to keep my aunt's identity a secret. Out of everyone in this family, she is the only one who has a whole other life under a fake name, so it makes sense dad sent her here. I'll never admit it but I am glad to have her here. I drag my feet the whole way to Artemis's office. I want to flee to my room but the urge to force him to his knees and ride his face is too fucking strong for me to deny. I burst through his office door without knocking, acting like I own the place.

"Honey, I'm here..." I snap my mouth shut at the sight of a blonde bimbo in a tight little black dress perched on the edge of his desk. They snap their heads toward me and their laughter cuts off. Unfiltered rage burns inside me at the sight of the bitch. Artemis climbs to his feet and moves to round his desk but the cunt darts her arm out and places it on his fucking chest halting his movements. Before I can even think, I pull the dagger from the side of my boot and grip the blade ready to hurl it at that bitch, but Artemis darts in front of her with his arm out wide.

"London, drop the fucking knife!" I shift to the side to get a better shot but he moves with me.

"Unless you want a fucking blade in your skull, I suggest you move so I can kill your whore." I spy Cronos and the triplets entering the room from the corner of my eye. The four of them don't seem worried, they all look like they are on the verge of laughter.

"Weapons are forbidden on the school grounds!"

I scoff. "Fuck you, asshole, don't try to play the headmaster card now after you've already eaten me out." The three idiots choke on their laughter while Artemis turns a bright shade of red from his anger. "Move now," I demand as I step forward ready to slit that bitches throat.

Artemis actually looks worried now, he should be because I plan to kill him next. He darts his gaze to Cronos and implores him with a look. "Cronos, now isn't the fucking time to let your hatred for Blake overpower you." I close the space between us, Artemis stiffens when I brush up against him.

"Baby, are you worried I'm going to hurt you or your little tramp?" I purr. His gaze turns ravenous and heat swirls in my gut but I ignore it and focus on my task when he grabs my waist. I tilt my head to the side exposing my neck and just like that I have him eating out of the palm of my hand at my fake show of submission. The second his mouth latches onto the side of my neck, I shove him to the side and lurch forward burying my blade in the top of the blonde bitches thigh. Her scream pierces the air as Artemis wraps his arm around my waist and yanks me back against him. "You like that, you fucking whore?" I scream, as he continues to drag me backward. "Might want to get that dirty snatch checked, babe, our boy over here has the clap."

"Shut the fuck up, London!" Artemis growls from behind. I slam my elbow into his side then throw my head back. He shouts in pain from the force of my headbutt. I maneuver out of his hold. He tries for me again but I dodge him and land a roundhouse kick to his chin that has him staggering to the side and gripping the bookshelves to keep on his feet.

"You stay the fuck away from me, don't you ever touch me again," I scream as I race from the room, ignoring the screams of the blonde and the shouts of the others. I push through the school doors, needing to get the fuck out of here. I hear footsteps behind me, so I spin around ready to go another round with my headmaster but freeze when I see it's Cronos. He doesn't stop moving until he is directly in front of me. He reaches out and cups my cheek. The tenderness in his eyes and touch has a strange feeling brewing inside me, it almost feels like... holy fuck, was I jealous of the blonde?

"Come on, Lon," he says as he grabs my hand and drags me toward the garage on the other side of the school. I don't question him because as crazy as it sounds, I trust Cronos.

Nos brought me to a hidden lake with a small wooden jetty. There's nothing out here aside from mountains, trees and this beautiful still lake. The stars light the evening sky, the moon is high and shines a stunning reflection off the water's surface. This place is fucking... magical for lack of a better word. The instant he ordered me out of the car and led me down here my anger and... I hate to admit but the hurt I felt disappeared at the sight of this place. We haven't spoken a single word for hours but just having him here beside me is more than enough. All my life it has just been me and my family, I've never had a friend I could talk to or depend on. All I have ever had in the way of friends is Aunt Meelz. I love Aunty Nell, I do but I also know I can't share everything with her because of her loyalty to my dad.

"I have only ever brought one person here," Nos says quietly. I turn to face him but he keeps his gaze on the water. The painful look that mars his face tells me there is a story there but it's a painful one.

"Who was she?" I ask. He lulls his head to the side with a cunning smile on his full lips.

"Who said it was a she?"

I purse my lips and pin him with a deadpan look. "There is always a *she*, only a woman can have a man sitting out here in the middle of nowhere all up in his feels."

He nods soberly and faces the water again. "Her name was Aida." It doesn't escape my attention that he said *was*. "She was fucking beautiful, too beautiful for this world." Anguish laces his tone. "She was pure and innocent, fuck she was so radiant that each time she walked into a room you couldn't help but stare. Every time I saw her she would steal the air from my lungs. I remember the first time she spoke to me, I couldn't even form a sentence or string two words together. She was my angel." He drops his gaze to his lap, his shoulders hunched forward and without thinking I shuffle closer to him and rest my head on his shoulder, offering him comfort. He wraps his arm around me and places a kiss to the top of my head, that small gesture has warmth spreading through me.

"It sounds like you loved her very much."

A whoosh of air escapes him. "I've never stopped loving her, Lon."

"What happened to Aida, Nos?" I hesitantly ask, being cautious of someone else's feelings is new to me but with Nos, I have this strange urge to protect him and never intentionally hurt him.

"I was going through the trials with Artemis, we were neck and neck through the whole thing, but on the knowledge challenge I managed to best him and won which meant he needed to complete the final trial without a single mistake in order to take over for Costa. The final trial is the one that separates the men from the boys the Godfathers say, but the truth is, it's for the sick and black hearted bastards." The anger that coats his tone seeps into my bones and my own rage for the pain that was inflicted on my friend rises inside me.

"What's the final trial?"

He ignores my question as he continues. "If Artemis completed the final trial, he would take over but what I didn't know at the time was if he won, I would die. Costa knew Artemis couldn't kill me, so he made sure that neither of us would win the trials and used Aida to do that. I was forced to watch... they fucking brutalized her and destroyed the most beautiful thing I had ever seen in this world. When it was all over, I took her out of there and tried to fix my fuck up but I knew the moment we left that room that her soul died in there and only her body remained with me." The watery tone of his voice has the need to hold him close forcing me to wrap my arms around his waist and nuzzle into his side. His hold on me tightens as if I am his anchor. "She killed herself two days later."

"Nos, I'm sorry." I'm surprised at how much I mean that. Feeling sorrow for someone else is fucking strange.

"She left a note. She blamed me for everything and wished she had never met me and honestly, I wish I never met her either. If I had left her alone she would still be alive and happy, living her life with some guy who actually deserved her and could keep her safe." In one of the boldest moves I have ever made, I shift and straddle his lap, gripping his face between my hands and forcing his gaze to mine. The sight of unshed tears in his eyes fucking kills me. He's my dark entity and I will do anything in this world to keep that haunted look from ever entering his gaze again.

"This is all your father's fault, not yours."

"That motherfucker isn't my father," he spits.

"All the greatest loves in history are designed to be painful, Nos. Most people think love should be easy and comfortable but that isn't the type of love people like us crave. We want painful, soul shattering, groundbreaking love that consumes us and drives us insane. What you shared with Aida is something that can never be replaced. She was your first love and don't you dare push me in the fucking lake for saying this but... she wasn't your greatest love, your soul breaking, death craving love."

A frown works its way across his handsome face, his hands grip my waist in a vice-like hold. "How do you know that?"

Leaning forward I rest my forehead against his. If anyone were to see us in this position it would appear like we are two lovers sharing a private moment but this is just... *us.* "Because you're still here," I whisper. "Romeo couldn't live without Juliet and vice versa. Your Juliet is out there, Nos, you just need to find her and let her break down your walls and destroy the fuck out of your heart until she owns every goddamn fucking piece of it. If it doesn't hurt then it isn't worth it."

"Is that how you feel about my brother?" The air whooshes out of me, I guess it's time to practice what I preach.

Chapter Seventeen

Artemis

"She is fucking crazy, Art!" I spin around and face Blake just as Cronos shoulders past me to go after London. I fight the urge to chase after him and tell him to fuck off and stay away from her.

"What the fuck did you expect, Blake?" I shout.

"So, we're just gonna go," Ares says but I pin the three of them with a look that has them standing taller and shutting their mouths.

"I have a fucking dagger in my leg, Artemis! She fucking stabbed me because she thinks I'm fucking you," Blake shouts.

"You still wish you were," Adonis mutters. Blake shoots him a scathing look but I ignore my brother.

"I'll take you to the nurses office and get a car to return you to your apartment," I say tiredly.

"I'll spend the night here," she fires back.

"Please do, then we can see London kill again," Ares says gleefully.

"She'd look so good covered in blood," Apollo adds.

"Fuck yes, go to Artemis's room and when Cronos brings her back, I'll send her right there," Adonis says with a wicked smile. I know what the three of them are trying to do and it isn't going to work. Blake and I used to fuck but that shit has been over for years, we're just friends now and I feel like a fucking dick that she got hurt because London can't control herself.

"Don't you three have some girl to molest?" The triplets and I stiffen, no one outside of family knows about that and rape being a trigger for our entire family after what happened, fuck.

"Take her to Max's office and get her patched up and sent home. I need to go after Cronos," I order the triplets.

"You can't leave me here. I'm fucking injured," Blake shouts.

"I'm sorry, B, my brother needs me and isn't in the right space to be alone with my girl." The moment the words leave my mouth, I regret it. The triplets eyes are wide and their smiles are fucking wider. I ignore them as I race after Cronos. The moment I break through the doors, all I see is his taillights. "Fuck!" I race to the garage and bypass my car, heading straight for my Ducati. I slam the helmet on and peel out of the garage, chasing down Cronos and London. I have a feeling he's taking her to his spot. He thinks I have no idea about that place but each night he would run away to feel closer to Aida, he would go there and I would hide in the woods. He has no idea I was ever there but I never wanted him to be alone. It's my fault why he is the way he is.

"I have only ever brought one person here." The sound of my brothers voice rouses me from my daydream. I push off the tree I was leaning against and peer around it to see him and London sitting at the end of the wooden dock. The fucking thing is so rickety and looks like it's going to break.

"Who was she?" London asks, I creep closer so I can hear them better.

"Who said it was a she?"

She looks over at him and pushes her lips to the sides. "There is always a *she*, only a woman can have a man sitting out here in the middle of nowhere all up in his feels."

"Her name was Aida." Holy fuck, is he going to tell her? Cronos has never told anyone this story, not even our brothers. I was forced to give them the cliff note version. "She was fucking beautiful, too beautiful for this world. She was pure and innocent, fuck she was so radiant that each time she walked into a room you couldn't help but stare. Every time I saw her she would steal the air from my lungs. I remember the first time she spoke to me I couldn't even form a sentence or string two words together, she was my angel." Jealousy rears its ugly head inside me when she moves toward him and they hold each other but when he places a kiss to the top of her head, it takes everything inside me to keep still and not march down and punch his teeth down his throat.

"It sounds like you loved her very much."

"I've never stopped loving her, Lon." My anger eases at his declaration.

"What happened to Aida, Nos?" she asks.

"I was going through the trials with Artemis, we were neck

and neck through the whole thing but on the knowledge challenge I managed to best him and won which meant he needed to complete the final trial without a single mistake in order to take over for Costa. The final trial is the one that separates the men from the boys the Godfathers say, but the truth is, it's for the sick and blackened hearted bastards." Shame washes over me.

"What's the final trial?"

Tension riddles me as I pray for him to keep his mouth shut and not tell her. "If Artemis completed the final trial, he would take over but what I didn't know at the time was if he won, I would die. Costa knew Artemis couldn't kill me so he made sure that neither of us would win the trials and used Aida to do that. I was forced to watch... they fucking brutalized her and destroyed the most beautiful thing I had ever seen in this world. When it was all over, I took her out of there and tried to fix my fuck up but I knew the moment we left that room that her soul died in there and only her body left with me. She killed herself two days later."

"Nos, I'm sorry."

"She left a note, she blamed me for everything and wished she had never met me and honestly, I wish I never met her either. If I had left her alone, she would still be alive and happy, living her life with some guy who actually deserved her and could keep her safe." My breath lodges in my throat when she straddles his lap and grips his face between her hands. My grip on the tree turns punishing as I watch on like a masochist waiting for the moment she seals her lips against his signing her death warrant. If she crosses that line with my brother, I will have no qualms in strangling the life from her.

"This is all your father's fault, not yours."

"That motherfucker isn't my father," he sneers.

"All the greatest loves in history are designed to be painful, Nos. Most people think love should be easy and comfortable but that isn't the type of love people like us crave. We want painful, soul shattering, groundbreaking love that consumes us and drives us insane. What you shared with Aida is something that can never be replaced. She was your first love and don't you dare push me in the fucking lake for saying this but... she wasn't your greatest love, your soul breaking, death craving love." His hands grip her waist and my vision blurs, I grind my teeth so fucking hard they begin to ache as I wait for my brother to betray me in the worst possible way.

"How do you know that?"

She leans her forehead against his. I will myself to turn away and not watch as she kisses my twin but I can't. I need to see her do it and watch as my brother stabs me in the fucking back like a pathetic piece of shit! "Because you're still here. Romeo couldn't live without Juliet and vice versa. Your Juliet is out there, Nos, you just need to find her and let her break down your walls and destroy the fuck out of your heart until she owns every goddamn fucking piece of it. If it doesn't hurt, then it isn't worth it."

"Is that how you feel about my brother?" My eyes snap wide at his question, my breathing accelerates. Everything she just described about love is us. No way am I in love with her or anything like that, but the fighting, the hurt, the pain and all the baggage that comes with us sleeping together is her way of seeing me worthy. Am I fucking crazy for thinking that or was this just a game to her to bag the headmaster?

"I don't know how I feel about him."

He reaches up and tucks a loose strand of hair behind her ear. Standing I watch with rapt focus as the two of them sit there looking so comfortable with each other but there is something wrong with this picture. When she's with me there's a fire that burns in her eyes but with him, she just looks... *safe*.

"But you do feel something for him, don't you?" Cronos pushes.

"If I say no will you believe me?" She tries to lighten the mood but Cronos isn't having it.

"Lon, he is a good guy and if these trials weren't a problem, then I swear you would see a different side of him."

"He's a dick and was fucking some blonde bitch!" The bitterness that coats her tone has a smile pulling at my lips.

My little demon is jealous.

"Blake wishes he was still fucking her."

London scrunches her face. "What?"

"Lon, he will never admit it but you have gotten under his skin. You make him feel and that isn't something my brother is used to."

"All he feels for me is anger and hatred."

"You're wrong, these trials are going to test his loyalty to our brothers."

"What do you mean?"

"He's going to have to choose between saving you and saving them."

"Oh please, he's going to save them and make sure I lose."

"If that were the case, darlin', he would have killed you the moment he met you like he was meant to." My phone begins to vibrate in my pocket. I fish it out to end the call and continue listening in but when I see it's Costa, I know I have to answer so I quickly dash away from them and head back to my bike.

I answer the call when I am far enough away that they won't hear me. "Yeah?"

"The trials begin tonight, get your twin and be ready for the call." He ends the call as I stand here at a loss for words, I thought we had more time. Adonis, Apollo and Ares aren't ready. I give myself a minute to sort my fucking head out before I call Cronos as I get on my bike.

"What?" he snaps.

"Get her back to school now."

"Why?"

"She needs to prepare."

"They begin tonight?"

"Yes," I clip out in annoyance.

"We'll be back in an hour." Before he can end the call I speak.

"Cronos?"

"Yeah?"

"Don't ever fucking touch my girl like that again. I'd hate to have to kill my own twin." I end the call and break every speed limit known to man as I race back to Blackwood to warn my brothers and try to prepare them for the first trial.

God help us.

I push every thought of London from my mind and focus on the need to protect my brothers, they are my main priority here and not her. She has her own family to worry about her, not me... But, they aren't here, or maybe...

I race through the side door of Blackwood that the staff use and ignore some of them sitting around eating dinner in the staff room as I head for the nurses office. I burst through the door without knocking. Max spins around and glares at me.

"Mr Argyros, I am with a patient right now, you need to wait outside." I look over her shoulder and see it's Blake who is sleeping, I grab Max's arm and drag her from her office leading her toward mine ignoring her protests. I push her inside my office and close the door behind us. "What the fuck do you think you are doing?" she shouts.

"Trying to save London's life." Her mouth snaps shut, she tries to mask her worry but I see it in her eyes.

"Who is she to you?"

"No one."

"You answered that way too quickly, you either tell me now or she is on her own."

"Why the fuck should I trust you?"

"Because she reacted to you today. London doesn't react to anyone but today she did. I could see the happiness in her eyes when she saw you. Her mask fell and I saw everything. Now, I am going to ask you again, who the fuck are you to her?" I can see the war in her eyes, she is debating if she should tell me or not so I give it one last shot. "The trials begin tonight, Miss Kingsley. I cannot protect her and save my brother's at the same time but I can swing it so I can bring the school nurse, in case of an injury."

My words seem to be her undoing. "What assurance do I have that you can keep my identity a secret and not betray me?"

"Max, I know you know that I am sleeping with a student." She purses her lips and narrows her eyes. "At any given moment you could call her father and rat me out, he would be well within his rights to kill me. The only reason I can think of why you didn't do that today is because you don't want to hurt her by killing me."

"How do you know that?"

"I overheard some of your conversation when I left today until I was called away."

She takes a deep breath and lifts her shirt, alarm riddles me until she stops at the top of her ribs showcasing a tattoo, no, not just any tattoo but the exact same one London has.

Η ελευθερία είναι δική μου.

"I believe given the horizontal dance you performed with

her that this ink work may look familiar to you?" I ignore her snark and nod.

"Why does she have the same tattoo as you?"

"Because London Murdoch is my niece." My eyes widen. "My name is Amelia Murdoch and I was sent to keep an eye on her and help her however I can through these trials."

Before I could stop it, the question burst out of me. "Why did she get that tattoo and why in Greek?"

"Because *freedom is ours for the taking*, believe it or not. London didn't want this life and nor do I but we are prisoners of our own blood. Why Greek? No idea, but now I feel like given the nature of your relationship with my niece it was cosmic if you will."

I nod. "She'll be back with my brother soon. I need to get the triplets ready. I'll come for you when the time is right." I turn to leave but she stops me with her question.

"Wait, what is the first trial?" I peer at her over my shoulder.

"Escape. She will be hunted through the woods and will need to escape her hunter before he kills her. My father wouldn't allow the first time she escaped the woods to be a trial."

"Who is the hunter, Artemis?" The edge to her voice tells me she already knows but I answer anyway.

"Me. She needs to escape me and make sure I don't find her or I'll have to kill her."

Chapter Eighteen

London

The moment we arrived back at the school grounds, I ditched Nos and raced back to my room to change and prepare for tonight. I have no idea how this all works but I know I need to be prepped and ready to go at a moment's notice. I sheath my blade inside my boot just as a knock sounds at the door. I tie my hair into a ponytail then answer it. Rolling my eyes I step aside and let Artemis in, he's changed as well. He's wearing jeans, combat boots and a black hoodie.

"What an unpleasant surprise. Come to reprimand me about stabbing your bitch?" I deadpan.

The bastard just smirks and wags his brows. "Jealousy looks good on you, my little demon."

I scoff. "I'm not your little anything, asshole."

"Oh but you are and it's about time you learned to deal with that shit because I'm not letting you run off with my brother and get that fucking close to him again!"

"You son of a bitch!"

"Hey, don't call my mom a bitch, she was a lovely woman," I growl.

"You listen to me—"

"No. You fucking listen to me, I've let you have your fun and tried to be nice but now, you will fucking submit to me, London." I lurch forward, ready to nail this motherfucker and break his nose but just as I get within striking distance, he darts to the side and I feel a sharp prick in the side of my neck. Reaching up I place my hand against the spot and spot the needle in his grasp.

"You drugged me," I say groggily.

Regret churns in his gaze. "I'm sorry, Omorfia, there is no other way but I swear, London, I will try to save you." Call me fucking deluded but I kind of believe him. When my knees give out, he darts forward and catches me, swinging my legs up to carry me bridal style. "Don't die on me, little demon," I hear him whisper before I pass out in his hold. I am getting so fucking over these twins and drugging me!

Chapter Nineteen

Artemis

She has no idea that these trials are designed to tear a person apart and separate the weak from the strong, those who are of sound mind from those clouded by self-doubt. These fucking trials are designed to break even the strongest of people, no one comes out of these unscathed. She may not break on the first or second trial but I guarantee that she will break by the end of it. Everyone gets told a cliff notes version but never the whole story of what actually transpires during the trials—nothing is off limits. If you kill another competitor you are not punished, in fact you are rewarded with a head start in the next trial.

Costa has given strict instructions on what I am to do—under no circumstances is London Murdoch to finish the trial. He knows the triplets don't have it in them to take her out. Cronos is a wildcard and listens to nothing Costa says, so that leaves me to kill her. Amelia is here with the other leaders and Costa. My father was pissed I brought someone else but I just played him off and said we needed to make sure that it looked like we did everything to save her so her family couldn't use that against us when a war started. Once I am situated in my vantage point, in one of the trees, I pull my phone from my pocket and dial Costa.

He answers on the third ring. "Is the bitch in position?"

I keep my anger in check as I answer. "She has her compass, canister of water and knife." Those are the only three things each person is allowed. The triplets will have the same as London, each of them will have a hunter on their asses. Unlike London, I put measures in place to protect them. Cronos may not listen to Costa but will listen to me. He is watching over the triplets.

"You strip the bitch?" I grind my teeth and grip my phone so fucking tight I fear I may crush it.

"Yes." His laughter grates on my fucking nerves. The triplets are fully clothed but that courtesy didn't apply to her, she is in nothing but her bra, panties and an oversized shirt of mine. That move will cost me if he finds out I gave her my shirt but fuck him, she will freeze out here before she even has a chance to make it out.

"You know the rules," he says in a curt tone. He can't say more with the others listening but I hear him loud and clear—make sure she doesn't make it out of here alive. Costa doesn't give a shit if his own sons die, it would work in his favor since Cronos and I never passed our trials, which means he gets to continue to lead. I don't bother responding and just end the call as I see her begin to stir awake. She's groggy and shivers as she slowly sits up and grips her head between her hands. It takes her a moment before she slowly lowers her hands and begins to look around, she won't be able to see much thanks to the darkness of the night.

Unlike her, I'm decked out in all tactical gear with night vision as well. It's fucking freezing out here, the wind carries an icy chill.

"Motherfucker!" she shouts as she slowly climbs to her feet unsteadily using the tree near her for support. She spots the canister, knife and compass. She collects the compass off the ground and stares down at it for a moment.

Let's see how well the Bloodhound and Hellhound trained you.

She gathers the other items and moves east, I smirk to myself. Clever girl can read a compass and she clearly knows which way to go. I wait a few minutes before I climb down and follow after her. She has until midday tomorrow to make it out of here or she loses. A part of me wishes I could help her but as the older brother to Adonis, Apollo and Ares, I can't allow her to make it out even though the idea of killing her makes me feel sick to my stomach.

I follow her for hours making sure to keep enough distance between us so she can't pick up on being followed. We're not even halfway or near it when she comes to a stop and I duck behind a tree to watch as she drops her items and starts doing jumping jacks to get her blood flowing. She has no shoes, I can see blood coating her feet but she doesn't complain. This girl is a fucking mystery, no woman has ever been deemed worthy to be a part of the Godfathers Of The Night because they are seen as weak. Women are supposed to be seen and not heard as Costa says. They cook, clean and carry our heirs, that's all they are good for.

"I'm going murder each of those cocksuckers. They have no idea who they are fucking with!" I bite my lip to keep from smiling at her outrage. I'll be honest, the sight of her in my shirt with her hair wild and in disarray, along with that angry snarl on her full lips, has my cock twitching in my cargo pants. When she finishes, she gathers her things and jogs away with me trailing after her. She descends an incline and I wait a few minutes before creeping forward to peak over the edge to make sure she is out of sight. I take one step forward, but then feel the distinct edge of her blade pressed against my back and freeze. "You're heavy on your feet, your breathing gave you away three miles back, Artemis." I raise my hands and slowly turn to face her, keeping my hands up, she looks lethal.

"You knew I was following you the whole time?" She presses the tip of the blade against my stomach and presses in closer.

"I know this may shock you but I'm not stupid. I may come off as arrogant and full of myself but one thing I have always taken seriously is my training and believe me, pretty boy, I was trained by the fucking best, so don't go easy on me because you want to fuck me." I open my mouth ready to bait her but the bitch makes her move. Before I can prepare, she shoves me backward, sending me down the incline. I grunt and growl the whole fucking way down. I feel like I'm rolling for hours but it must be mere minutes before I smack into the side of a tree with a loud grunt.

I breath through the pain and grit my teeth as I force myself to my feet ready to make my way back up there and strangle her fucking neck, but when I look up, I notice she isn't there.

"Fuck!" I roar as I take off in a sprint through the woods to track her. She may have caught me off guard that time but I won't give her a chance to do it again. My anger is riding me hard, now the idea of killing her does fucking appeal to me.

It has taken me hours of scouring the woods trying to pick up on her trail but there isn't one to be found, if it wasn't for a snapped branch a mile back I would think I was going the wrong way. She is fucking perfect at covering her trail, there isn't a single footprint. The sun is cresting the horizon. Costa has called me twice to check on my status, I ignored his calls knowing what waits for me when I get back regardless of if I kill her now or not. She was supposed to be dead hours ago, but I failed.

I drop my backpack and take a second to rest, I know she is already miles ahead of me so I may as well rehydrate and take a breather. Dropping down on the hard cold earth I sigh, Costa underestimated her and so did I. Clearly her aunt was right, Chanel warned us not to underestimate her because she would prove us wrong and she has proven that point a couple times now. When my phone vibrates in my pocket I pull it out of my pocket ready to face my father but frown when I see it's a random number. I answer.

"Who the fuck is this?" I snarl.

"Darling." I jump to my feet and dart my gaze around me at the sound of her voice.

"Little demon, how did you get a phone?" I try to sound lax and uncaring.

"Oh, well it's a funny story actually." I grab my bag and start moving whilst keeping her talking.

"Tell me about it, baby, I'm curious now."

"Well, I had this fucker tailing me from the moment I woke in the middle of the woods naked except for his shirt." I smile and hum out a laugh. "I got rid of that dead weight and took off only for some other fucker to try take me down."

"Where the fuck is he?" I snap before I can stop myself, the thought of one of the other trackers touching her sends my blood boiling.

"Baby, don't worry," she says in a mocking tone.

"Did you kill him?"

She chuckles. "Darling, you know how hot and heavy I get when you talk about murder."

I come to a halt and grit my teeth. "Either you killed the cunt for touching what is mine or I find him and make you watch as I slit his fucking throat."

"What's yours?" The joking tone of her voice is gone and replaced by anger.

"Yeah, Omorfia, what is mine."

"I'm not yours, Artemis."

"Yeah, you are."

"You're out here to kill me and make sure I never make it to the finish line."

I curse. "You pumped him for information before you killed him." It's not a question.

"I stole his clothes and map, I'm making it out of here, Artemis, and when I do, I'm killing your father."

"Don't make promises you can't keep, little demon."

"After I kill him, I'm going to kill you and make Nos the head of the Greeks. You want to stop me, then come find me, baby, because I'm a sore loser."

"I'll find you, baby, and when I do, I'm going to fuck you right before I kill you."

"Hmmmm, now that sounds like a good time, pretty boy, except there's a problem with that." I frown.

"What's that?"

"Look down." I do as she says and my eyes snap wide when I see the red laser pointed at my chest. "I didn't just steal his clothes and map, I took his rifle and started a hunt of my own."

"You gonna kill me?" I ask, then gulp loudly, my life is in her hands right now.

"Goodbye." I slam my eyes closed and wait for her to end it all, when the shot rings out I wait for the feeling of numbness to overcome me but when a thud comes from behind, I spin around to see Cooper in a crumpled heap on the ground with a hole in his forehead. The sound of footsteps behind me draws my attention. I watch as London saunters toward me in clothes way too big for her, she has her rifle cocked and aimed at me.

"You missed," I tease.

She scoffs. "I never miss, you weren't my target, pretty boy, he was," she says cockily while I frown.

"What?" She moves past me and crouches down next to Cooper, she pulls something from his ear and that's when I notice it's a com. She cleans it off on her pant leg before placing it in her own ear. "What the fuck are you doing London?"

She rises and turns to face me. "Surviving. If you want to do the same thing then I suggest you follow me because I have already taken out four men and there are more scattered throughout the woods." I stare at her in shock, shaking my head.

"There are only three men out here hunting aside from me."

"No, Artemis, there are at least a dozen more. The first fucker I took out squealed like a pig before I gutted him. From the information he supplied, you should have killed me within the first hour of me waking, they are going after your brothers now to teach you a lesson." My blood runs cold. "Pull yourself together, I don't like the little fuckers but I also won't allow your father to get what he wants, so for the next twelve hours you have my word we are on the same side." She turns to leave but I snake my hand out and grip her wrist, halting her escape. She glares up at me.

"You aren't doing this for the triplets, what's your real reason?" Her upper lip twitches, I can see she is pissed off that I saw through her mask but I know better than to believe she would do anything to help those three, she has made it clear she hates them.

"Your father has Cronos." Those four words change everything. I release her and nod. I make no complaint as she begins to jog, I keep pace with her and follow her lead, too stunned by the fact Costa knew I had Cronos out here guarding the triplets. It should take us hours to cover the ground we have but we do it in half the time. I loathe to admit it, but she is clearly in better shape than I am. The sun is shining but it does nothing to force the chill from my bones, dread churning inside me. I need to get to the triplets and then go after Cronos.

London is a couple feet in front of me when the sight of a red laser shines on her back, I don't overthink it as I leap forward and tackle her to ground just as the shot rings out. She rolls beneath me but I don't move, using my body as a shield. She grabs the handgun from my side and lifts it, a deafening shot rings out sending a high pitched ringing through my ear.

"Fuck," I roar as she pushes me off her and runs back the way we came to scout the area. I rub my ear but it does nothing to ease the ringing. I spot the body of one of Costa's men a few feet away. "Mother fucking cunt," I snarl as I punch the dirt and push to my feet. I snag the gun from the dead guy just as London comes back into view. She rushes to me and grabs my face between her hands, turning my face to the side so she can inspect my ear.

"You'll be deaf for a while but your eardrum didn't burst," she says loud enough for me to hear. I mimic her move and clasp her face between my hands and bend at the knee so we are eye level.

"You saved my life."

"Don't mention it," she says as she steps back.

"You could have saved yourself a lot of problems and let me die."

"And you could have killed me while I was knocked out but you didn't. We're even now." I stare at her for a moment before nodding stiffly.

"I would never have hurt you." I'm surprised at how much I actually mean that.

"Yeah, you would have if it meant saving your brothers and I respect that but right now, if you don't shut the fuck up and run, your brothers will be dead soon." She turns to leave but my question stops her.

"Why do you care about Cronos so much?" She keeps her back to me as she answers.

"Because he sees through the bullshit and doesn't care who I am beneath it. He's a realist and I respect that." I say nothing because what the fuck do you say to that? She hates me but continues to allow me to touch and fuck her but she loves my brother. I check my watch, it's ten in the morning, we only have two hours left to get back or she loses and... I won't be able to pull the trigger.

"London, you need to go back now." She ignores me and carries on trudging through the woods. I close the distance between us, grab her arm and yank her back. She tries to fight free but I maneuver us so she is pressed against a tree and use my body to pin her in place.

"Get the fuck off me." She sneers.

"You need to go back, follow the trail east and keep going. It will take you down the mountain. I'll go after my brothers."

She shakes her head. "I won't leave Cronos."

I cup her face between my hands. "Cronos won't be out here, he will be at the head of the trail with Costa. You need to go now, little demon. If you aren't back in time, Costa will force me to put a bullet in your head." Her features show nothing but eyes flick between mine, searching for something.

"You really don't want to kill me, do you?"

"I don't tend to fuck people I want to kill," I say, trying to lighten the mood but fail.

"And here I thought you would still be salty over me stabbing your whore." I can't help the laughter that bursts out of me. She stands here looking like she sucked on a lemon.

"Blake is not my whore."

"Blake is such a dumb fucking name for a chick."

"Just as dumb as you having a daughter and naming it Paris." Her face contorts in disgust. "Calm down, killer, it was a joke." The urge to kiss her overcomes me so I don't overthink it, I smash my lips against hers. She stiffens for a split second before she relaxes and begins to kiss me back. It's all teeth and a fight for power but she needs to learn. She may be a boss in her daily life but when it comes to sex, I will always be the one in control and calling the shots. I drop my hands and begin tearing her pants down her legs. Gripping the backs of her thighs, I lift her. She moans into my mouth when I press my cock into her, she breaks the kiss and looks me directly in the eyes as she says,

"This means nothing."

Chapter Twenty

London

I say it with enough conviction that there is no way he is able to misconstrue my meaning, this is just our bodies needing a release and nothing more.

"*This*, does mean something, little demon," He bites back before silencing me with another kiss that robs me of air. I grind against his hard length, needing friction to ease this ache he has caused inside me. Being around Artemis is like being turned on twenty-four hours a fucking day. He is toxic and no good for me. Seeing him with that blonde whore had a tsunami of rage warring inside me. All I could see was red and the need to kill her for being near him. I have never had that type of reaction before. He reaches between us and frees his cock from the confines of his cargo pants, pushes my panties to the side and rubs his length through my folds, groaning. "Fuck, you're drenched for me."

"No, not for you, for your cock." I push down onto him

trying to force him inside me but the fucker uses his size against me and presses his chest to mine to keep me still. "I'm gonna stab you."

"Tell me you want me and I'll fuck you so hard you'll forget where you begin and I end." I shake my head and open my mouth ready to tell him to fuck off but then he presses the tip of his cock against my entrance and derails my train of thought. "Say it," he growls as he pushes in further drawing a strangled moan from me. I try to fight against him and drop down but the motherfucker holds firm. "You don't get this cock inside you until you admit that you want me."

"Never," I force out, feeling proud of myself until he pulls all the way out leaving my pussy to clamp down on air. "Artemis–"

"Let go of your fucking pride and admit you want me. I can see it in your eyes, little demon. You don't stab a woman over a man you hate."

I scoff. "You do realize who I am, right? I would stab you if I was bored—" He presses inside me just enough to prove his point, the fight drains from me and I fucking give in. "Fine, I want you." The self-satisfied smirk that crosses his face makes me want to stab him in the jugular.

"About time," he says cheerfully before gripping my waist and slamming me down onto his waiting cock. I scream so fucking long and loud that he has no choice but to kiss me to mute the sound before I give away our position. God's honest truth, I would murder any fucker that tried to stop this, I need him to make me come so fucking bad that I might actually cry if some cunt tried to kill us right now. He draws almost all the way out of me before slamming back inside me. I scream into his mouth, I can feel him smiling.

I break the kiss and drag in some much needed air. I wrap

my arms around him and bury my face in the crook of his neck. An idea strikes me as he continues to fuck me so well I can already feel my orgasm cresting. I bite his neck and suck the soft salty flesh into my mouth, relishing the thought of leaving my own mark on him.

"Artemis, just like that," I moan as I throw my head back, he uses his teeth to pull my shirt down and bites on the soft flesh of my right tit, sucking it hard enough that I know it will be bruised for days. I want to tell him to stop but then he thrusts inside me and my orgasm rips through me like a tidal wave. He quickly covers my mouth with his to silence my cries of pleasure, then works me down slowly as I become dead weight in his arms.

"I want to come down your throat, let me." It isn't posed as a question when it fucking should have been but honestly, I have been so curious about the taste of him that I nod my agreement. He pulls out of me and forces me to my knees. I fucking love that he doesn't ask me for shit and demands what he wants. All my life no one has dared to demand things of me or order me around, well everyone except my father. I ignore the sticks stabbing into my knees as he pumps his cock in his hand. "Open your mouth." I obey without complaint.

He doesn't glide inside my mouth slowly, he rams his cock down my throat causing me to gag. I try to pull back but he grips my hair and holds me in place as he fucks my face like a man possessed.

"Yeah, baby, fucking your mouth feels amazing," he moans when I swirl my tongue around him. I can't stop gagging. I flick my gaze up to him and the smirk I see on his face tells me he loves that I can't take him all the way into my mouth without choking. "Fuck, Omorfia, I'm gonna come. Swallow every fucking drop of my cum or next time I'm fucking that ass over my desk." His words have heat blooming inside me, the whole forbidden aspect of what he just suggested has me clenching my thighs and wanting to defy him just so he'll honor his threat. "Fuck!" he roars out as I feel him swell inside my mouth a second before I feel his cum begin to fill my mouth leaving me no choice at all but to swallow.

Swallowing around his large girth is fucking difficult and I gag a few times but manage to swallow every last drop of him. A moan escapes me at the taste of him. He shudders and slowly pulls back. Spit drips down my chin, so I reach up to wipe it away but he swats at my hand and bends down in front of me using two of his fingers to swipe most of the mess before he shifts and moves those same two fingers to my pussy and pushes inside me. I hold his blissed out gaze as I moan. He pumps in and out as his other hand wraps around my throat forcing my head back.

"I can feel your greedy cunt clamping my fingers. You want to come don't you my little demon?"

"Yes," I say huskily.

"Beg me." My eyes widen as he shifts forward so I can see him, the dark look in his eyes shows me that he won't accept anything less than me begging and right now I need to come so fucking badly.

"Make me come, please."

"You can do better than that," he growls, then curls his fingers inside me hitting that sweet fucking spot, drawing a cry from me.

"Please, fuck me and make me come. I need you to do it." His eyes darken further.

"Tell me you need me."

"I need you!" The words blurt out before I can stop them. He presses the pad of his thumb against my clit as he continues to work his fingers in and out of me, two seconds tops and then his mouth is on mine muting my screams as I come all over his fingers. I break the kiss, needing to breathe. He pulls his fingers free and I smirk at the sight of my cum covering them. He holds my gaze as he brings them to his mouth and sucks them. My jaw unhinges and my eyes widen at the sight of him sucking my cum off his fingers.

"You taste fucking delicious," he growls when he pulls his fingers free, meanwhile I'm still stuck in a trance-like state, just staring at him. That was the hottest fucking experience of my life and the fact I got to watch him enjoy the taste of my own release has my pussy throbbing to feel him inside me again.

Greedy slut!

"Get dressed, we need to move now," he snaps, pulling me out of my stupor. Acting on autopilot I do as he says. I turn to grab the dagger I dropped on the ground and flinch at the sight of the body—I forgot all about him while I was fucking Artemis. "You're lucky I didn't use his corpse as a mattress so I could fuck you." I spin around and balk up at the cocky fucker as he stands smirking down at me. "What's wrong, baby, my cock finally silenced you?" I snort and ignore the fucker as I turn to go in search of his brothers but he darts in front of me. "You need to go the other way."

"I told you I would help you," I answer.

"Help me by not forcing me to kill you, make it back alive and you would have helped me more than you know."

"What are you going to do?"

"I need to find my brothers."

"What makes you think they aren't back there yet?" I clap back. He scrubs a hand down his face and sighs.

"If they had made it back, Costa would have alerted me." There's a hint of worry in his tone and I kind of feel bad for him but then he turns his head away and I spot the hickey on his neck and feel smug at the sight.

Put that in your fucking pipe and smoke it, Blake, you whore!

"What happens if they don't make it back?" He pulls his gaze back to me and frowns.

"Same rules apply. I'll be forced to do something I won't survive." I nod in understanding but the reality is that disgust rolls through me, not toward him but his father. How the fuck could someone create a child and then carelessly throw that away for power? Not to mention the fact he expects his other child to take the life for him. What a fucking coward.

"What happens if the four of us were to arrive back at the same time?" His face contorts and I can see the cogs of his mind turning as he thinks about what I've just said.

"I honestly don't know, no one has ever done it before." The skepticism in his tone is clear.

"Well, I guess it's time to find out, but on the next trial, they are on their own. I'm only doing this because I know Nos loves those dicks." Artemis's face morphs into one of anger and his upper lip twitches.

"Cronos isn't as fucking great as you make him out to be!" I ignore his outburst and spin on my heel heading in the direction of the triplets. I'd bet my inheritance on the fact those idiots managed to find each other but not the way out. I'm tired, hungry and dying of thirst so these dumbasses better not be far. The longer it takes for us to locate them the more antsy Artemis grows, I can feel his stress wafting off him in waves. I get him being worried about what may happen to us if we make it back after the allotted time but what are they going to do, kill the four of us and stop the trials from continuing?

For like the sixteenth time in the past twenty minutes Artemis sighs beside me and I can't take it any longer, I dart my arm out stopping his movements as I turn to him and scowl. "Would you stop that, it's not like it's your fucking life on the line here!"

His nostrils flare as he glares down at me. "No, I'll just be forced to kill you and my own flesh and fucking blood, so please, Omorfia, take your fucking time." The sarcasm in his tone pisses me off.

"What the fuck does *Omorfia* mean?" I don't know why I blurted that out but my anger seems to be riding me so hard whenever he is around that I just blurt random shit.

"It means..." He releases a loud exhale and stabs his hand through his hair clearly feeling uncomfortable. "*Beauty.*"

My heart stops.

Bellezza.

He used to call me beauty.

I will never leave you, I'll always come back.

My breaths come in short rapid pants as the last words my favorite person said to me run through my mind. I can feel myself falling but I see and hear nothing as I'm transported back to the day he left and I snuck into that fucking car thinking I was strong enough to protect him.

Havoc died that day because of me!

I killed my favorite person.

I'm not beauty, my soul is black and tainted because of the life I took, the life I stole. My cousin will never know his father because I fucked up thinking I was stronger than what I am. I cost Havoc everything. Uncle Chaos has every right to hate me, I fucked everything up.

I killed Havoc.

The ace of Diamond is no more, the *Memento Mori* lost their back bone. I ruined it, I made him leave just like everyone who ever cares about me leaves. It's only a matter of time for my family to figure out what my birth parents did, I'm not worth shit and unworthy of love.

Chapter Twenty-One

Artemis

Before she can hit the ground, I dart forward and catch her, panic is thrumming through me. Her eyes are open but unfocused as if she has gone into a trance-like state. I jolt in shock when a scream filled with so much pain tears its way out of her. I try to cover her mouth with my hand to quiet her down, when that fails I even try to kiss her but the sound continues. I can hear footsteps pounding the ground from the north and carefully lay her on the ground hating that I have to leave her unprotected for a minute as I dart behind a tree and draw my gun ready to take out any fucker who tries to touch her. I flip the safety off when I hear them closing in. London's scream dies off as they burst into the small, wooded area where she lays motionless and I dart out from behind the tree.

"Ares, Apollo, Adonis, you're alive," I breathe out as I rush the three of them pulling them all in for an awkward hug. They shove me back and mutter about me being a pussy.

"Of course we are," Adonis smugly says.

"They can't take us down," Ares inserts.

"They nearly did, you dumbasses," I snap.

"What?" Apollo asks as he looks to the other two.

"London and I have been taking them down. I don't have time to explain. We need to get the fuck back to Costa now before the time is up and he does something to Cronos."

"He has Nos?" Ares asks in shock.

I narrow my eyes. "Since when do you call him *Nos*?" He purses his lips and shrugs.

"It kind of suits him." I scoff and turn my back to them, scoop London into my arms and peer down at her. Her eyes are open and unfocused still, did she have a mental breakdown?

"What happened to her?" Apollo asks.

"I don't know, just keep moving and don't stop," I bark as I begin to lead the way back down the mountain, suddenly feeling like I can take a deep breath for the first time since this trial started knowing they are alive.

"Why are there guys out here hunting us?" Adonis asks.

I shift London in my arms as I answer him. "You knew that each of you would be hunted but Costa upped the stakes and positioned men out here to take the four of you out. They're on our tail as we speak so stay sharp and shut the fuck up." We continue on in silence, every few minutes one of them will branch off to scout around us and make sure the path is clear before rejoining us. It has pride swelling inside me that these three, although they act like idiots most of the time, did pay attention to everything I have taught them. They managed to evade their hunters and find each other out here, that was something Cronos and I couldn't even do.

"There," Apollo says, pointing toward a worn trail at the base of the mountain. I come to a stop and turn to face the three of them. Each of them looks confused but say nothing as I pass London to Ares who takes her without complaint.

"You follow that trail back—"

Adonis cuts me off. "Where the fuck are you going?"

"I can't exit with the four of you. Take her back and make sure Cronos looks after her."

"Where are you going?" Ares asks, the worry in his tone guts me.

"I'll be right behind you, do not fight what will happen. You three get in the car with Cronos and London. Do not come back for me no matter what."

"What the fuck!"

"Fuck you."

"We're not leaving you!" The three of them shout in unison. London steals my attention when she begins to stir in Ares's hold. Her head lulls to the side and when her gaze finally focuses on me she frowns, then looks around and when her gaze locks on Ares who smirks and wiggles his brows, she thrashes in his arms leaving him no choice but to release her. She lands in a crouch before quickly pushing back to her feet.

"What the fuck happened? Did you drug me again?" she shouts at me. I raise my hands as if surrendering and shake my head.

"No, but something did happen and I don't think now is the time or place to discuss this considering we have at least six men on our asses." I heard the fuckers a couple miles back trailing us.

"Well, let's go then," she snaps, clearly pissed off because she is missing some information but I would bet my testicles on the fact she wouldn't want the triplets to know she had a fucking mental breakdown.

"I'm not leaving my brother!" Adonis growls as he steps up to London, she doesn't back down and presses in closer to him.

"What the fuck are you on about?" she grits out.

"Artemis isn't coming with us," he answers. She flicks her gaze to me and studies me intensely for a minute. When her face scrunches in confusion, I breathe easier but then her features smooth out and understanding dawns in her gaze before she steps away from Adonis and moves to close the space between us. She reaches out and places her hand on my chest. I can feel my brothers gazes on us the whole time but ignore them.

"He can't know you helped, can he?" She poses it as a question for the benefit of the triplets but her and I both know that I'm fucked for helping her.

"No, you need to take them back now and make sure they don't do something stupid like come back here for me." She nods while the triplets curse me out behind her.

"You helped me, so I'll help you." I stare at her skeptically for a moment trying to gauge her meaning. That second costs me. A roar of pain rips free as I feel the blade of her knife imbedded in the side of my thigh. I drop to my knees as my brothers rush forward trying to subdue her but she fights them off. "Shut the fuck up!" she screams, silencing them.

"You fucking stabbed my brother, you bitch!" Ares yells, his hatred for her is clear in his gaze.

"He can't walk out of here uninjured, you dipshit! Me stabbing him just saved his life. Do you really think your father would have let him live if he walked out of here unscathed with the four of us?" They open their mouths to fight back but I cut in before they can.

"She's right." Their gazes swing to me. I use the tree beside me to help me to my feet. "Go with her, if you run you will make it on time, I'll follow behind." I can see the unease in their gazes. "Run, get back to Cronos. I'll come find you when I get back to Blackwood, I swear." It takes them a minute but they reluctantly nod. I turn to London next, asking her without words to protect my brothers. She doesn't owe me a thing but she is my only option right now. I can see she is still haunted by whatever the fuck happened before but she pushes past it to nod.

"You have my word."

"Run. The four of you need to make it back together." I stand here, gritting my teeth to hide the pain I'm in as I watch them run like their asses are on fire. I failed to mention that if I'm caught out here by Costa's men, I know without a doubt they are ordered to kill me so, I hobble like a cripple down the trail. I have to stop every couple steps to catch my breath, the pain is blinding and robs me of breath each time I take a step. Sweat coats my forehead, I can feel the blood trailing down my leg and soaking my boot but I try as hard as I can to ignore it. It's taken me nearly thirty minutes to get as far as I have. Granted, it's not fucking far at all and I know without a doubt that I'm about to be caught.

"You look pale." I snap my gaze up to see London jogging back toward me. I push off the tree I'm leaning against and flinch in pain.

"What the fuck are you doing here?" I snarl.

"Easy tiger," she says as she reaches my side and wraps my arm around her shoulders, taking some of my weight to help me. I feel like a prick but I lean on her more than I should, I need her help and right now she isn't mocking me about it so it's a win for me.

"Why are you here?" I ask again after a minute.

"I passed the finish line, shot your father the middle finger and made it known to who I assume are the other leaders that there was a team out here trying to kill us. Your father acted the part and said his men had gone rogue. I high tailed it out of there and came back to help."

"Why?" I ask as I force us to a stop, she huffs.

"I was hoping if the sex didn't get me an A that saving my headmaster's life would at least get me an A+." I can't help the laughter that bursts free. She shoots me a wink and not a second later joins me.

As we finally exit the woods I'm drenched in sweat and feeling dizzy and light headed. London is bearing most of my weight now, she grunts with each step and doesn't make a single complaint. There is no doubt in my mind that if she didn't come back I would have died by the hands of Costa's men or been eaten by rabid animals when I passed out. I spot a line of Escalades in the parking lot. I ignore the Godfathers as I run my gaze over the faces of people only coming to a stop when I see the four of my brothers standing off to the side with Amelia. Cronos is the first to spot us. One look at me and he sprints toward us, coming to my other side to help London. He's careful not to knock the blade that is sticking out of my leg. Amelia shouts for him to bring me to the back of the car.

When we reach the back door, London releases me and tries to step back. I reach for her but she shakes her head and darts her gaze over my shoulder, warning me that Costa and the others are watching. I release a sigh and nod stiffly as Cronos helps me into the back seat.

"Cronos, you drive and London can ride shotgun while the

others get in the back. I need to patch his leg and stabilize the knife until we get back to the clinic where I can get a better look," Amelia–Max orders. Everyone jumps into action, obeying her orders. I reach for my door but a hand darts out stopping it from closing. I turn to see Costa standing there, his eyes burn with indignation.

"Get patched up, the club is closed for the night so meet me there, we need to talk," he forces out through clenched teeth.

"He won't be going anywhere tonight," Max says from beside me. Costa doesn't spare her a glance, keeping his gaze on me.

"Don't make me wait," he snarls.

"We'd love to meet you there tonight to discuss how the trial was botched, Mr. Argyros," London says from the front seat. Costa stiffens, I can see his jaw ticking with rage so I cut in.

"I'll be there as soon as I'm done." At my agreement he steps back and slams the door closed. The only reason we are able to drive out of here still breathing is because the other Godfathers are here and he can't outright kill us in front of them, they would band together and overthrow him. I may be in pain now but I know without a doubt, I will be in even more when Costa is finished with me.

Chapter Twenty-Two

London

I sit in the chair opposite the bed Artemis currently is asleep in. Max had to remove the blade, clean the wound and stitch him up. He lost a fair amount of blood and was instructed to rest. He tried to argue and fight, so I sedated him. I know that knocking him out will make things worse for him with his father but the moment he wakes I know he will leave and go to him, only for him to come back here bloody and beaten again. He doesn't need to say it but I've pieced it together that he takes these beatings so his brothers don't have to.

I rest my forearms on my thighs and lean forward, staring at him. His long lashes would make my mother jealous. His hair is a tousled mess with leaves and other things stuck in it but even with dirt caked on his face he still looks... good. Fuck, am I more than just attracted to Artemis Argyros?

"You like him, don't you?" I push to my feet and spin

around to see my aunt standing in the doorway with a crooked smile on her face.

"No," I defend. Aunt Meelz quirks a brow as she makes her way into the room and checks over Artemis while I stand here awkwardly, suddenly feeling like a dick for being in here with him when I shouldn't be. I should be in my room trying to catch up on the shit I missed in class today. I decide it's better if I leave and just check on him later but Aunt Meelz clears her throat, halting my escape. I slowly turn to face her and hate the sight of the smile on her face.

"Why are you running away?"

I balk at her. "I'm not running."

"Fine, why are you *walking* away?"

"Because... I have things to do and he is clearly not gonna die so I'm off the hook with Dad having to find another head-master." She places her hands on her hips and cocks her head to the side.

"So, you're not in here because you're concerned for the guy you actually like, but to make sure you didn't kill the headmaster?"

I nod. "Exactly, see you got it all figured out." I try to escape again but she calls out to me.

"London." I slowly turn to face her and pin her with a bored look. "Why are you hiding it?"

"Hiding what?" I snap.

"Your feelings for him. I know you and you don't sit at anyone's bedside unless they mean something to you. So, I will ask again, why are you hiding it?"

"He calls me Omorfia," I say barely above a whisper.

"What does that—"

"Bellezza." Her eyes widen and her mouth parts on a gasp. "Yeah, he brought it all back today and I can't do that shit, not again." This time when I make my escape, I don't stop when she calls out to me. I practically run down the hallways, heading toward the entryway. I round the corner and slam to a stop when I crash into someone. Hands grip my shoulders. I dart my gaze and the moment his brown eyes collide with mine the tension that was mounting moments ago begins to ease. Whatever he sees in my eyes has him wrapping his arm around my shoulders and leading me out of the doors of the school and heading toward the garage. We ignore the looks and the whispers of the students milling about. I know they are wondering if Cronos is Artemis or not and I don't care enough to tell them the difference. Those nosey fuckers can think what they like because let's be real, it's not like it's not true. I am screwing the headmaster.

Nos doesn't say a word or pry as he drives us out of the school grounds, I know without him needing to say it where he is taking me. I haven't slept or even showered and I can't find it within myself to give a fuck. Something is happening to me and I don't know how to stop it. These feelings inside me are fucking with my head, I'm not that girl that gets caught up in her feels. When Nos finally reaches his spot, exhaustion is weighing heavy on me but I push through it and follow him down to the rickety dock where we sit side by side. He wraps his arm around my shoulders and draws me into his side. I breathe him in and instantly relax.

"Last time we were here I told you about Aida. I'm only guessing here but something tells me there was a guy in your life that broke something inside you." I keep my gaze ahead, unsure how to answer him or if I even want to. I have never spoken to anyone about this. Aunt Meelz only knows a small amount. I told her what I had to do in order to keep her off my back when my mom sent her to check on me when I went into a dark hole. I had to claw my way out of that fucking hole and swore I would never go back there, that shit nearly killed me. "I will never judge you, Lon."

A whoosh of air escapes me. "I can't," I say barely above a whisper, feeling guilty that he confided in me and trusted me enough to share his story but I can't do the same.

"If you ever need to get that shit off your chest, I'm here." I nod, a yawn escapes me. "Come on, I'll take you back." I shake my head even though my eyes begin to droop.

"A couple more minutes," I say through another yawn. He chuckles and places a kiss to the top of my head.

"I'll carry you back to the car when you fall asleep." How can I feel so at ease with him and trust him so much in a short amount of time but I'm screwing his brother? They are identical twins but I don't—I can't look at Nos the way I do Artemis because somehow they look nothing alike to me. Artemis is an enigma. He commands attention when he enters the room and carries this asshole aura with him that reels me in but Nos, his aura is dark and broken and that shit has me needing to be close to him and fix him in a way.

"Lon, it's time to wake up." I slowly blink my eyes open and frown when I realize for the second time today I am in another Argyros's arms. "I need you to open your room door, darlin'." I turn to the side and sure enough I'm met with the sight of my bedroom door. I lean forward in his hold so the retina scanner can scan my eye, the door opens with a click. Nos shoulders it open and instantly frowns. I turn my head to the side and follow his gaze to find none other than his twin brother sitting on the edge of my bed with a pissed off look on his face. It's not the angry look on his face that has me pushing away from Nos so he'll put me down, it's the bruises on his face and the blood seeping through the back of his shirt. I rush toward him and reach for his face but he flinches back and I immediately feel like a fucking asshole, I shouldn't have left him.

"Where the fuck have you been?" I ignore the bite in his tone and force myself to remain calm.

"Why did you go?" I counter, his eyes narrow. I can see he is trying to mask the pain he's in but he isn't fooling me.

"You think I get a choice?" He doesn't give me a chance to answer. "I don't get to decide shit, I was forced to be here. You think I fucking love this shit?" He's starting to lose it and right now I don't have the mental capacity to deal with his meltdown and what the fuck is going through my head.

"Get up, you need to shower and so do I." He recoils as if I have said the most outrageous thing in the world. "It's not like you haven't seen me naked before, pretty boy, get your ass up now and if you're a good boy, I might stitch those wounds on your back." He drops his gaze to his lap in shame, I don't pity him because I know if I was in his position that shit would piss me off. I turn to Cronos who is glaring holes into the side of his brother's head. I move to stand in front of him forcing him to look at me. "I need you to go and grab me the first aid kit from his office and some clothes."

"Just take him to the nurse."

"No," both Artemis and I say in unison. I shoot him a look over my shoulder, why the fuck is he avoiding the nurse?

"Please, just do what I asked." He begrudgingly nods and turns to leave but Artemis calls out to him. Nos turns to his brother and catches the keys he tosses him.

"The gold one is the master key, use that to get back in." My jaw unhinges.

"I want that key," I snap. Artemis ignores me as he climbs to his feet, flinching in pain. I can see exhaustion is weighing heavy on him. That is the only fucking reason I don't push him on using that freaking key to constantly break into my room. I lead him into the adjoining bathroom and turn the shower on. The cubicle isn't big and it will be a tight squeeze but I mean, the dude literally squeezed inside my pussy so I'm sure we can make it work.

"I'm gonna need your help." I spin around to see him struggling to remove his shirt. I help him remove it and cringe every time he grunts or hisses in pain. The moment his shirt is removed my eyes widen. Purple and black bruises cover his entire front. I move to the back and the sight of the four slices down his back has my hand shooting up to cover my mouth. "It looks worse than it feels." His tone is laced with pain, I circle around him and bite my tongue not trusting myself to speak as I unbutton his jeans and push them and his boxers down his legs. The wound on his leg is patched but blood has soaked the gauze. I slam my eyes closed at the sight of boot print bruises that litter his legs.

I push to my feet and stand before him. He reaches out and grips my face between his hands. "Why did you go?" I ask without thought.

A sad smile graces his face. "Killing him isn't as easy as you think. If I take him out then the laws state that me and my brothers will be taken out by the other leaders. I don't have a choice but to weather his punishments because I would rather it be me than them."

"If I were to win the trials, what happens to you and the brothers?" Rather than answer me he places a soft kiss to my lips then releases me as he steps into the cubicle. I strip off and follow in after him, it's a tight fit but we make it work. He hisses when the water touches the cuts on his back. I grab my loofa and gently wash the cuts. They aren't deep enough to need stitches but they will leave scars, as I was cleaning the third cut it's then that it hits me. "He cut you four times because the four of us passed the trial." It's not a question but he still answers me.

"It was meant as a reminder that I can't save them or... you." I move to stand in front of him, ducking under his arm where he has them both resting flat against the wall. His hair has flopped onto his forehead. I reach up without thought and use my fingers to brush it back, his eyes close briefly at the feeling of my touch. When his eyes open they hold a haunted look in the depths.

"I don't need you to save me, Artemis," I whisper, this moment feels so different from all the others, there are no masks in place to shield our feelings from the other.

"Yeah, you do and you won't believe me until the final trial. Believe me, London, I doubt my brothers will even pass it."

"Why do you say that?"

His eyes harden as he stares down at me. "Cronos and I failed, our rings don't hold the Anyolite ruby because we failed to complete the final trial." I fucking knew it! The rings the five of them wear mean something.

"Do I get one?"

He smiles and shakes his head. "No."

"Why not?" I huff out.

"Because we are made to wear these by our father as a constant reminder of what we lost. The triplets got theirs this year. Their rings will never be complete, Costa will make sure of that."

"How?" I push.

"He won't allow them to finish the trials," he says somberly.

"What happens when they don't pass the trials?" A shadow clouds his features.

"They are the last chance to save us all. If they win, they can spare our lives but if they fail, Costa has the right to end the five of us because we all shamed our family by failing."

"If I win, can I spare you five?" My voice is firm.

He drops his hands to my waist and pulls me flush against him, it takes me a second to realize that he wants me to hug him, I wrap my arms around, careful not to touch the cuts on his back. This feels weird, I've hugged people but not like this. I've needed comfort from someone before but this feels strangely okay... better than okay actually.

"I wish it was that simple, baby, he won't let you pass the trials."

I take a shuddering breath and speak my truth, I can't allow him to think that whatever this is between us will derail my plans.

"If you try to kill me to save them, I will fight back and kill you, Artemis, I have my own family to fight for."

He places a kiss on the top of my head. "I know, no matter who he sends after you, even if it's Cronos, you fight, London, and don't allow him to break you. Make it the fuck out of here alive and take the Greeks down. End the trials and spare the lives of all future male heirs."

Why does it feel like he is telling me he isn't going to make it out of this alive?

Chapter Twenty-Three

Artemis

Cronos dropped me off some clothes and the first aid kit. He wasn't happy about the fact London told him I would be spending the night here with her. I can tell my brother doesn't approve of my relationship with her, he also doesn't realize that I can see through his bullshit. He likes her. London patched me up and helped me dress before we fell into bed. She tried to scoot as far away from me as she could but I wasn't having that. I fixed that issue by pulling her into my side so she could rest her cheek on my bare chest and I could hold her close.

Whatever this is won't last, Costa made it clear tonight that she is to die. He wants the war with her family. Her death will cause her family to break the alliance resulting in the other families coming to his aide to take out her entire family, giving Costa the power he needs to take over the US. My brothers and I won't be alive to see that, I saw it in his eyes tonight he has something planned. If I could run away with them and never come back, I would. Deserters are chased to the ends of the earth and brought back to Mykonos to stand trial before the Godfathers, they never make it out alive. They see the trials as an honor. They love pitting all the heirs against each other and watching them kill off each family line—it's fucking sick.

"Bellezza," London whispers, pulling me from my thoughts.

"What does it mean?"

She takes a shuddering breath, I get the sense that whatever she is about to tell me is fucking important and hard for her to speak aloud.

"It means *Beauty*." My heart lurches.

I take a deep breath and force myself to ask. "Who called you Bellezza?"

She remains silent for so long I begin to think she won't answer until she finally does. "Havoc." My eyes widen but I remain silent. Havoc is the twin that died years ago. We heard the rumors that the *Memento Mori* and Murdoch Mafia went crazy, they killed federal agents, Albanians and anyone who was there the day Havoc Murdoch was murdered. His brother Chaos took out an entire family for hiding his brother's son from them. The rumors about Chaos are a fucking worry, the guy is said to be fucking ruthless and just happens to be the uncle of the girl currently wearing my shirt and tucked into my side. "He used to call me Bellezza, I was his beauty." The pain that laces her words is so thick I can feel it.

"He isn't wrong, you are beautiful," I say quietly.

"He was the first person aside from my mom to love me unconditionally. He treated me like an equal and loved me for who I am. He never pushed me away or tried to change me. He told me to embrace who I am and never change for the world, he said the world could change to fit in with me."

"He isn't wrong, you are amazing the way you are. You don't give a shit what anyone thinks about you and that is a quality a lot of women don't have."

"Is that why you're sleeping with me and not someone your own age?" I can't help the snort that breaks free.

"Yeah, something like that." She chuckles. We remain silent for a while lost in our thoughts until she speaks again.

"Do you plan to use my own dagger against me tonight?" I stiffen beneath her.

"What?" I rasp out.

She remains nestled into my side and doesn't move an inch as she speaks. "I felt it the second you gripped the handle under my pillow after we got into bed. I may lose control of my emotions when you are around but the one thing I never lose is my senses. I told you about Havoc because he is the only person who I have loved without restraint. It's the closest love I will ever know to having a sibling. If you plan to use that blade to save the lives of your brothers, make sure you kill me because if you don't, on the life of my fucking uncle, I will dismember your brothers in front of you, piece by piece and make you watch the entire ordeal."

I ignore the pain radiating throughout my body as I move so I am on top of her and nestled between her legs with the blade pressed against her throat. Her blinds are open so the moonlight casts enough light for me to see the relaxed expression on her face, she isn't even fazed that I'm holding a blade to her throat.

"All I would need to do is prod the stab wound on your thigh so your grip on the blade would loosen enough for me to disarm you and then plunge the blade into your side, your lung would collapse and you would drown in your own blood."

"I never should have allowed you to get in my head. I had

one job, to save them and it seems I can't even kill the person who holds the fate of my brothers' lives in her hands."

"What about your life?"

"My life was over the moment I agreed to serve the devil in order for them to remain unharmed."

"You want to save them then, do it, but you and I both know my death won't stop theirs."

"How are you so calm right now?" In a move that shocks the fuck out of me she reaches up and cups my face between her tiny hands.

"I don't fear death, believe me when I tell you being reunited with Havoc in the next life is more appealing then living in this fucked up world."

"What about your family?" I blurt out unsure of why the fuck I said that.

A devilish smile graces her face. "They would wage war on the fucking world to avenge me. My death would seal the fate of every cunt that ever wronged them. It would be the greatest war the world has ever seen."

"You are fucking insane!"

"And yet you still see through my crazy and that is the fucking reason why you can't glide that knife across my throat, because in your attempt to try and seduce me so you could kill me, you forgot to keep your feelings out of it." A whoosh of air escapes me, she has just called me on my bullshit.

"You want the truth?"

"Nah, I want you to lie to me," she deadpans.

"I should have killed you the first time I met you, the second time you should have for sure been dead but still, I couldn't bring myself to fucking kill you because for the first time in my life I saw a light in the darkness. You may not realize it, but you didn't only shine a light on me, you brought

Cronos back. I was there the day he told you about Aida. He's never told anyone about her." She doesn't seem shocked about my revelation, she knew I was there. "I also know you have feelings for me too."

"I do." Her honesty floors me. "But unlike you, I can switch those feelings off in an instant and take your life if it means saving my family."

"I can't do this with you anymore, it's clouding my judgment and I need to remain focused on saving my brothers."

"Then leave, Artemis. I'm not gonna stop you or chase you." I take a shuddering breath and nod. I attempt to move but her words stop me. "Maybe if I met you under different circumstances, things may have turned out differently."

I smile sadly down at her, then toss the blade to the side not giving a fuck about the consequences, and kiss her. She kisses me back with a hunger I've felt from her before, she may not say aloud but I can feel it in this kiss. She likes me and given the choice to kill or not, she would flounder. I break the kiss, gasping for air. I roll back to my side of the bed flinching in pain, my fucking leg is burning and my ribs are protesting but that kiss was worth it.

It's been about three weeks since I walked out of London's room. I haven't spoken to her or forced her to work out of my office since then. From what I hear from her teachers she is doing well in classes which shocks the hell out of me. I expected her to fight back and rebel but I'm pleasantly surprised at the turn of events. The only worry I have now is Costa's silence. The second trial should have begun last week and I haven't heard from him. I push that thought away as I continue to reply to emails until my office door bursts open to reveal an angry looking Max.

"Mind telling me why the fuck my cousin is threatening to come here and murder your brother?" I shove back from my desk and stand.

"The fuck do you mean?" I snap. Max–Amelia moves toward me and shoves her phone in my face. My brows jump to my hairline when I see a picture of London and Cronos, each seated on tattoo chairs with an artist each tattooing them.

"Royal is going to kill your brother."

"Why?"

"He thinks Cronos is you!"

"Fuck," I snarl as I snag my keys off the edge of my desk and rush to the garage. There is only one tattoo parlor in town so I know exactly where they are. I planted my foot the whole way, the past three weeks have been great. I haven't had to deal with London's father since he found out about the first trial. The fucker blew my phone up and when I refused to answer his calls, he started forcing Max to write down threats and leave them on my desk promising me he would inflict as much pain as possible when I finally *grew the balls to leave the school*, his words not mine.

I park my car behind Cronos's and dash into the store, my anger is riding me. I have more important shit to deal with right now instead of worrying about London cutting class and getting tatted up with my fucking brother. At the sight of me they both smirk.

"Told you he would snitch," London says to Cronos.

"I didn't snitch on anyone!" I snap, she rolls her eyes.

"Wasn't talking about you, pretty boy." I move toward them. One guy tries to stop me but I pin him with a fucking look that promises pain if he touches me. He wisely backs up and lets me pass, I open my mouth to rip the pair of them a new asshole but snap my mouth closed at the sight of their tattoos. London has a portrait of some guy... No, not some guy. I met Chaos Murdoch and I know without a doubt that isn't his face on her forearm, it's his twin, Havoc with the Ace of Diamonds card in the background. Cronos has a portrait of... Aida on his forearm.

"Planning on getting inked mate?" the guy tattooing London asks. The she-devil looks up at me and smirks before answering for me.

"Nah, he's the headmaster of my school, so no tats for him."

"Oh, so not your boyfriend then?" The hopeful tone of his voice has me grinding my teeth, she shoots me a wink before looking back to the dick head tattooing her.

"Nope. I'm young, free and single."

"Want to hang out later?" the motherfucker with the death wish asks her.

Before she can answer I cut in. "No, she has a date riding her headmaster's dick for the remainder of her schooling." For once I manage to catch London off guard, she chokes on air while Cronos laughs and the cunt tattooing her scoffs. "Problem?" I snarl, he stops his gun and turns to look up at me.

"You know that shit is illegal, right?" The cockiness in his gaze and the smug lilt to his voice has me clenching my fists at my sides.

"So is me murdering your family while you watch but that still won't stop me from doing it if you try to flirt with her again."

"Calm down, pretty boy, he was only joking." The fucker gulps loudly and forces himself to nod before returning to his task. If he knows what's good for him he'll keep his fucking mouth shut until we leave, make no mistake, she is leaving with me tonight.

It's about an hour for them both to finish. They get their arms wrapped and high five each other before making their way toward where I sit on the faux leather couch. I say nothing as I wait for them to get a rundown on after care from their artists. I tune them out until I hear that motherfucker try his luck again.

"Hit me up when you finish school and riding him." I spin around ready to fuck him up but London beats me to it.

"His dick's too good to give up and I don't shit where I eat, so unless you want me to travel the three hours out of town for my next tattoo, I suggest you shut the fuck up." He stares at her with an open mouth, Cronos just laughs and dumps a stack of cash on the counter before wrapping his arm around London's shoulders and leading her past me. I shoot the cunt a glare before I follow after them. She tries to head to my brother's car but I dart my arm out and snag her wrist pulling her with me.

"I'm assuming you want to get laid?" she snarks. I growl in response before opening her door and shoving her inside. "Oh, I like it when you get rough." I glare down at her.

"And I like it when your mouth is full of my cock so you can't speak but we can't always get what we want," I snap before slamming the door closed and heading around to my side. Cronos stands there scowling at me but I ignore him as I climb behind the wheel and burn rubber. I spy her pulling her phone from her pocket, then scrolls through her messages and laughs before placing a call.

"Block your ears," she says as she puts the call on speaker and grins, the person answers on the second ring.

"Are you out of your fucking mind?" My eyes widen slightly at the sound of her father's voice, she laughs in response. She is a fucking maniac! "You think this is fucking funny?"

"Calm your tits, old man, it's just a tattoo."

"You got a fucking tattoo of some guys face on your arm!" I see her turn rigid beside me.

"He isn't just some guy," she grits out through clenched teeth, without thinking I reach over and place my hand on the top of her thigh, I feel her begin to relax under my touch and that notion fills me with a sense of pride that I am able to calm her.

"Who the fuck is the cunt? I'm gonna fucking kill him." He doesn't give her a chance to answer. "Chaos, Chanel, we leave first thing in the morning," he shouts.

"Pretty hard to kill him when he's already dead." The bitterness that laces her tone has me feeling anger toward her father for upsetting her.

"What?" Royal barks clearly confused.

"He isn't just some guy, Dad. I'm not stupid contrary to what you think."

"Who the fuck is the guy then?"

"Havoc," she snaps before ending the call and dropping her phone on her lap, she turns and stares out the window ignoring the incessant ringing of her phone. I'll give Royal that, he is fucking persistent. When her phone stops ringing and mine begins, she snaps her head toward the stereo and sees her father's name come up on the screen. Before I can stop her the little shit hits answer on the steering wheel.

"The gates to that school are supposed to be fucking locked but yet my daughter somehow managed to get out—"

"Why the hell are you calling Artemis?" London snaps.

There's a pause on the other end of the phone and I can only imagine the thoughts running through his mind at his daughter answering my phone.

"What the fuck are you doing with him?" Royal snaps.

"Well, creating you a grandchild of course, Daddy." I choke on my own fucking spit while he shouts out curses and screaming for his wife.

"Give me the fucking phone," I hear a woman demand. "Karma, what did you do this time?" The smirk on my girl's face tells me all I need to know, it's Chanel not her mother.

"Aunt Nelly, I missed you."

The woman snorts. "You have like a minute to get your side in before your mother gets here and your father goes on a rampage."

London sighs. "I got a tattoo."

Chanel whistles. "Yep, that'll do it. R.I.P to you kid. I'll make sure to pick out a nice casket and outfit to bury you in." Before London can respond she speaks again, "Here's your mom, good luck."

"Baby girl." Comes through the speaker next, London deflates beside me.

"Hi, Mom."

"Why is your father threatening to murder the new headmaster of your school?" London glances at me and smirks. I shake my head and tell her with a look not to be a brat but of course she ignores me.

"He isn't happy that I got a tattoo and decided to try to give him a grandchild, can you believe that? All I was trying to do is make him happy and then he goes off and has a tantrum, the nerve of that man, right?" I shake my head, this girl is a fucking quack!

"Jesus, you really are going to give your father a heart

attack! You know he can't deal with the fact you are growing up and drawing the attention of boys." I grip the steering wheel in a vice-like grip. "Why the hell do you think he hired female guards for you?"

"Not my fault he doesn't trust me," she snaps back.

"It isn't you he doesn't trust."

"Bullshit, he thinks I spread my legs for the team." Erika snorts but the sound of shit breaking in the background makes it obvious that Royal heard that.

"He told me you got Hav's face tattooed?" The love in her mother's tone is strong, it's clear Erika thought the world of Havoc.

"Yeah. I did."

"That's beautiful, baby. You know he loved you more than anything in this world, right?" London's eyes fall closed and she takes a deep breath.

"Yeah. Mom?"

"Yeah, baby girl?"

"I'm not a virgin anymore." *Oh sweet fucking Christ.* Before a reply can come through the speakers, a car rams into the side of us, London screams as the car begins to roll, I try to reach for her but the airbag deploys at the same time and everything goes black.

Chapter Twenty-Four

London

The pounding in my head rouses me. I groan as I try to sit up but I can't move anything aside from my head. I slowly peel my eyes open and cringe in pain as the light beams down on me, I slam them shut as the drum beat in my head intensifies. I try to recall what the fuck happened and that's when everything comes rushing back to me, I was in a car wreck! I push through the pain in my head and slowly blink my eyes open until they adjust to the light above me, it takes a few tries but when I finally manage to get them open I frown. I expected to be in a hospital room not... whatever the fuck this place is. It's a room but the concrete walls tell me I'm not in a place with people who care for my wellbeing and if that wasn't enough, the fact my wrists and ankles are shackled to this metal bed frame should do the trick.

I fight against my restraints trying to yank free but it's fucking futile!

I take calming breathes to keep myself in check, all getting hysterical would do is deplete my energy and show whoever the fuck has me that I am scared. I close my eyes and exhale as I recall what my dad taught me.

Never allow fear to become a factor, you shut everything down and focus. Pain is nothing but a second, it will go away, you just need to remember to shield your mind. They can break your body and you will survive but, if they break your mind that shit can't be healed.

I replay his words over and over in my head, it's strange to find comfort in something he said when at that moment all I wanted to do was escape and go be free. I wanted to be someone else instead of London Murdoch. I thought I could lead a normal life but since returning to Blackwood I've learned that I can never be anyone but myself. I am who I am and I'm good with that. There will never be a normal life for me because I am nothing like anyone else, I am the daughter of Royal and Erika Murdoch and I will survive this fucking place and conquer these trials to show my father I am worthy to take over and lead my family when the time comes.

When the sound of a key enters the key hole in the door, I force my body not to tense and remain relaxed in the bed. When the door opens, I lazily lull my head to the side and it takes a fuck load of effort not to allow the shock from showing on my face at the sight of the fucking triplets. Adonis walks in carrying a tray with food and water, Apollo keeps his head down but the sight of the scissors in his left hand has me on edge. Ares, he is the one to hold my attention, his gaze is focused on me and unrelenting. I try to decipher his emotions but all I can see in the depths of his gaze is guilt and shame. An angry man can be controlled but a guilty man is unstable and ruled by his emotions. Ares is the wildcard at this point so I'm going to have to work the other two to keep their brother in line.

Adonis places the tray on the ground beside the bed I am chained to, Apollo comes to the other side of the bed, refusing to meet my gaze as he looks to Ares as he stands at the foot of the bed. I raise my chin to show them even in this weak position that I am still superior, I am not a weak bitch. I will never scream, shout or beg for mercy. If I am to meet my maker, then I will go out with my fucking dignity.

"London Murdoch," Ares says in a tone filled with loathing. "You have been sentenced by the Godfathers Of The night to complete the trial of innocence."

I snort for show. "Innocence? Pretty hard to do anything when I am chained to this fucking bed," I snap. The three of them share a look before Ares finally nods to Apollo before turning back to me.

"You will be bared for all to see. Given the fact you are the first woman to *ever* enter into the trials, you will become the trial and we will prove our worth by taking the innocence of our foe." The second he finishes speaking, my attention is snagged by Apollo as he leans down and grips the shirt I wear, fear spikes inside me when he begins to cut my shirt open with the scissors, I keep my breathing even and mask of indifference in place. Once he cuts the shirt away he tosses it to the ground leaving me in my bra and pants, he reaches for the waistband of my jeans but hesitates.

"Do it," Ares orders but Apollo remains frozen.

"If you don't, he will," Adonis whispers. I watch as Apollo closes his eyes and takes a deep breath before cutting from my waistband all the way down to my ankle, he does the same on the other side and yanks the material out from underneath me leaving me in nothing but my bra and thong. I dart my gaze between the three of them as fear slowly works its way through my body, I'm not stupid, I know what comes next. I need to mentally prepare myself for it because without a doubt, I know having them rape me will destroy something inside me.

"The hair," Ares mutters. Apollo slowly turns back to me and does everything he can to keep his gaze from meeting mine as he leans over me to grip my ponytail. I don't fight when he reaches around with his other hand. When I hear the distinct sound of the scissors cutting through my hair I close my eyes, I know it's just hair but that isn't the point. This haircut isn't something I wanted and they just took that from me.

"I'm so sorry, London, if we don't do this he'll kill him," Apollo whispers as he draws back with what used to be my ponytail in his hand. Ares nods to his brothers and the three of them turn to leave. I slink into the bed grateful that they didn't rape me but when a voice filled with glee sounds out around the room and the three of them go eerily still. I dart my gaze above my head and narrow my eyes, there are two cameras on either corner and a speaker concreted into the wall above my head.

"Take it all," the voice says. I can see the muscles in their backs bunch as they slowly turn back to me, the resolute look in their eyes sets me on edge. A feeling in my gut tells me they were actually trying to be nice before but now, they have no choice but to do whatever it is they have to. Ares nudges Apollo but he doesn't move. The distraught look in his eyes has my breaths coming in rapid pants. Then Adonis pushes him aside, plants his feet and shakes his head.

"I can't!" Apollo snaps.

"You don't do it, he dies. You want that?" Ares shouts in his face.

"Give it to me." At the sound of his voice, everything inside me freezes. The triplets part to make way for Artemis. My gaze runs over him. His face is bruised and he walks with a limp. I can see he is shielding his brothers from seeing the extent of the real pain he's in. He keeps his gaze on me as he holds his hand out for Apollo to place the scissors in the palm of his hand. "Get out," he barks. The triplets practically run from the room at his order. He stands there just staring at me. As the seconds tick by, I watch as he slowly locks away his emotions until his eyes become nothing but an empty void.

"Make it count, pretty boy, whatever you planned better kill me because if it doesn't…" I let my threat trail off, he knows what will happen if he does something to me, it will cost him his life.

"Believe me, you will wish that I had killed you by the end of this." The regret in his tone gives me pause as he slowly eliminates the space between us. He comes to a stop at the edge of the bed, looming above me. I see the torment of emotions splayed across his face. Realization crashes into me, he isn't here to kill me.

"Artemis?" He swallows loudly and gives me his full attention. "If it comes to *that*, make sure it's you." Shame casts its shadow across his features.

"I can't," he whispers as he slowly bends down and glides the scissors through the center of my bra cutting it open. I suck in a sharp intake of breath.

"Look at me," I grit out through clenched teeth, he slowly lifts his gaze to mine. "If it is anyone else, brothers or not, I will slit their fucking throats." His gaze searches mine for a second before he tears it away from me to cut my underwear away exposing me to the cameras.

"I should have killed you and saved you from this pain," he whispers before gathering the scraps of my clothes and undergarments and walking out. The moment the door clicks shut the speaker above my head crackles. Grinding my teeth, knowing without a doubt that Costa is the one speaking. Artemis wouldn't be doing this for any other reason than his father forcing him to do this in order to save the lives of his brothers.

"You will be nothing but a broken little doll after this."

"Maybe, but didn't your whore of a mother ever teach you that broken things can be fixed?" I clap back, the speaker crackles again but no reply comes. Taunting him probably isn't a good idea but fuck it. Artemis and Cronos never told me that this trial—Oh fuck! Artemis did but I didn't figure it out until now.

"There are five trials in total. Kill. Take. Escape. Describe. Steal. The final trial is the hardest, you may think you are strong and can take on the world but believe me, this trial will break you. I don't say this as a threat, I say it as a warning, London. That trial is not for the faint of heart, if it doesn't break you physically, it will destroy you mentally and emotionally."

If this is the final trial then does that mean I skipped one or something? I can feel it in my bones that something really bad is going to happen. You know when you have that feeling in your gut that you can just sense evil and you begin to feel nauseous because your body can sense the danger before your mind? I can feel that in my soul right now. I close my eyes to try to ease the pounding in my head. I try to get lost in my thoughts to distract myself from the fact I am naked and on camera. I don't know who is watching but if they expect to see me break then they will be waiting a long fucking time, I would rather die than allow anyone the satisfaction of thinking they could break me.

I must have fallen asleep because the sound of the door opening draws my attention. I watch as two men enter the room with robes on, followed by another four in similar robes but theirs have the hoods down. When their gazes land on me their mouths hang open. The surprise on their faces is all I need to know that they didn't expect to enter this room and find me shackled to this bed.

"I'll fucking kill you!" My eyes widen at the sound of Cronos's voice. He's dragged into the room by four men, fighting with everything he has until his gaze meets mine. He freezes at the sight of me, his eyes wide and filled with horror. "Aida," he whispers brokenly. I gasp as the guards drag him further into the room to make room for another to enter flanked by the triplets.

The sinister smile on his face is pure evil. I make sure Costa can see the hatred I feel for him all over my face. Unlike the other robed figures he wears a plain black suit that fits him like a second skin, the sight of him in a suit tells me this is why Artemis doesn't dress like a headmaster because he doesn't want to appear anything like his father. Costa moves toward me with a sparkle in his eye.

"Don't you fucking touch her!" Cronos roars. Costa peers back over his shoulder and nods to his men. Two of them land blows to his face and stomach. I bite my lip to keep from screaming out for them to fucking stop. He looks like a dark angel in his black jeans and black hoodie with his hair a tousled mess on his head. I look at the triplets thinking they will help their brother but when I spot Ares sporting a busted lip and

Apollo clutching his side I know they must have faced the same treatment.

Costa perches his fat ass on the edge of the bed beside me and smiles when I try to shift as far from him as my restraints will allow. He reaches out and glides his fingers down the column of my throat and pauses between the swell of my breasts. I breath through my nose trying to tamper the disgust rolling through me. Without any hesitation he skates his hand the remainder of the way down my body and cups my pussy, I snap my head to the side and my gaze collides with Cronos. Tears fill his eyes and I know he isn't seeing me, this is what happened to his Aida and he is being forced to watch it happen again to a girl who forced him to let her in and made him care. I ignore the feeling of Costa's finger prodding at my entrance as I focus on Nos.

"I'm not her," I whimper as he plunges a finger inside me.

"I can't!" Adonis snaps as he stumbles back a step. I cut a glance to three of them. Each of them stare at me with regret, humiliation for their part in this and guilt.

"I'm so sorry," Ares mouths as he closes his eyes unable to stomach the sight of his father fingering me. I turn back to Cronos needing him to distract me from what is happening. The four guards release him and focus on me, the hunger in each of their gazes has bile rushing up my throat. The lights cut out and Costa withdraws his finger from inside me.

"What the fuck happened?" he barks. I can hear the sound of footsteps and the guards barking orders for one of them to check the breaker. Rather than focus on them I take the time to train my mind, *Pain is nothing but a second, it will go away, you just need to remember to shield your mind.* I focus on the sound of my father's voice and replay his words trying to build walls around my mind. They are going to break my body but I will not allow them to break my spirit.

I can't.

When the lights come back on, I spot Cronos on the ground with two guards behind him, his hood is up now and the sight of him still in here brings me comfort. "No interruptions, I want this recorded," Costa barks as he reaches for my pussy again.

"I'll do it." My eyes widen, as Costa freezes his movements and snaps his gaze to Cronos.

"You going to fuck the bitch so you can complete the last trial?" The anger in his tone is clear. He moves his head so only his eyes are visible beneath the hood and I want to cry at the sight.

"I agree to the terms of Sanctum in front of *all* the Godfathers, I will complete this trial." Costa's lip twitches but he says nothing as he pushes to his feet, then snarls when he looks down at me. The motherfucker spits right in my face, and it takes so much restraint that I didn't know I had to keep my mouth shut. I watch as my dark angel pushes to his feet and shoulders his father on the way to me, my breaths come in fast and hard as the reality of what's about to happen slams into me.

"This is out of turn, she is an heir and to compete not be the target of the trial," some guy says to Costa.

"She has a cunt, she will never lead us and she should never have been given the opportunity to compete alongside my sons," Costa claps back.

"She was to be given a fair chance," another robe dude says. I tune out their conversation as he slowly climbs atop me and nestles himself between my legs, the material of his jeans chafes against my bare pussy. His gaze bores into mine as he rests his elbows on either side of my face and leans down to whisper in my ear.

"I'm so sorry, Omorfia." I slam my eyes closed as the first tear falls.

Chapter Twenty-Five

Artemis

Cutting the power was easy, dragging Cronos out of a crowded room was fucking hard until I told him my plan. He knew it was the only way even if he hates it. I can't let them do this to her. I can't kill them so this is the only way I know how to keep her safe.

Switch places with my twin so it's me inside her.

"I'm so sorry, Omorfia," I whisper in her ear, shame like I have never felt before slams into me when I feel her tear land on my cheek. I pull back and look down at her, her hair is cut and she is bare beneath me, this trial is designed to break men, it broke my brother and me when I refused to rape Aida. I've spent the past two hours since I've seen her convincing myself I'm not raping her because she asked for it to be me. Without it being spelled out for her, she already knew what was to come front his trial.

"Come on, boy, fuck the whore," Costa shouts. London

slowly blinks her eyes open and stares up at me with a look of...
fear. That is a look I never thought I would ever see in her eyes,
yet I am the one to put that look there.

"I wish there was another way," I whisper.

"I'm going to kill them." I nod.

"I'll help," I say quietly as I reach between us and begin to
undo my jeans. Her body stiffens and I hate myself more than I
ever thought possible. Self-loathing isn't something new for
me, especially after what happened last time in this room. This
time it's different because the person strapped to the bed is
someone I care about and there isn't a fucking thing I can do
about it to save her. I'm about to do something to her that I
can never take back or change. What is about to happen is
going to destroy the both of us for the rest of our lives. When
my cock is free I have no choice but to pump it in my hand to
get it up, if I don't do this Costa will make sure he takes his
time raping her and then passing her onto his men to take
turns, just like he did with Aida.

I line my cock up with her entrance and she stiffens, tears
flow freely from her eyes as she stares up at me with a blank
look. "I hate you," she sneers. I slam my eyes closed as I slowly
push inside her, the sounds of her whimpers shred what was
left of my soul to pieces. When I'm balls deep a sob works its
way out of her, the laughter behind me makes me sick. I clasp
her face between my hands and rest my forehead against hers.

"Open your eyes, baby." She obeys but the look in her eyes
kills me. "It's just me, me and you, just us." Her gaze flicks
between mine for a second.

"Just us."

I nod. "I'm so sorry, baby, I tried to save you from this but I
failed." Another whimper escapes her as I thrust inside her. I've
never fucked a woman before and felt nothing. I continue to

move inside her wanting to come as fast as I can so this can be over. Do you know how fucking hard it is to come when you aren't even aroused or into the idea of having sex? The vacant look in her eyes as I continue to move inside her kills something inside me!

This strong beautiful fearsome woman has been reduced to nothing but a shell because of me. I did this. I broke her and destroyed what I had left of my soul in order to save the lives of my brothers. I would give anything for there to have been another way but killing Costa outright would mean certain death for myself and my brothers.

"I hate you," she cries. I nod and place a kiss on her lips.

"I know, hate me all you want and come after me my little demon but never give up. I'm so sorry it had to be me," I whisper against her lips as I slam inside her one last time before I finally come. Instead of feeling sated or relieved, I feel disgusted. I cup her face between my hands and stare into her eyes.

Broken, that's what I see when I look into her eyes.

"Who's next, she looks like she's got at least twelve more rounds in her." Anger sores inside me at Costa's declaration. I pull out of her and cringe when she flinches, she wasn't even wet so I know that shit hurt her. I discreetly tuck myself back into my pants and remove the hoodie I wear covering her nakedness. "What the fuck do you think you're doing, take that off her!"

I slowly turn back to face Costa and the other leaders with my head held high, the triplets eyes widen at the sight of me. Unlike them and London, Costa can't differentiate the difference between me and Cronos.

"I, Artemis Argyros, hereby declare the completion of my

final trial." The outrage on Costa's face is priceless, the other leaders appear just as shocked as he does.

"You are not permitted to take part in these trials, boy," my father snaps. I keep my gaze on the other leaders as I answer.

"Nowhere in the rule book or guidelines of the GOTN does it state that I cannot participate in a selected trial. I have not broken any rules here and what you just witnessed is the final trial, which all you sick fucks just watched me do." They bristle at my insult but say nothing. Costa moves to stand before me, but I keep my gaze focused over his shoulders and watch as the other leaders form a huddle and mutter amongst themselves.

"You think you have outwitted me, you think because you fucked some whore that you can overthrow me?" I don't bother answering him. "You will never take my place at the head of this family, I'll make sure of that, you little cunt." He turns away from me. I reach forward and snag the keys from his pocket, he wheels around and tries to reach for me, but I jump back a step.

"The trial is complete. She was my conquest and weakness to conquer so therefore she is no longer needed," I say in a tone that dares these fuckers to argue with me.

"Get in here!" Costa yells for more guards and I tense in preparation for a fight. The triplets begin to shout and beg for him to just let me go but their arguments fall on deaf ears. The other leaders do nothing to intervene or say a fucking thing in fear of what Costa might do. I rush to London and use what little time I have to free her, I manage to get one hand unshackled before the guards swarm the room with their guns trained on me. I discreetly press the keys into her palm as I stand to my full height and look directly to my father. The bastard stands there with a wicked smirk on his face, he knows he's won and everything I just did to try and overthrow him was for nothing!

"Do your worst," I grit out. Costa may have had his men beat me in private before so the other leaders never found out how he kept his best soldier in line, but now that I have crossed a line in their presence he is within his rights as the leader to exact his pound of flesh. The guards await their signal from their master like good dogs, the odds aren't in my favor, nine on one.

"Teach him a lesson," he says with a smile. I dart forward and tackle the one closest to me to the ground. I manage a single hit before I'm hauled backward and thrown to the ground. I know the drill. I curl into a ball and cover my head and face, the stitches in my leg already tore earlier, the pain has become a constant reminder that I'm living in hell.

"Get the fuck off him!" I hear one of the triplets scream. I shout in pain when one of the motherfuckers stomps on my ribs and I feel it crack. Tears blur my vision as pain explodes in every part of my body. This is one of those times where I wish I would pass the fuck out. When a gunshot sounds out, the beating stops. I groan in pain and use all the strength I have left to roll over. The sight of Cronos standing there with a gun pointed at our father has my blood turning to ice.

"Enough of this, you will release him and allow him to walk free," Cronos orders, I hear the shackles behind me clink and bang as London finishes unchaining herself. "Come here, darlin'." A second later I see her limp past me, wearing only the hoodie I left draped over her.

"You are not walking out of here," Costa snarls. I chance a look at the other leaders and glare when I see them standing there with pale faces. How are men of their stature scared of Costa? Combined they have the power to overthrow him and force him from his position, but they are too fucking scared and weak to do it. I was a fucking fool for thinking that completing the trial would garner me their backing, they will never turn against him out of fear. "Drop the gun before I drop them." Horror washes over my twin's face. I flick my gaze toward Costa and my heart stills in my chest at the sight of Ares on his knees with a gun pressed to the back of his head.

"Artemis," he whispers, the pain is forgotten as I push to my knees and stare up at Costa.

"He's your son," I shout. Costa scoffs and rolls his eyes like holding a gun to his child's head is nothing.

"You want to save his life?" he taunts with a smile.

"Yes," I answer without hesitation.

A dark gleam enters his eyes. "It wasn't supposed to be you, it was supposed to be him." He spits as he flicks his gaze to Cronos scowling. "You are easy to control, he isn't." He sneers as he returns his gaze to me.

"Then kill me and let them go, you have my word they will disappear—"

"No!"

"Artemis."

"Fuck no."

"Stop!"

The four of my brother's shout but I ignore them and push on. "I am the oldest and the next in line. Cronos is weak and will never lead, the triplets want their freedom and will never come after your crown. You kill me, you son of bitch, and let my brothers go! You hear me, you fucking let them go!" I scream hysterically, the feeling of being trapped and backed into a corner is suffocating. I'm grasping at straws right now to ensure that they all make it out of here alive.

"You want them to live?" he asks.

"Yes," I answer.

Costa smirks and holds his hand out to one of his guards, the fucker places a hunting blade in his hand. "The four of them will live but you will not." My brothers begin to shout and spew threats but their fight will do nothing, I see it in our fathers eyes. He may rule the Greeks and have all the leaders in a chokehold but he won't allow me to live after what I did tonight in case there is a slim chance I could rise against him. Costa flicks his gaze to London and smiles wide. "You get to kill your rapist." I flinch in shame, hearing him call me that has bile rushing up my throat.

"No." My gaze snaps to London in shock. After what I just did to her I would have expected her to jump at the opportunity to slay me and bathe in my fucking blood. "You want me to kill that bitch then you need to tell me what the fuck is in it for me, you fat fuck." Cronos snorts to mask his laughter while I kneel here with wide eyes—she has a fucking death wish.

"You worthless bitch, you will do it because I fucking ordered it. Now, do it." He sneers in disgust, London flicks her gaze to me and I can see it in the depths of her eyes that she is fighting to remain in control of her emotions. "Kill him or I kill the four of them and make him watch." His threat pushes me into action.

"Do it, you let them die and I will fucking carve the skin from your body and lay it across your worthless dead uncles grave." Her emotions evaporate from her features as a cold emotionless mask overtakes her. She attempts to take a step forward but Cronos darts his arm out and grips her wrist.

"Don't do it, darlin', I can't let you hurt him." London says nothing as she reaches down and pries his fingers from her wrist.

"My mother once told me that *only in madness do you find*

a beautiful death," she says in a monotone way. She keeps her gaze on Costa as she closes the space between them and snatches the blade from his hand. "You may think you have won but let me assure you of this, Costa, you won the battle but you will not win the war. I will wipe you and your people from the fucking map."

Costa laughs but there is little humor to it. "You will cause a war that will end your family, you stupid cunt." To my utter surprise, London smiles showing her teeth but it's the unhinged look in her eyes that sets me on edge.

"You broke the agreement with the families the moment you decided to touch me, you worthless piece of shit." Costa strikes out and slaps her. I lurch forward but the guards push me back to my knees. Cronos is restrained by a new set of fuckers and disarmed. London staggers but doesn't fall, she just smirks and spits blood at his feet. When she finally turns to me with that mask in place, I realize I am in the presence of the heart of the reaper.

Chapter Twenty-Six

London

I keep my gaze on him as I lower to my knees, his brown eyes shine with resolution and understanding. I fight with everything I have to keep hold of my anger, I want to hate him for what he did and said about Havoc but I know he only did those things so I wouldn't be raped by Costa and his men. What he said about my uncle was to push me over the edge so I would save the lives of his brothers. I grip the hilt of the blade in my hand and place the other on the top of his shoulder. He smiles sadly and nods. I should run this knife through him and not give a second thought to my actions but... I hesitate and he sees it in my gaze. He gently reaches out and cups my cheeks between his hands, offering me comfort when he shouldn't.

"Remember how much you hated me when we first met?" I nod stiffly. "Latch onto that, draw on that hate and let it fester until it controls you... then run that fucking knife through me so you can save the life of your best friend and my little brothers."

I press the tip of the blade against his stomach and stare into his eyes. "I don't hate you," I whisper, he smiles and nods.

"I know," he whispers placing a soft kiss to my lips as I ram the knife into his abdomen. He gasps and as his brothers begin to fight to get to him, he flops forward and rests his forehead against my shoulder. His breathing is labored, I slam my eyes closed and will my fucking emotions to remain in check.

"I'm so sorry," I whisper in his ear as I feel his blood begin to coat my hand that still holds the knife.

"Don't be, you saved them when I couldn't," he rasps out. I release the blade and grip his face between my hands pushing back until I can meet his gaze. The look of pain and comfort in his eyes kills me. He only feels comfort because he knows his brothers will live thanks to his sacrifice. A lump forms in my throat and tears begin to cloud my vision as I watch his skin slowly turn pale.

"Aunt Meelz was right, I wasted time hiding how I felt because I was scared," I force out past the lump ignoring the fighting going on around us.

"Don't say those three words, Omorfia, save them for someone who is worthy of them," he gasps out.

"You are worthy," I choke out.

He weakly lifts his hand to cup my cheek and I nuzzle into his touch. "No. I'm not worthy of your love. I was supposed to kill you and save them but then that plan changed when I met you. I fell in love with the daughter of my enemy." I gasp at his declaration. I feel arms wrap around my waist and yank me back. I scream and fight against the fucker as I watch Artemis slouch forward, the sight of him lying there in his own blood has tears breaking free.

"Artemis, I'm sorry. I'm so fucking sorry! I love you," I scream as I'm dragged from the room kicking and screaming, sobs rip out of me.

"Hold on, killer, your dad's outside." I still and snap my mouth shut at the sound of Uncle Chaos's voice. I blink a couple times to clear my vision and that's when I notice the bodies of Costa's guards littering the ground around us. I see men dressed in black with masks covering their faces rushing down the concrete hallways. I know they are part of my dad's crew and begin to relax in my uncle's hold. As we climb some steps, I realize I was being held in a fucking bunker! A man darts in front of us and shoves the door open for Uncle Chaos to carry me out. He keeps his arm around my waist as he lowers me to my feet and leads me out through some trees. I don't take in my surroundings I'm too fucked up in the head right now.

"London!" I snap my head up at the sound of my dad's voice and freeze on the spot at the sight before me. Cronos, Ares, Apollo and Adonis are all on their knees with four men behind them holding guns to the backs of their heads. Dad rushes to me and snags me from my uncle's hold and crushes me against his chest. "Fuck, I thought I lost you." The worry in his tone is clear. I wrap my arms around him and bury my face in his chest soaking up his warmth and comfort.

"Royal, we need to move!" I hear Aunt Sin shout from behind us. Dad reluctantly releases me and runs his gaze over me once before a deep frown mars his forehead.

"Take them with us," Dad shouts while keeping his eyes on me. I yank free of his hold and rush toward Cronos. The guys try to haul him away but I throw out my hands smacking one right in the nose and the other in the eyes, they both curse and drop their hold on my friend who drops to the ground. I follow him to my knees.

"Are you okay?" The haunted look in his eyes shreds me in half.

"Just let them kill us, if they don't Costa will." I frown.

"Costa got away?" Cronos nods and I flop back on my ass.

"London, we need to move now," my dad barks, snapping me out of it. I look up to see him looming above me and shake my head.

"No. They come with me and I'm not leaving him down there," I shout as I push to my feet and take a step in the direction of the bunker, but dad snaps his arm out and stops me.

"The bunker is rigged to blow in three minutes, get the fuck in the car." My dad's words have my head spinning and I sway on my feet, he wraps his arm around my waist and draws me into his side.

"I can't leave him," I scream as he drags me away. I fight with everything I have to get free of his hold but he is unrelenting and clings to me. "Let me go!" I scream.

"London, calm the fuck down," Dad chastises me but I can't, a need so strong has overcome me with the need to get the fuck back to Artemis. "Get her in the car, we need to move." Before I can comprehend what is happening I'm shoved into the back seat of the car and the door is slammed closed behind me. I reach for the handle.

"London?" I spin around in my seat and the sight of her sitting there looking terrified and worried for me stops my heart.

"Mom," I choke out, she lurches across the seat and wraps me in her arms.

"I'm here, baby girl, I've got you, baby." No tears come as I hold my mom, I feel destroyed and confused but I can't cry.

Something inside me has shut down and I beg it to close everything else inside me away inside a black box so I feel nothing. I want to feel numb and rid myself of this crippling pain in my chest, it feels like I'm dying. "We'll get you through this, baby."

There is no getting through this because I just killed him.

I step beneath the spray of the shower in the hotel room my dad put me in. I feel numb and empty. I frown at the sight of the water turning red and draining away, I gasp and drop to my knees covering the drain with my hand as I reach around blindly to shut off the shower.

"No, I'm sorry, no, no come back, I'm sorry," I scream as I try to stop the bloody water from leaking between my fingers into the drain. "Come back, I'm sorry."

The door to the bathroom bursts open to reveal my mom and dad. At the sight of me naked and on the floor, my dad falls over his feet to escape while my mom rushes to yank the glass door open and drops to her knees in front of me. "What is it, honey?"

"Turn the shower off," I shout at her. She leans over me and shuts the water off.

"No!" I cry out as the water continues to drain away. "Get me something to stop it, I can't let him go like that."

Mom grabs my face and lifts my head. "London, What's happening?"

I shake free of her hold. "I let him go, it's all I have left and he's draining away." Confusion mars her features.

"Erika!" My mom turns toward the door and catches the robe my dad tosses her, she wraps it over my shoulders as the last remnants of water slip through my fingers. I stare at the specks of blood that still cling to my skin and feel relief, he's still with me. Strong arms lift me from the floor and I know it's my dad, he gently places me on the bed as my mom darts forward and secures the robe around me as I continue to stare at the blood staining my nails.

He's still with me.

"Royal, what the fuck happened?" I hear Mom ask.

"I don't know," he answers dejectedly.

"Something happened to our daughter," she whispers brokenly. I peer over at them and frown at the sight of them both standing there staring at me.

"He's still with me." Mom looks like she's about to cry while Dad looks murderous.

"Who is?" Mom pushes. I cut my gaze to Dad and watch as he studies me for a moment before his gaze hardens. He says nothing as he reaches into his pocket and pulls his phone out. He dials someone before bringing the phone to his ear.

"Get to London's room now." I cock my head to the side, confused for a second until I push that away and go back to staring at the blood on my skin and smile.

He's still here.

I bolt upright screaming. Hands grab at me and I scream louder as I fight to push them away in the dark. "Get the fuck away from me," I shout as I shuffle backward, falling off the side of the bed. I continue to crawl on my hands and knees until I reach the corner of the room and huddle there. A light flickers on and I bury my face in the top of my legs.

"London?" The voice sounds familiar but I don't look up, this is just a dream.

"Royal, let him talk to her." I know that voice as well.

"Why the fuck would I do that, Chaos? His family fucking clearly tortured my daughter."

"You didn't see what I saw when I brought her out."

"What did you see exactly?" That's my dad's voice. The sound slowly begins to penetrate the fog.

"Your daughter breaking her own heart, let the boy in to see her. He's a twin and seeing him will help her, trust me, I know." The room grows quiet for a long time until I feel someone growing closer. I don't dare look up, but the person stops a few feet away and I hear them sit on the ground. I don't move or say anything for a while but curiosity gets the better of me and I slowly lift my head to see him sitting a few feet away from me. A sob claws out of my throat as I crawl toward him and straddle his lap, burying my face in the crook of his neck as his arms band around me, holding me tight. I wrap my arms around him and hold him close, soaking in his warmth and relishing in the feeling of having him here with me in the flesh.

I don't know how much time passes before I can feel my lids drooping shut from exhaustion, but I'm scared that if I close my eyes that horrible nightmare will come back, it was so real. I felt the blade tear through his skin and sink into his stomach.

It felt so real.

"No one can find Amelia."

"How the fuck can they not find her, Sin?"

"I don't know, Royal. She was with us when we went to get London and that was the last time we saw her."

"Fuck, send men out to find her now. I've put off calling my dad but he needs to know what I did."

"No, this isn't on you. Chaos and I knew what we were doing when we agreed to come with you, this is on all of us." I peek my eyes open to see my dad standing there with his arm around my mom's shoulders, Aunty Nell and Uncle Kacey both stand with them but my gaze zeros in on Uncle Chaos, who stands there staring directly back at me.

He takes a step toward me and I shrink back. He pauses and crouches down keeping plenty of space between us. I scan his face and feel a pang of longing, I drop my gaze to my arm. "Can I see it?" His tone is calming and a stark contrast to the dark aura that clings to him like a second skin. I dart my tongue out to moisten my lips and slowly extend my arm, exposing the tattoo I got. His breath hitches at the sight, I expect him to get mad at me for daring to get his brother's face tattooed on my arm but he shocks me when he smiles. "If we weren't identical twins, I would say that tattoo is hideous but given that we are, I must say that is the most handsome face I have ever seen in my life." I snort as my parents creep in closer to get a better look. I expect my dad to be furious at the sight but all I see is pride in his gaze.

"He would be honored," Mom says with emotion thick in her tone. I say nothing as I wrap my arm back around his neck and hold him tight. Dad frowns but says nothing, Mom looks concerned but Uncle Chaos just looks like he understands.

"London?" I turn to Uncle Chaos and hold his gaze as he speaks. "You need to really look at him and see he isn't the one you want him to be."

"What the fuck—"

"Shut up, Royal. I know what I'm doing and she needs to deal with this so she can process what the fuck happened." I cock my head to the side confused. "London, look at him," he urges, the arms around me slowly slacken allowing me the chance to lean back but I don't move.

"No," I bite out. Uncle Chaos opens his mouth but he speaks, cutting him off.

"Darlin', look at me." I slam my eyes closed and shake my head trying to force my mind back into the place where everything was okay and he's here with me. Hands cup my cheeks and force me back. "Open your eyes, darlin'." I fight it, I don't want to because I know the moment I open my eyes I will see the difference and I don't want it not to be him beneath me. "I'm not him."

I snap my eyes open and the sight of Nos looking up at me with anguish in his eyes makes it all real. He isn't Artemis, identical twins or not they look nothing alike to me. My face contorts in pain, Nos strokes my cheeks with his thumbs and smiles brokenly. Cronos doesn't push me, he just sits there giving me time to process and work through the thoughts plaguing my mind.

"Artemis," I whisper, at the sound of his brother's name he sucks in a shuddering breath. I hear the others around me gasp and murmur but my focus is on Nos.

"You gave him an ending fit for a man of his ranking," he says that to comfort me but I can tell it's hurting him.

"I didn't have a choice, he was baiting me to do it, that's why he threw Havoc in my face," I say in a rush.

"You told him about my brother?" I dart my gaze back to Uncle Chaos.

"I...I... He saw the tattoo and—"

"He knew it would push you and force you to react. He made sure you would be the one to do it because he knew me and the triplets couldn't. You were stronger than us, darlin'." I shake my head denying his words.

"No. I was weak and I killed him—" Cronos cuts me off by getting right in my face, I hear my family close in around us but the angry look in my besties eyes keeps me captivated.

"You did what he asked of you, what you went through..." Disgust rolls through him but he forces himself to carry on. "Your kill was warranted," he mutters.

"What the fuck happened, London?" Dad snaps.

"Royal, now isn't the time," Mom begs but he ignores her.

"The four of these Greek fucks live because your uncle thinks they mean something to you." At the mention of my dad harming Nos and the triplets I snap my head up to glare at him.

"I killed him to save them, don't you fucking touch them," I scream.

"Why the fuck do you care about your headmaster? He was pitted against you—"

"Royal, that's enough!" Aunt Sin shouts. Dad turns to the side and looks from her to me a couple times before his eyes widen.

"Chanel, I forgave you for lying to me about Kacey but I will not forgive you for lying to me about my own daughter." Aunt Sin's face is a mask of indifference.

"Ask me."

"Was my daughter fucking her headmaster?" he forces out through clenched teeth. Aunt Sin darts her gaze to me and I see it, she is about to lie for me and I can't let her do that, so I answer.

"No." Dad's shoulders sag with relief. "I fell in love with my headmaster and slept with him." Dad's face turns a shade of red but I push on. "Hate me all you want but I couldn't stop feeling something for him. I let him in and all that got me was fucking pain that I can't escape because I killed him." My hysteria begins to rise. "I stabbed him and then he told me he loved me, he fucking saved me from being raped by all of them," I scream as horror clouds my father's features. "He saved me and I killed him." Tears break free and roll down my cheeks, the sight of my tears has an unreadable look on my dad's face. "It hurts, it fucking hurts, Daddy." Within a fraction of a second I'm torn from Cronos's hold and crushed against my dad's chest as he holds me while I cry.

"I'll slaughter every single one of those fuckers," Dad vows. I cling to him as my chest feels like it's ripping open. I can feel his hands on me stroking my hair—or what's left of it.

"We go to war," I hear Uncle Chaos say behind me.

"Sin, call my dad and tell him I want him on the first flight here. We go to fucking war and take out every single Greek cunt, none of them are to remain breathing." Dad is in don mode and that brings me some comfort knowing that I will get the chance to avenge Artemis.

Chapter Twenty-Seven

London

Three weeks later...

I sit out on the back patio of my house. Since arriving back in Miami three weeks ago things have been different, *I'm* different. I can't explain it but something inside me has changed. I used to be plagued with nightmares about Uncle Havoc's death every night but now, I am plagued with the constant nightmare of that night. Every time I close my eyes, I see him on his knees and feel the blade tear through his flesh.

"You got a second?" I peer over my shoulder to see Ares standing at the back door with his hands stuffed in his pockets, rocking back and forth on his heels looking uncomfortable as fuck.

"Yeah," I breath out before facing forward again and soaking in the view I never appreciated before. Ares drops down beside me. Having the triplets and Cronos in my childhood home feels weird but my dad agreed that they could stay with us until the war is over. Dad has been scouting for Costa everywhere—the other heads of the families refused to be involved in the war between the Greeks and my family. After I told them what happened that night they all agreed that trial or not, Costa went too fucking far with what he did to me. Ares, Cronos, Apollo and Adonis backed my story. The four leaders agreed to remain neutral and would not aid either my family or Costa.

"My brothers and I aren't going back to Blackwood." I snort and pin him with a deadpan look.

"It was our last year, somehow I don't think I will be going back either."

He shakes his head. "No, you don't get it."

"Get what Ares?"

"We can't go back because your father went to the board and told them Artemis seduced a student and broke the school's code. We are being sent to a different school here in the US."

"He what?" I snap, Ares reels back.

"He told them Artemis prayed on you, my brother's name is being dragged through the fucking mud right now." I don't stick around, I shove to my feet and storm inside heading straight for my father's office. I push the door open and ignore the shocked looks of my aunts and uncles and even my grandparents and I stalk toward my father's desk and slam my palms down on it. He leans forward in his chair and scowls at me.

"We're in the middle of a meeting," he reprimands me.

"I don't give a fuck. You call that fucking board and tell them Artemis didn't seduce me." Dad's lip twitches and his eyes darken as he pushes to his feet and lays his hands flat on his desk, then leans forward so we are eye level.

"That sleezy fuck manipulated you—"

I scoff out a laugh and pin him with a look that says he's dumb as fuck. "I was the one who begged him to fuck me in the locker room showers, not the other way around." Dad stumbles backward until he smacks into the wall behind his desk. I can hear the others around us speaking in hushed voices but my focus is on my dad. When Mom comes to stand next to him I snort. "Taking his side are you?"

"No. I'm taking the side of my daughter who is clearly heartbroken over the boy she lost. I'm on the side of her father who is doing everything within his power to hunt down the man who hurt his little girl. I am on the fucking side of the two people I love most in this world because it is killing me every day to see the two of you avoiding each other."

"Erika—"

Mom snaps her angry glare to Dad, forcing him to shut his mouth or face her wrath. "You need to learn she isn't a little girl anymore. She fell in love, Royal. What that boy did will always be viewed as unforgivable in your eyes but not in mine."

"He fucking raped my daughter!" Dad roars, my eyes widen. I've never seen my dad so unhinged before. He stands there heaving with his hands clenched into fists at his side as he glares down at my mom. I expect my mom to shrink away from him but she reaches out and places a hand on his chest and smiles sadly up at her husband. "He hurt my little girl, Erika. I will never forgive that." My mouth dries, all this time I thought he was angry at me because I had sex and disobeyed him but it turns out he's been angry because he thinks the man I fell for hurt *me*.

"He chose to weather her hatred for what he did to her because he loved her enough to not allow another to touch the woman he loved. He saved her from..." Mom takes a shuddering breath. "We couldn't be there to protect her, Royal. That boy saved our daughter from having multiple men violate her. He saved her."

"He fucking used her to get to me, that's why they never fucking let her out of the trials. Costa wanted her dead because he knew I would start a fucking war for her!" he shouts as he blindly points toward me. When he jerks his gaze to me I stiffen and stand up straight. "Do you see now, I would start a fucking war for you and force our entire family to fight alongside me because that is what you mean to me. You are mine to protect and love, not that fucking cocksuckers."

When a hand lands on my shoulder, I look up to see my grandpa standing there with a stern look on his face, my grandma comes to stand on my other side. Dad looks between his parents and shakes his head sighing in defeat.

"Royal—"

"Don't, Dad," he says as he drops his gaze to the floor. "She may be your granddaughter but she is my daughter and no matter what you or her mother say, I will never forgive that cunt for what he did to her." He slowly lifts his gaze to me and the sight of unshed tears in his blue eyes has my breath lodging in my throat. "If I didn't have a tracker implanted on you, I would never have gotten to you in time. I should have been there to protect you. I fucking failed," he grits out before storming out of the room, leaving me standing here reeling.

"Go to him, honey, he needs you," my mom urges. I shake my head to snap me out of it as I go after my dad. I don't have to look far. I walk out the back door and smile at the sight of him sitting in the spot I just occupied minutes ago. Dropping down beside him, I gaze out over the view of the landscape.

"I don't think I have ever thanked you and Mom for giving me this extraordinary life." I feel his gaze on the side of my head but I keep mine ahead. "I never knew what it felt like to be a part of something until Mom brought me back here. I found a home, people who cared for me and most of all, I found my family."

"London—"

I push on needing to get this out or I never will. "That was all I needed. I never wanted for anything else until *him*. At first I wanted to ruin him and send him packing like all the rest, but he wasn't like the others. He was sure and confident in who he was. He didn't bend to my will and run scared when he learned what my last name was." I slowly turn to my dad and see I have his full attention. "He didn't see me as Royal Murdoch's daughter, he saw me as London, just London nothing more, nothing less. For the first time in my life I felt seen. I toyed with him and fucked with his head for a while and even stabbed his best friend."

Dad's brows raise. "London—"

I wave him off. "The whore is fine, she'll have a little scar to tell her friends about, but she'll be fine." He quirks a brow at me. "What?"

"You can't stab people because you get jealous."

I scoff. "Coming from the guy who threatens his guards for saying *hi* to his wife."

He shrugs. "I don't stab them though."

"Mmhmm. You keep telling yourself that, old man." He scowls at me and I smile, some of the tension between us eases.

"You liked him didn't you?" he asks after a moment.

"I... I loved him, still do honestly, and I hate that I can't stop it because it fucking hurts. Seeing Nos every day makes it harder and better at the same time."

Dad nods as if he understands. "Chaos hated that." I cringe, I didn't even think about my uncle. "He knew we all saw Hav through him and for a while he allowed us to until we laid him to rest. Chaos forced us to see him and not his brother and that was the best thing he could have done because without Havoc by his side, we didn't really know who Chaos was on his own."

"Cronos is avoiding me."

"Because he can't be who you want him to be." My brows draw in, Dad scoffs and rolls his eyes. "You see him as your *bestie*," he tries to say in a voice meant to mimic mine.

"I don't sound like that!"

"You really do." I nudge him with my shoulder. "He doesn't see you in a friendly way."

"He does, he knows we're besties and he can't get rid of me."

Dad looks serious suddenly. "London, you may view him that way but he doesn't look at you like a friend should. Your bestie wants more than... friendship." My face contorts in disgust.

"No, he knows—"

"He knows his brother is dead and that you're grieving that loss but believe me, daughter, he is waiting in the wings for you to move on and he plans to swoop in." I stare at him with my mouth open, my mind reeling, could that be true?

I shake my head. "I can't think about any of that until the Greeks are dealt with. I want them gone and these fucking barbaric trials abolished."

He nods. "I get that but we also need to talk about Blackwood."

"I'm not going back!" I snap.

He sighs. "Well, you're in luck because the families agree it's better for the school and other students if my daughter doesn't return." I roll my lips over my teeth to keep from smiling. "Don't look so fucking smug, you little shit." Laughter burst out of me. Dad sits there smiling at me with love in his eyes. "I'm sorry." My laughter dies out as I frown at him.

"For what?"

Sadness fills his blue eyes. "For not being there when you needed me. When I heard your scream through the phone when you crashed, I knew something was wrong and got on the first plane out. I know you have struggled with being adopted and wondering if I would come for you or wage a war in your name." My breath hitches. "The answer to that question, London, is I would burn alive for you if it meant you got to survive. You may find a man that loves you but he will never love you like I do. You gave my life a purpose I never knew it needed. This thing with the Greeks will cost us lives on both sides but you have my word, daughter, that Costa Argyros will fucking die slowly."

"I want to be the one to do it." He looks at me intently for a second trying to gauge if I mean it or not.

"Can you handle that?"

"I loved Artemis, Dad, and he forced me to take his life. I want to drive a fucking knife through Costa's heart and watch him die slowly as I cut off the finger he used to touch me." His eyes darken. "I know you don't want to hear it but he really did protect me, Dad. He was beaten and cut open by his own father for not killing me. He protected me even when I didn't know he was doing it."

"Jesus, he isn't a fucking saint, you know, and that fucker was only a couple years younger than me! He's also a whiny bitch and ungrateful as fuck—"

"Wait." He snaps his mouth closed and tries to look innocent but I see it in his eyes. I leap to my feet and peer down at my dad. To the rest of the world he may be unreadable but not to me. I cross my arms over my chest and stare him down. "How do you know he is whiny and ungrateful?"

"Sir, Miss Murdoch is at the gate," Marco says from below us on the lawn. Dad slowly stands in front of me but I refuse to back down.

"Remember I love you."

"That doesn't answer my question," I grit out through clenched teeth.

"I will always love you more than any fucker, now follow me before your mother fucking kills the both of us." He turns and begins to walk away.

"Wait, why the hell is Mom mad at us? What did you do?" I shout as I chase after him. He pauses in the doorway and peers over his shoulder at me.

"I kept a secret and you are going to act like you knew the entire time so I don't go down alone."

I balk up at him. "Hell no!"

He narrows his eyes. "You'll change your mind." He clips out before heading toward the front door with me hot on his heels. "Erika," he shouts as he pulls the door open and moves outside. I look over my shoulder to see my mom, grandparents, uncles and aunts looking just as confused as me. I spy the triplets and Nos out of the corner of my eye when I turn to follow after my dad. I stand beside him as we watch a sleek black pick-up truck head toward us.

"Who the fuck is that?" Aunt Sin asks.

"I found Amelia." All of us turn and stare at my dad but he refuses to meet any of our gazes.

"When?" Uncle Chaos snaps.

Dad shrugs and steps forward when the car draws near. "She was never missing," he says it so casually like he didn't do something wrong. The tint on the windows of the truck are so dark I can't see inside it. When it comes to a stop we all stand here waiting as Dad heads around to the other side of the truck out of view while the driver's door opens and Aunt Meelz climbs out. She shoots everyone a smile but when her gaze lands on me a flicker of guilt flashes in her eyes which stumps me.

"You move and I will fucking slit your throat while she watches. You have one purpose of being here and that is help find the fucking Greeks." I frown at hearing my dad's threat and it annoys me. I can't see who he is talking to. I feel Nos at my back and the triplets form a semicircle around us.

"Who is it?" Adonis whispers.

"No fucking clue but I'm about to find out." I take a step forward and slam to a stop when my dad rounds the hood of the truck. He stares at me for a second looking torn, before blowing out a breath and stepping aside.

"Hello, Omorfia."

Chapter Twenty-Eight

Artemis

She looks like a fucking angel standing there, the shock is evident in her eyes but so is the love she feels for me. My attention is snagged when Cronos steps forward and places a hand on her shoulder. I glare at the hand.

"Artemis," Ares shouts as he, Adonis and Apollo rush toward me. I tense and prepare for the onslaught of pain that will ensue when they tackle me but Amelia darts in front of me at the last second stopping them.

"He's still healing and needs to take it easy, so go easy," she warns. The three of them nod and smile wide at the hot nurse.

"Yes, ma'am," Apollo says with stars in his eyes. They dash around Amelia and carefully wrap me in a three-way hug. I close my eyes and exhale. I knew they were alive but seeing them safe with my own eyes is another thing altogether. Adonis and Ares release me, stepping back with stupid grins on their faces while Apollo keeps his arms locked around me. I wrap my arms around him and hold him close.

"I'm fine," I say, trying to ease some of his worry but all my words do is have him tighten his hold to the point of being painful. Amelia shoots me a disapproving look but I ignore it.

"I watched you die." Guilt churns inside me. I wanted to reach out to them and tell them I was alive but I wasn't afforded that opportunity. The one time I ignored Amelia's warning and climbed my broken ass out of bed, I tore the stitches and she snitched to Royal who threatened to kill my brothers if I tried again.

I gently push him back and hate the sight of tears leaking from his eyes. Gripping the back of his head, I pull him into me and press my forehead against his. "I'm not going anywhere, brother, I'm right here." He nods and I smile trying to reassure him without words that we'll be okay, I'll make sure of it. "Now, want to let me pass so I can see my girl?" He grins and steps back allowing me to see her again but this time it isn't just Cronos with her, Chaos, Kacey, Chanel, Bishop, Kiara and a woman I assume to be Chaos's wife, Cassandra, stand around her. I dart my gaze to the side to see Royal standing there with his wife at his side and an unyielding look in his gaze.

The rational side of my brain knows I should bypass her and follow after her father to do what I was brought here to do and give them the secret location of the Godfathers, but the other part of me, the part that has done nothing but dream of the moment I would be able to finally see her again, urges me to go to her.

"Believe it or not, the choice you make right now is the choice that will shape your future with both of them, choose wisely, Art," Amelia warns. "Make the right choice, Artemis, because neither of those two offer second chances." Steeling my spine, I make my choice. In a lot of eyes this may be the wrong thing given everything I have done to protect my family, but this is something I can't give up—no, I won't give up. My life has been nothing but bleak, nothing mattered aside from Cronos, Apollo, Ares and Adonis. But now, I care about someone just as much and I am not letting go of that. I can feel their gazes on me as I approach but I only have eyes for her. She stands there shrouded in the protection of her family but what they don't realize is, she doesn't need them to protect her. I don't stop until the top of my shoes hits hers. I'll admit having all her family this close and them clearly knowing that I have been with her is unnerving, but I'm making a choice and I'll choose her every fucking time.

"You need to give her space." I meet my twins stare and it fucking hurts, I can see it written all over his face. He's fallen for her and my miraculous resurrection from the dead has thrown a wrench in his plans to move in on my girl.

"You need to back the fuck off because she isn't your concern," I bite out. Cronos doesn't back down or move an inch.

"You think she is your concern?" I slowly turn to the other side and meet the sinister gaze of Bishop Murdoch. This man is fucking lethal, he's the guy you warn your children about, he makes the boogeyman look like a daydream.

"With all due respect, yes, she is my concern and not yours or your sons and definitely not my fucking brothers." Kiara purses her lips to keep from smiling, Bishop's nostrils flare in outrage, but his wife calmly steps in front of her husband, claiming his attention, affording me the chance to focus mine on my girl who still refuses to look at me. "You gonna keep acting like I'm not standing right here?"

She scoffs and shoves me back. I grunt in pain but weather

it as she comes at me again, this time she punches me across the jaw sending me staggering back a step.

"Karma, he's injured," Amelia shouts, but London isn't hearing a word she says. She stands there with her fist clenched at her side. I stand tall and stare her down, daring her to come at me again. I let the first hit slide but I won't allow a second.

"Come on, little demon, you know you missed me," I taunt.

"Fuck you!" she screams as she charges forward. I dodge her right hook and jump back when she throws an uppercut with her left.

"I would love to," I say with a smirk.

"Motherfucker is gonna die slowly," I hear Royal say but I don't dare take my focus off of the killer in front of me.

"I hate you."

"A part of you does but that other part of you that hesitated for a split second before driving that knife through me doesn't." Her eyes slam closed at the reminder. I take a huge risk and close the space between us and tentatively reach out, cupping her cheeks in my hands. She sucks in a ragged breath at the feeling of my hands on her again. I force her head back so she can look at me, I see it in her green eyes. "That part of you loves me," I say low enough for just her to hear. A deep groove forms in the center of her brows as she mulls over my words.

"I can't do this." She rips free of my hold and turns away from me but fuck that, I'm not letting her go. I strike out and grip her wrist, yanking her back to me. The males around us begin to shout but fuck them. I keep an arm locked around her waist and grip a fistful of her hair, tugging on the strands, forcing her to look at me.

"I know you are running because what happened brought back memories you thought you could evade." Her eyes widen in surprise that I can see through her bullshit. "I'm not him, London, I'm still here with you. I'm so sorry for what I said about your uncle, it was uncalled for and wrong but I had—"

"I know why you did it," she whispers. I'm not used to seeing this side of her, she's quiet and controlled and I don't like it.

"Can we talk?" She frowns.

"We are talking."

I make a sound in the back of my throat. "Maybe somewhere more private so your dad, grandfather and uncles aren't standing there plotting my death loud enough that I can hear." She darts her gaze toward them and they all keep their glares on me.

"You think I'm letting that motherfucker anywhere alone with you, *you* are out of your fucking mind," her father spits.

"You saved him!" she rebukes.

"She has a point," Bishop tacks on, earning a scowl from his son.

"Stay out of this," he snaps at his father before he breaks away from the others and steps forward, eyeing me up and down like I'm nothing and he isn't wrong. What I did cost us everything, we have nothing and nowhere to go now. "You live because of what I need to know, she is not part of this so you stay the fuck away from my daughter."

"Royal, enough," Erika says as she eliminates the space between us. As she draws near, I release London and stand beside her. Unlike her husband, Erika doesn't eye me with disdain or disgust. "You may escort my daughter out back but be warned, her father, uncles *and* grandfather will be around so do not insight their wrath any further."

London laughs. "But, Mom..." she whines, "annoying Dad is my favorite thing to do, you know this."

Royal rolls his head back and sighs up at the sky while Erika purses her lips. "Take him out back. I need to have some words with your father about keeping secrets." That has Royal breaking his neck to look at his daughter.

"She knew," he accuses. London's brows raise as Erika slowly turns to face her husband placing her hands on her hips.

"Her right hook to his jaw suggests otherwise, now you can take it like a man out here or we can have this conversation in your office."

"Out here!" Bishop and London both say at the same time. When Royal pins London with a look that begs for her help, she grabs my hand and pulls me after her.

"You dirty little traitor! Next time, I won't save the little bitch," he calls after us.

"For that I won't stop Mom from killing you!" London shouts as she drags me around the back of their massive house. She leads me up the stairs and walks over to the edge of the patio where two wooden chairs sit looking out over the golf course at the back of the property. She drops into one with the grace of a toddler while I slowly ease into mine, wincing a couple times. I can feel her worried gaze on me.

"I'm fine," I say once I'm finally seated, the slight sheen of sweat on my brow would suggest otherwise but fuck it, fake it till ya make it right.

"The fact you look constipated tells me you're full of shit." I choke on air, clearly she still hasn't found a filter for her mouth.

"Well, getting the shit beaten out of you and stabbed does have that effect," I say jokingly but she doesn't laugh, instead she looks like she ate a lemon. "I'm sorry, I was trying to lighten the mood."

"You coming back from the dead ruined the mood."

"Ouch, I thought you would be happy to see me."

"What the fuck would give you that notion?"

"The fact I wasn't dead when you screamed out that you loved me." Her face slackens and she slouches back into her chair with a huff.

"Heat of the moment had me all up in my feels, we all say shit we don't mean." Her dismissal annoys the fuck out of me.

"Don't do that."

"Do what?" she bites back in an angry tone.

"Hide." She balks at me.

"I'm not hiding."

"Yeah, you are."

"Coming from the guy who avoided me for weeks before that night!" Yeah, I can't exactly fight her on that one.

"I was trying to keep you safe."

"By what, being a fucking pussy?"

"How the fuck do you go from saying you love me to calling me a pussy?"

She shrugs. "Easily. I had weeks to get the fuck over you and forget you ever existed."

That knocks the fucking wind out of my lungs and hurts more than I want to admit. "Right. Well, I guess I will be the one saving your father from your mother's wrath then," I say as I grip the handles of the chair and prepare to stand.

"That's it?" I turn to her and frown.

"You made your point. I fell for you and you said what you did out of guilt. It's fine, I'll help your father and then me and my brothers will be out of here." I grit my teeth and stand grunting in pain as I feel my stitches pull. That pain is better to feel than the other. I thought coming back here she would be excited to see me and for the first time without the trials in our way and my father in the picture that we could give whatever this is between us a real go, but I was fucking delusional. There will never be a future between us after what I did to her, she has every right to hate me but she will never hate me as much as I hate myself. "For what it's worth, I'm so sorry for what happened." I ignore the pain exploding in my chest as I walk away from her.

She is a wildfire, the best way to describe her is like warm honey on your tongue, her beauty is as bright as the sun. London Murdoch is someone so unique you will never meet another person like her in your lifetime. She exudes darkness but that isn't what she was to me, she was a light at the end of a long dark road but I fucked it up.

"You should know by now I never say shit I don't mean." I freeze on the spot and force the hope blooming inside me to abate as I slowly turn to face her. She stands there with her hair billowing around her like a curtain. The short hair actually suits her, it enhances the bone structure in her face.

"Don't play games with me, London, say what the fuck you mean before I walk out and this time I won't come back."

The little shit smirks and slowly saunters toward me with the swagger of a wet dream. I stay where I am, forcing her to choose to either come to me or walk away. I made my stand and showed her what I want. Now it's time for her to stop hiding behind her fear of losing someone else she loves. She keeps a foot of space between us and cranes her head back to look up at me.

"I don't want to play games with you but you have to know I will kill your father, it isn't a debate, it's a fact that it's going to happen."

"I wouldn't be here if I was opposed to him dying. Was me nearly dying to save the lives of my brothers, not indication enough for you to see that I hate him. I want him to rot in fucking hell for what he did to you." She exhales loudly at the reminder of what happened. "Don't get me wrong, I know I also have a first class ticket to hell because of what I did to you."

"What?" she says confused.

"Don't play dumb, it doesn't suit you."

"I'm not playing anything, asshole. I don't understand what the fuck you mean, which is why I said *what*."

"What I did to you that night..." I close my eyes and force the shame away so I can get through this. "I will hate myself forever for doing that shit to you, London. It was fucked up and disgusting and it makes me sick knowing that—"

"You stopped him and everyone else from running a fucking train on me." I reel back in shock. "I told you to do it, I wanted it to be you because I knew..." she drops her gaze to her feet, "you wouldn't hurt me and would make sure I was okay." I reach out and brush my knuckles along her cheek.

"I would never have hurt you," I say barely above a whisper.

She clutches my shirt in her hands and hauls me against her. "I know and that is the exact reason I wanted it to be you." I search her gaze for any sign of deceit but don't see any.

"You don't hate me?" She smiles and shakes her head.

"No. I don't blame you for anything that happened, pretty boy. I'm grateful you saved me from what could have happened." Hearing those words come from her mouth is like a weight being lifted off my chest. For the past three weeks I have spent every waking moment praying that she wouldn't hate me, but another part of me thought it was just wishful thinking. "Now this is the part where you kiss me and we find a dark corner where you can rail me without my dad finding us and killing you."

She doesn't need to tell me twice, I lean down and seal my lips to hers. She opens for me without hesitation. The moment the taste of her invades my senses I groan, gripping her waist I pull her in so she can feel how much I want her. She moans into my mouth when she feels my hard cock pressed against her.

"You want to fucking die?" We jerk apart at the sound of Royal's angry voice. He stomps up the stairs toward us and doesn't stop until he pushes London out of the way and gets right in my face. "You don't touch her."

"Fine, but I'm going to touch him."

Jesus Christ! She really does want her father to fucking kill me! Royal doesn't look at her as he answers.

"You touch him, I kill him. He touches you, I torture him. My house, my fucking rules."

"Fine. I'm telling Mom I'm moving out and you can explain to her why." Royal's eyes widen a fraction before he schools his features, not wanting to fuck things up with him further I cut in.

"Okay," I say.

"What the hell do you mean, *okay*?" London shouts. Royal smiles and takes a step back as I spy the rest of the family coming to join us, yippee.

"He clearly wants to live." London turns a bright shade of red.

"So just to clarify, he can't touch me and I can't touch him while under your roof?" He smiles wide and nods like he won the fucking lottery, dumbass should know better than that. "Perfect." She swings her gaze to me and bats her lashes. "Choose a car."

I frown in confusion. "Why?" I ask hesitantly.

"Because I can touch you all I want in the back seat of a car without him killing you."

"The fuck you can!" Royal shouts so fucking loud I jerk. "You fucking lay a single finger on her, you little cunt, and I'll slit your fucking throat, feel me?" Being the smart man that I am, I keep my mouth shut, raise my hands and take a few steps backward. London rounds on her father and the two of them begin to bicker and fight. The triplets come to stand by me as we watch the scene in front of us. I tune them out and focus on my brothers.

"You guys good?" I ask.

"Yeah, thanks to you we live." Adonis tries to sound nonchalant but I hear the undertone of sadness in his voice.

Placing a hand on his shoulder I say, "No, you live because you fought and did everything I taught you to do."

"How is that going to work out for you?" Ares says, flicking his gaze toward London and Royal.

I deflate. "Very painfully." The three of them snicker at my expense.

Chapter Twenty-Nine

London

Dad and I are officially at a *Stalemate*.

I'm fucking fuming at the audacity of him. He thinks he can lay down the law and I will just abide by what he says—wrong! I plan to push every one of his fucking buttons until he learns he cannot forbid me from seeing Artemis. Thinking he was dead destroyed something inside me. For the past three weeks I haven't felt like myself but now seeing him again, the part that I thought died is slowly breathing life back into me.

"Snooping?" I jerk around and glare at Cronos.

"No."

He rests his shoulder against the wall and pins me with a dry stare. "Why are you standing outside your father's closed office door then?"

I growl and stomp my foot. "Because he fucking locked me out and won't let me in there!" I am fucking livid right now. Aunt Sin, Uncle Kacey, Aunt Meelz, Uncle Chaos, Grandpa, and Artemis are in there with him but I'm locked out here. Aunt Cass and Grandma went back to their place with Mom so Aunt Cass could show them the renovations she did to the twins' rooms.

"You mad because you were not included in the plans or because you're worried your dad is scaring Artemis off?"

I huff. "Never mind," I grit out as I stomp past him and head for the kitchen. The sight of my phone on the counter sparks an idea. I grab it and quickly dial Marco's number, I can feel Nos behind me watching my every move.

"Miss Murdoch?" he says when he answers.

"Marco, come quickly there is someone trying to break in." I end the call for dramatic effect and smile at my bestie as I perch my ass on one of the breakfast stools and pat the one next to me. He shakes his head but I can see he's fighting to keep his smile hidden as he claims the seat next to me. "3...2...1.."

"London!" my dad roars from down the hallway. I hear their feet pounding the ground as they rush to find me and rescue me from the intruder.

"In here!" I singsong. I snort at the sight of all of them with their guns drawn except for Artemis and Aunt Meelz. Artemis shoves past everyone and ignores my dad's threats as he comes to me. He doesn't hesitate as he pushes between my legs and cups my face, I smile.

His eyes narrow. "You little shit," he mutters.

"The fuck did you just call my daughter?" Dad barks out followed by the sound of his gun cocking. We ignore him as I reach out and grip Artemis's waist.

"I was scared," I say in a nasally voice trying to sound scared.

"Bullshit, everyone in this fucking house is scared of *you*," he claps back, earning a gasp from me.

"Darling, how could you say such a thing?" Artemis rolls his eyes before he is shoved out of the way and I'm met with a very angry Royal Murdoch standing before me. "Daddy, thank goodness you're here, I was so scared—"

"Cut the shit, London," he snaps.

"Fine." I slouch back against the counter and cross my arms over my chest.

"Chaos, call Marco and call off the hunt, tell him my daughter was being a brat."

My jaw unhinges. "I was not being a brat!" I shout.

"Were too!"

Happiness erupts inside me at my dad's reply, everyone around us groans. "Were not!"

"Yes, you were."

"I love this game, Daddy! Was not."

He grinds his teeth so hard I think he may actually break them, then releases a growl before spinning away from me and looking at my grandfather. "See, she isn't a fucking sweetheart, you deal with her while I finish planning this shit."

"I vote Artemis deals with me," I say as I raise my arm into the air like I'm a student in school trying to ask my teacher a question. I spy Artemis out of the corner of my eye shaking his head and fighting not to laugh. When Dad takes a single step in my man's direction, I leap off my chair ready to intervene until Cronos yanks me back by my wrist. At the sound of my grunt, Artemis snaps his head toward us and a cloud of darkness shrouds him as he focuses his gaze on where his brother is touching me. Artemis shoulders past my dad, not giving a fuck that he is pointing a gun at him. He smacks Nos's hand away from me and pushes me behind him as his twin climbs to his feet and gets right in his face.

"She doesn't want you!" Artemis forces out through clenched teeth.

"You don't fucking own her," Nos snaps back. I look around the room to see my family are all standing around watching this unfold.

"What's the problem, *Nos*, you angry because she doesn't want you or are you pissed that we are identical and she still sees me as more than you?" I reel back in outrage.

"Hold the fuck on—" They ignore my protest as Nos steps into his brother so they are eye to eye.

"She will see soon enough that you only care about taking over for Costa and she was nothing to you but leverage to garner the support of her family because you were too weak to overthrow him by yourself." I balk at Cronos, his twin literally nearly died to try and save their lives and this is how he repays him.

"At one stage that was all I wanted because it meant giving you and the triplets your freedom from our fucking father!" Artemis shouts in his face. It's at that moment the triplets enter the room looking worried at the sight of their brothers.

"We didn't need you to protect us," Cronos shouts. I slam my eyes closed because the four of them haven't seen the scars he saved them from.

"And I didn't need you to move in on my girl the moment you thought I was dead, but yet you did." My eyes widen to the size of dinner plates.

"He doesn't—"

Cronos cuts in before I can finish. "I'm the better choice." I stumble backward and dart my gaze to my dad who shoots me an *I told ya so* look, it pisses me off that he looks so smug about this situation.

"Yeah you are," Artemis's reply stuns every person in this room, even Cronos.

"What?"

"You are the better choice, brother, I know it, she knows it and so do you." I shake my head denying what he says without words. "You offer her safety, comfort and will bend to her will. I can't offer her those things because as long as Costa breathes, she will never be safe with me. I can't offer her the comfort you can because I have demons of my own that haunt me. I can never bend to her will because she doesn't need someone who will submit to her every whim, she needs a challenge and I do that for her. I'm the wrong choice but she still chose me. I have given my all to doing everything for you, Adonis, Ares and Apollo. I've never taken something for myself or had anything of my own—"

"You have Blake," Cronos says smugly. Artemis lazily rolls his head to the side to look at the triplets who suddenly find the ceiling and floor more interesting.

"Oh my God, you three ran a train on the blonde whore!" I say gleefully, they all cringe and shoot their brother a sheepish look. Fuck yes, that blonde bitch is gone, no coming back from that one, you dirty little rat.

"Blake was never something I wanted. She was just a constant and someone outside of the four of you to speak to. But *she* is different, I want her more than anything and I won't let her go without a fight. I have given the four of you everything you have ever wanted but I'm keeping this one thing for myself."

"You've never done anything for us!" Cronos roars. I've had enough of this whole being talked about while I stand here and not say anything, so I push between the twins ignoring the protests of my family as I stare up at my best friend. I can see the hurt in his eyes and I hate that I didn't realize sooner that our friendship meant something different to him and I was too dense to see that. I tentatively reach out and place my hand on his chest, he instantly softens at my touch, I feel Artemis tense behind me.

"Nos." A shuddering breath leaves him and I feel like an utter bitch but I've never had to deal with anything like this before. "I love you." I feel Artemis deflate behind me but I can't worry about him right now. I can feel everyone's gaze on us, the most noticeable being my dad's because I can feel his trigger finger itching to shoot both guys just to make sure I don't have a chance of being nailed by one of them. "I meant everything I said to you when I said I wanted us to be besties. You are the only friend I have ever had outside of my family. Shit, I've never wanted a friend until I met you."

"Just a friend?" he says quietly. I suck in a deep breath and force myself to carry on. I don't know how people can deal with this shit all the time, it's fucking exhausting and awkward and I don't like it.

"You think because he's your twin that I will see him through you but the truth is, you two look nothing alike to me. Neither do the triplets. I can tell the difference between the five of you with ease. To the outside world they may confuse the both of you but not me. I see you as my best friend but I see him as..." I bite my lip unsure how to continue.

"See me as what?" Artemis huskily whispers behind me. I close my eyes for a second before slowly opening them again and doing what Aunt Meelz and Artemis have told me, I won't hide my feelings anymore.

"My friend." I hear him scoff behind me in annoyance. "My partner, someone who will push me to never change to fit the world. He sees me as me, not as Royal Murdoch's daughter or Bishop's granddaughter, he's always just seen me. Can you say the same?" I see he wants to lie so I pin him with a look begging him to be straight with me.

"I knew who you were the moment you walked into the club." I nod.

"I know, I saw it in your eyes when you served me."

"What if I didn't see you as that anymore and I saw you?" Fuck, this shit sucks!

"You do see me now but you see the side of me no one else gets to see. You saw me break, no one has ever seen that, Nos, I mean that honestly." His brows raise at my declaration. "My own father and mother have never seen what you did in that hotel room."

"You thought I was Artemis," he says bitterly.

I shake my head. "I saw you. Did I wish it was him? Yes. But at that moment, it wasn't my family or your brother I needed, it was you, my best friend. I've never had someone I could rely on and call to talk about shit except for my aunts but I know there is only so much I can tell them. With you, I never have to hide anything. I love you, I really do, but not in the way you want me to."

"This whole her being sweet thing is fucking weird." I peer around Nos and glare at Uncle Chaos.

"Just so you know, he isn't a saint." I roll my eyes and turn my back to Cronos to face Artemis, his gaze bores into mine, the lustful look in his eyes has me fighting back a groan and forcing myself not to clench my thighs to ease the ache beginning to form between my legs. I push all thoughts of him pinning me against the wall and slamming inside me from my head.

"Take your shirt off."

"London!" Dad shouts. I turn to him.

"It's not what you think, Dad, just trust me." I turn back to Artemis who looks torn. "Show them, let them see what you sacrificed." He shakes his head.

"I can't," he mutters.

"What is she talking about, Art?" Ares asks as he and the other two creep in closer to us.

"Nothing," he clips out.

"Pretty boy, either you take it off willingly or I jab you in the gut and rip it off you."

"You need therapy," he grits out.

"I've said that for years," Dad mutters. I shoot him a glare but notice even he has crept in closer to us.

"I'm telling Mom." He screws his face up.

"Snitch." I ignore my dad and focus back on Artemis.

"Show them. They think you are some selfish prick who does everything Daddy says. Make them understand that isn't who the fuck you are or I will." He takes a deep breath and nods.

"Can you help me?" I reach for the hem of his shirt and fight the smirk from breaking free at the sound of my dad, grandpa and uncle's muttering curses beneath their breath.

"He can't do it on his own because of the stitches!" Aunt Meelz scolds them. the moment his shirt is off, I shoot him a reassuring smile and step out of the way so his brothers can see. He slowly turns so they can see the scars that litter his back and chest, even my own family gasps at the sight. My eyes are glued to the bandage around his abs, guilt churns inside me at the sight.

"What the fuck!"

"Who did that?"

"How long did this go on for?"

"I thought you said you fought in the underground?" the

four Argyros siblings fire off at once. Artemis runs his gaze over each of them before answering.

"I told you I fought in illegal fights so you would never know the truth about what Costa would do if any of us stepped out of line."

Adonis reels back. "What the fuck do you mean, if *we* stepped out of line?"

"It doesn't matter!" Art says in a firm tone.

"Yes the fuck, it does!" Ares claps back.

Artemis runs a hand through his hair, clearly feeling uncomfortable about this whole thing and having my family gawking at him and listening to what he's saying wouldn't help either.

"If any of us did something he didn't like, I got one of these and then the shit beaten out of me by four or more of his men. You happy now?" The four of them stand there with pale faces. I move in closer to Artemis's side and lace my fingers through his, some of the tension eases from him.

"If it makes it better, he got one of those on his back because of me," I say, the four of them swing their gazes to me.

"What?" Dad barks, drawing my attention to him but Artemis answers before I can, keeping his gaze on his shoes.

"I got four that night because I helped my brothers pass the first trial and refused to kill London." A range of emotions ripple across my dad's face.

"The day we came to meet with you all about the trials, you were injured?" Artemis lifts his gaze to meet my Dad's and nods.

"Yes. I got two cuts because I defied an order and failed to kill London for the first time." The bitterness that laces each of his words can be felt by all.

"Wow, so three of those belong to me." Artemis pins me with a bored look.

"Really?"

I shrug and smile up at him. "Hey, I'm totally into the scars," I defend.

"Put your fucking shirt on," Dad snaps. My family laughs at his expense.

"Help me?" Art asks.

"Of course!" I answer, only to be hauled backward by the back of my shirt by my dad. "Hey!" I protest.

"He has those four to fucking help his Edward Scissorhands looking ass." I gape up at my dad.

"I know who that is!" The asshole just winks at me, while I stand here and silently fume.

"Good, then you know the whole town hated him," he says smugly.

"Want to know where else he has scars and bruises?" I clap back, the smugness drops right off his face, triumph ripples through me.

"Want me to add to that collection of scars in your name?" Anger replaces my triumph.

"Touch him and I'll resort to my old tactics of trying to kill you in your sleep." I hear my grandpa, uncles and aunts choke on air behind me.

"You little shit—"

Artemis cuts in before Dad can finish. "Costa will be with the other leaders in Mykonos at the cove of the founding fathers." Dad and I remain in a glare off, ignoring what Artemis said. Even though I can see my dad wants to jump into action, he refuses to bow out and let me win.

"I won't let you hurt him," I say.

"My rules apply, touch him he dies, he touches you I torture him," he fires back.

"Oh, he has already touched me." Anger like I have never seen before roars to life in his eyes.

"Chaos, Kacey, take that motherfucker to the basement!" I turn to the side, keeping my uncles and my dad in my view.

"Any of you touches him and I promise you I will burn this fucking house down and make all the shit you did to Grandpa look like child's play." I see both my uncles hesitate but not my dad.

"He just gave up his only form of leverage, he is worth nothing to me now!" Dad yells. We have had spats in the past but not like this. We've never gone this far to the point where our anger has taken control and we hurt each other.

"But he's worth everything to me!" I yell back. We're both breathing hard and fast, ready to fight at a second's notice if that is what it comes down to. I don't relish the idea of fighting my family but I will if it means protecting Artemis.

"London, stop. I'll go with them."

"Shut up, pretty boy," I snap.

Chapter Thirty

Artemis

The tension between Royal and London is so thick you can taste it on the tip of your tongue, her body is coiled tight and ready to strike at any second. The fact she is standing here ready to face off against her family means more than she will ever know. She's shown me twice now that she chooses me. Not wanting to cause anymore problems between her and her father, I make a decision to end this shit between them. I grip the back of her neck and haul her back to me, she doesn't fight me as I tighten my hold and force her gaze to mine.

"Get your fucking hands off her," Royal roars.

"Royal!" Chanel warns.

"Listen to me, little demon, I knew the second I touched you that if I lost against our father that this is where I would end up for daring to taint the Murdoch's prized heir."

"You didn't taint me," she protests.

Smirking down at her I nod. "I did a little but let's be real,

you were already tainted by the devil before I touched you."
She chuckles. "Point is, I was in a position of power and to
everyone else it would appear as if I used that power to seduce
you." She opens her mouth to argue but I push on. "I don't
regret it for a single second but you need to come to terms with
this, he has every right to do what he wants because I fucked
up. I don't have the army of the Greeks behind me or their
protection. I'm just a man who fell in love with the girl who
turned his whole fucking world upside down." Fuck it, I smash
my lips against hers, needing to taste her one last time. If she is
the last thing I taste in this world aside from my own blood
then I will die happily. Before she can deepen the kiss, I pull
back and step away from her turning to face a pissed off
looking Royal. "Do your worst."

He takes a single step forward only to be halted when his
father comes to stand in front of me, flanked by Amelia and
Chanel.

"We have a war to plan, Son."

"Dad, you need to get the fuck out of my way right now. If
I have to shoot you to get to that motherfucker who thought
he could touch my daughter, then I will." The pure hatred in
Royal's tone is palpable.

"You are not going to touch the boy," Chanel says in a
deathly calm voice.

"Sin, stay the fuck out of this," he snarls.

"You want to hurt her and make her hate you? Then go
right ahead and kill him, we won't stop you, but if you want to
have a relationship like the one I share with my dad because of
what he did to the man I loved, then you just need to pull that
trigger." Amelia steps aside, Chanel follows her lead but Bishop
doesn't budge.

"Being a father is hard. You gave me so much shit for being

hard on you and all we did was fight until I saw the errors of my ways. You hurt my granddaughter by hurting that prick, then I'm gonna have to hurt you as well, Son. Make no mistake though, the moment your mother and wife find out what you have done they will both raise hell." If this wasn't such a serious moment I would laugh at the way his face contorted in pain at the mention of his wife and Mom. I love how these men are all badass and ruthless but when it comes to facing the wrath of their women, they drop their nuts. It's a sight I have never seen because women aren't viewed the same way where I come from.

"I won't touch him," London says with the grace of an opera singer as she moves to stand by her grandfather. "I'll stay away from him, you win." The anguish in her tone spears me, she shoulders past her father as she dashes from the room.

"You're a real dick," Amelia bites out before following after her niece.

"You remind me so much of my dad right now. Learn from his mistakes, Royal, and don't fucking hurt that girl because if you make her cry, I'll mark your fucking ass so fast and put you out of your own misery." Chanel shoulders past him, he grunts and stumbles but says nothing. A look of shock flashes through his eyes when Kacey follows after Chanel and Chaos steps up to him.

"Not you too," he whines.

"Fraid so, brother. You know London doesn't do feelings, she's fucking allergic to them." I snort and quickly clamp my mouth closed when the three Murdoch's shoot me a scathing look. "She has been different since Havoc died, she barely smiled, never touched anyone freely and always hid away but now, since that dick came along, she actually seems... happy. She even laughs now. You didn't see her that night when she thought he died, she was a wreck with Havoc but with him, she was destroyed. Don't take away her chance of happiness, if that prick is what makes her happy, then let him live."

"You don't even like him," Royal fires back.

Chaos shrugs. "The fact he's willing to die for her and be cut up at least proves he is somewhat worthy of her time." Chaos turns to face me and being the sole focus of his attention is fucking unnerving but I've dealt with worse so I stand tall and hold his gaze. "You so much as make that girl shed a single fucking tear and I'll rip you limb from fucking limb and piss on your rotting corpse while I lie to my niece and tell her you ran away like a bitch." He leaves me standing here reeling over his threat as he goes after London.

"All of you get out." Bishop laughs, nods and orders my brothers out of the room, leaving me alone with Royal for the first time. We size each other up. If I wasn't injured right now, I know I could take him, we're the same height and similar build, we would be evenly matched in a fist fight. "I hate you."

"I know."

"You aren't good enough for her."

"I know."

"You will never have my blessing or acceptance of you wanting to be with her."

"I get that."

"You're too fucking old for her."

"It's not that big of a gap."

"You will never return to Blackwood as headmaster, I made sure of that."

"I never wanted the job to begin with."

"Why'd you take it then?"

"I didn't have a choice, either I took the job or my brothers paid the price."

"Why'd you save her?"

A whoosh of air escapes me. I stab a hand through my hair and try to think of the right thing to say but come up blank so, I decide to just tell him the story. "You've met your daughter, she's a magnet."

"No, she isn't. She's a fucking sour lemon and exudes fuck off vibes."

I snort and nod. "Oh, she did all of that. When I first met her I was awestruck. She didn't flaunt herself around, she fought me at every turn and when it came down to it she became an addiction. A need. I found any excuse to see her, speak to her or incite her wrath just so she would spare me a scrap of her attention for a fleeting moment." I take a deep breath and stop myself from rambling for a second before I pull it together and try a different way to explain it to him. "I would continue to take beating after beating and scar after scar if it meant I got to just catch a glimpse of her, hear her laughter from a distance. I know it's not what you want to hear but I fell in love with your daughter when I had no fucking right."

"No, you didn't, but you still did."

I nod. "It was out of my control. She literally stole the fucking organ from my chest and branded her name on the fucking thing."

"You must be higher than a giraffe's pussy if you think that shit will sway me."

"I don't know how to answer that."

"When your father is dealt with, and the Greek's appoint you the new Godfather what happens to her then?"

"What makes you think I will be chosen?" I ask in surprise.

"Because I will make sure you are chosen. I'll wipe them all out for standing back and allowing your cocksucker of a father to touch my baby girl. There is no saving any of them, there will be a new leader and Godfathers Of The Night, you will lead them and your brothers will be your council."

"Why would you do that?"

He looks pained as he speaks. "Because, you seem level headed and from what I have heard and seen, you cared enough about my daughter to go against your family and birthright to protect her when I couldn't. Accept what I am offering you and you have my word that you and your brothers will live and remain unharmed."

"What's the catch?"

He smirks and takes a couple steps toward me, leaving a foot of space between us. "The trials are to be stopped, you are to stop helping the others with transporting women for the skin trade."

I eye him warily for a moment, there's more I can see it in his eyes. "What else?"

"The law states that once you lead the Greeks, you can never rule another family."

I scoff. "Meaning London can never be with me as the heiress to the Murdoch mafia and *Memento Mori*, she would be forced to return home and leave me when that time came."

He smiles and nods. "Exactly, see, I can be a reasonable guy."

"Yeah, right," I mutter bitterly.

"This conversation is over, we leave for Mykonos first thing in the morning. I want this shit done before Christmas so I can spend it with my family while you spend it with yours thousands of miles away."

"She comes to Mykonos with us," I say just before he leaves.

"No." He turns to leave but I push on.

"Yes!"

He spins around and glares at me. "That shit isn't funny when London does it and sure as fuck isn't working in your favor playing her stupid game."

"It's not a game, Royal. She needs to be there because she needs to be the one to do it. She wants her pound of flesh from him because he stole something from her. You hate me because of what I did to your daughter, I hate myself too for it even if she refuses to hate me. I did it to save her the pain of having to endure all those other motherfuckers thinking they could touch my girl."

"She isn't yours!" he roars. "She is mine and Erika's, you will never take her from us."

"What if she chooses me?"

He scoffs. "She may think she loves you but her obligation to her family will always come first. Deny it all you want but you know it's true. She remains here."

"She'll follow us, you know it and so do I. She is safer with us than following behind on her own."

"Fuck off, you sleep outside tonight, bitch boy."

Chapter Thirty-One

London

I can't tamper down the rage inside me. Ever since my aunts and uncles left my room earlier, thanks to my dad ordering them away and telling me I am to stay put. I, of course, rebelled and tried to storm out of my room but the bastard locked me in here. I tried the windows only to see two guards stationed beneath them! I called my mom begging her to help me. I can hear her and my dad arguing from their bedroom but I can already tell he won't back down. I heard him yelling earlier that they are leaving for Mykonos in the morning and he plans to leave me behind. I'm not fucking staying here!

The sound of the lock clicking open on my door has me pausing in the center of my room. I wait with bated breath to see who it is because I know it isn't my dad. I can still hear him and my mom shouting. When the door finally opens, my jaw hits the floor at the sight in front of me. My two aunts and Uncle Chaos stand there with shit eating grins on their faces.

"What are you three doing?" I ask.

"Breaking in." I snort at Aunt Meelz's answer.

"I see that but why?"

"Oh, we're not breaking in, he is," Aunt Sin says as Uncle Chaos shifts out of view for a second and then the next thing I see is Artemis stumbling into my room. He looks just as shocked as I do.

"What's going on?" he asks.

"We're doing you a solid, don't be a brat and tell your dad we helped." I gape at Uncle Chaos. "We're all heading home, we'll be back first thing in the morning to kick dipshit out before Royal realizes he isn't sleeping under the patio."

"Don't rip his stitches!" Aunt Meelz warns as they close and lock the door behind themselves. Butterflies erupt inside me.

Since when have I ever had fucking butterflies?

There's tension between us, some of it awkwardness but most of it is sexual tension and right now all I want is to feel him inside me, owning me, claiming me as his like he's done before. I take a single step toward him but he takes one back.

"London, you need to know some things."

"I don't need to know shit right now, unless it's you telling me you don't want me then I don't give a fuck."

His features soften. "I could never say no to you but are you sure you're okay with this? Last time wasn't exactly—"

"Artemis, they saw me naked, they didn't touch me."

"Costa did," he grits out.

"And that motherfucker is going to die for that tomorrow but tonight, I don't want to talk." I grip the hem of my shirt and yank it over my head. His eyes blaze at the sight of the skin I've uncovered. I rid myself of my pants next, standing before him in nothing but my bra and panties. He drinks in the sight of me and the heated look in his eyes sends shivers down my spine.

"Lose the bra and panties." The husky tone of his voice has a thrill rushing through me. I do as he demands, tossing my bra to the side and kicking my panties away. "Fuck." He comes toward me staying just out of reach, the anticipation he is building inside me has me growing wet. "Undress me." I eagerly obey. He bends enough for me to get rid of his shirt. I keep my eyes on his as I pop the button on his jeans and slowly lower his zipper. His jaw works from side to side in impatience but he refuses to be the first to break. Crouching down, I peel his jeans and boxers down his legs, helping him out of them.

I kneel before him and stare up at him through my lashes, it's taking all my strength not to look at his cock, my mouth watering at the memory of what he tasted like.

"Suck it." I groan in delight as I finally drop my gaze to his hard length. "Hands behind your back." I do as he says. He reaches down. gripping himself, then pumps it a couple times until a bead pre cum can be seen. I dart my tongue out eager to taste him but he shifts. "Beg me." My gaze snaps to him instantly.

"Please."

"Please what?"

Need coils low in my belly. "Please let me suck your cock."

"That's better. Now open." I open my mouth for him. He doesn't gently enter my mouth, no, he slams almost all the way in, forcing me to gag around his girth. Tears instantly cloud my vision, his hand tangling in my hair as he holds me in place and fucks my mouth. "Fuck, baby, swirl your tongue just like that." I swirl my tongue along the underside of his dick and relish in the sounds tumbling from his lips. "Fuck yes," he grits out as his thrusts begin to grow erratic. I can feel him growing inside my mouth and know he's close. He tries to pull out but I'm not having that, I reach out and grip the globes of his ass, holding him in place as I bob my head up and down on his cock needing to taste his cum. "Fuck, London!" he grits out as he comes down my throat, shuddering. I swallow every fucking drop, loving the taste. I slowly ease off him and place a kiss to the tip of his cock, then shoot him a wink.

"Feel better, darling?" I taunt. His eyes darken, his grip on my hair tightens as he uses it to pull me to my feet. I stare at him open-mouthed and shocked at that move. "Did you just pull me to my feet by my hair?"

"Shut the fuck up and get on the bed, now." The throbbing in my pussy overrides my need to argue back. He follows me over to the bed. I watch as he positions himself in the center of the bed. "Sit on my face."

"What?"

"Bring my pretty fucking pussy over here and sit on my fucking face." Feeling kind of unsure and slightly embarrassed, I hesitate. "Now, or you don't come." Yep, that wipes away any doubts. I climb on the bed and straddle his face gripping the headboard for support as I hover above him.

"Will you be able to breathe?"

He tears his gaze from my weeping pussy to glare up at me. "Baby, if I'm able to breathe then you ain't doing it right. Now shut the fuck up and ride my face quietly so your dad doesn't hear me fucking his little girl."

Fuck it, I press down onto his waiting tongue and moan loudly before I clamp a hand over my mouth. He reaches up and tweaks my nipples as he runs his tongue from my clit to my opening. My body takes over and begins to grind on his face. I'm so fucking turned on that I know I won't take long to come, I just hope he is good at holding his breath because I'm not stopping, this feels too fucking good to stop.

"Artemis, just like that," I grit out, then bite down on my fingers to keep from screaming when he sucks my clit into his mouth. A shudder rips through me when he flicks the tip of his tongue against my clit. He catches on and continues to do that. I feel my orgasm building and begin to grind against him faster, chasing my release. He pinches my nipples, drawing a strangled cry from me, that feeling of pain and the pleasure he is inflicting on my pussy sends me over the edge. I bite down so hard on my fingers to keep from screaming as I come all over his face. Aftershocks tear through me as I slowly come down from my high, he continues to lap at my pussy forcing more tremors to take control of me.

When it becomes too much, I push off him, panting. He lolls his head to the side with the biggest grin on his face. "Fuck, you taste so good."

"I could say the same about you."

"Good, now get the fuck on my cock and reacquaint your pussy with the feeling of my cum inside you." I scurry down the bed to do as he says. He's already hard for me and I fucking love that. I straddle his lap, careful not to touch the bandage wrapped around his abs, and reach between us to line his cock up with my entrance. I dart my gaze to his, we hold each other's stare as I slowly sink down on him. I love watching his features change as I swallow each inch of him. When he is fully sheathed inside me we both moan at the feeling. He reaches out and interlocks his fingers with mine, locking his arms so I have something to hold onto. "Bounce up and down."

I follow his instructions and lift up until only the tip remains inside me before dropping down, a loud moan rips out of me.

"Shut the fuck up," he snaps.

"I can't," I whine as I repeat the same move, moaning again.

"Bite your lip or something." I balk at him, but he silences the argument on the tip of my tongue when he thrusts up inside me. When I lift up this time he meets me thrust for thrust. I bite down so hard on my lip I draw blood.

"I can't," I cry out when I can no longer remain silent. He growls and in a swift move I don't see coming, has me flat on my stomach. He grunts in pain as he slips off the edge of the bed. He grips my hips and hauls me back until the tips of my toes touch the carpet. He kicks my legs apart and slams into me at the same time his hand presses on the back of my head forcing my face into the comforter. I scream out but it's muted. He fucks me ruthlessly, the only sounds that can be heard are his heavy breathing and skin slapping against skin. I feel my pussy clamp down on his cock and without any warning I come so fucking hard I see little spots in the corner of my eyes. His pace doesn't slow or change for a moment until he starts to pound into me harder, forcing me into the mattress.

"I want your cum coating my cock."

"I can't," I mumble into the comforter.

"Give me that fucking cum, baby. I want that pussy milking the cum out of me." He uses his free hand to land two swift slaps to my ass. I yelp and lurch forward but the grip he has on my head holds me in place. "Come for me, baby," he grits out, then lands another slap to my cheek. As if he is a genie and can grant magic orgasms out of thin air, I come again but this time it's so fucking strong and intense that I can't breathe and my body feels like pins and needles are scattered throughout. "Fuck, yes," he grits out as he comes deep inside me, the feeling of his cum filling me has a sick sense of satisfaction rolling through me.

He releases his hold on my head and I turn to the side gasping for air, he's breathing just as hard as me. He slowly eases out of me and to my surprise flips me onto my back before reclaiming his place between my legs. I watch with rapt attention as he runs his finger through my folds and I jerk. I'm so sensitive. He keeps his gaze on mine as he pushes a finger inside me. I moan and fight to keep my eyes from rolling back into my head.

"This feeling right here of my cum inside you is what I want you to remember." I'm trying to focus on what he's saying but it's so fucking hard when he's fingering me so fucking good. "This pussy is mine."

"Fuck." I arch off the bed when he hooks his finger and hits that sweet fucking spot inside me.

"Say it."

"Yes, yes whatever you want just don't stop." I reach blindly for a pillow. I snag one and bite down on it just in time for him to insert a second finger.

"I love you, London." My heart melts, I knew I had one of them but I've never felt it beat like this before.

I yank the pillow from my mouth and stare deep into his eyes. "I love you too." He smiles cockily then leans down and captures my lips in a heated kiss. I moan when I taste myself on his tongue. He continues to finger fuck me and swallows my scream as I come all over his hand but this time when the orgasm rips through me, I pass the fuck out.

What a way to go, death by lethal Argyros cock.

Chapter Thirty-Two

Artemis

I woke this morning to the sound of Amelia entering London's room. I hated having to untangle myself from her hold. That was the best sleep I have had in years, well, we did manage to get a couple hours in between me waking her to fuck and her waking me with my cock in her mouth or her pussy on my face. My body is aching but in the best possible way. I snag my jeans off the floor and find my shirt across the other side of the room. Amelia says nothing as I walk past her shirtless and reeking of sex. I stand to the side and wait for her to quietly close the door. She motions for me to follow her down the stairs. She leads me out the back door and points toward the two wooden chairs London and I sat in yesterday. I nod my thanks but before she leaves I reach out and grab her arms.

'Thank you, Amelia, for looking after me and for last night."

She smiles kindly. "You're welcome. I love helping people

but about last night, don't ever mention it again, seriously." I chuckle and nod. She disappears back into the house as I make my way over to the seats. The sight of some blankets and a pillow brings a smile to my face, I bet this was all Amelia's doing. I get comfortable in my seat, I'm too wired to sleep so I decide to wait and watch the sunrise.

"You gonna let me in?" I snap my head to the side.

"How did you get out?" She rolls her eyes and lifts the blanket on my lap. She gently sits down, careful not to press against my stitches as she perches on my lap. I pull the blanket over us and wrap my arms around her, placing a kiss to the side of her head. "Seriously though, how did you get out?"

She laughs quietly. "Aunt Meelz didn't lock the door."

I groan. "He's going to know—"

"I don't care, he can't stop this, Artemis." I remain silent because she may not know it yet but he has made sure she and I can never be more than a moment in time. She will find someone else who will love and cherish her, someone who her family will welcome with open arms while I'll spend the rest of my life loving a girl I could never have.

"Is this a closed party?" I tense at the sound of my brother's voice. London smiles up at her bestie and waggles her brows.

"How could I ever have a party without my bestie?"

Cronos scoffs and shakes his head, dropping into the seat next to us. I grab the spare blanket and toss it to him.

"Thanks," he grunts. London and he fall into easy conversation like yesterday never happened. I know without a doubt that she cares about him but not in the way he cares for her. I start to wonder if he and I will ever be okay again. I love him but I won't allow him to try and steal my girl from me.

"Are you listening?" I shake my head and stare at London with a frown.

"What?"

"So rude," she says with an eye roll. I tighten my hold around her and bite down gently on the side of her neck, drawing a giggle from her. "Okay, stop. Nos was just saying he wants to travel."

I stare at my twin in surprise. "Since when?"

He shrugs. "Since now, I want something different from this life. I don't know what I want to do but I know it isn't this." Envy rears its ugly head inside me, I would love to choose to do something different with my life but that wasn't the card I was dealt.

"That's awesome, I'm happy for you." I mean every word.

"The triplets want this life, they want to rule over Greece and be kings." He and I both laugh, those three idiots have always loved the spotlight. We fall into comfortable silence as we watch the sunrise. I cement this memory in my mind, my girl in my arms with my brother by side as we watch the most stunning view. This will be a memory I'll draw on when they are both gone.

"Sweetheart." London leaps from my lap at the sound of her grandfather's voice.

"Grandpa." She tries to act unaffected but she isn't fooling anyone. Cronos and I remain seated and say nothing. "I was just... hanging out?"

Bishop snorts. "Is that what they call it these days?" She cringes. "Go shower and pack a bag.

If you want to be on that flight to Mykonos I would be quick." Her face lights up.

"You convinced dad?"

"No, I overheard a conversation yesterday and someone else convinced me that it was a good idea for you to come, plus it will piss your father off so I'm on board with that." They both laugh. London shoots me a wink before she rushes inside. I tense as I hear Bishop make his way over to us, stepping through the gap in the chairs. He wears a three-piece suit that fits him perfectly. The title of Don really does suit him. He runs his gaze over me and I can see the clear disdain in his eyes. "I heard the whole conversation between you and my son yesterday." I drop my gaze to my lap.

"Yeah," is all I manage to say.

"She is a once in a lifetime type of girl, don't be a fucking pussy and give into the demands of my son." I snap my gaze back to him in surprise. "You don't need the Greek army to stand behind you, all you need is his wife, his mother and me. The fact my granddaughter is free from her room, I would say you have her uncle and aunts on your side—"

"I broke in, they didn't help me—" He raises his hand stopping me, I clamp my mouth closed.

"I helped raise those three idiots. I know their tricks and they aren't as smart as they like to think they are." I roll my lips over my teeth to keep from smiling. "Know this, Artemis, that girl is all Royal has. He doesn't have siblings, only his cousins and he is fucking loyal and protective over them. He loves Erika as much as I love his mother but he loves that girl more, as any father should. You are a threat to that and he will fight you at every turn because she is all they will ever have until the day London makes them grandparents."

I pale. "That is not something—"

"Calm down, dipshit." I snap my mouth closed and force myself not to glare at him. "If you got her pregnant now, no one would be able to stop him from killing you, not even Kiara or Erika could stop that."

"Why are you telling me this?"

"Because unlike my wife who gave me a second chance

when I fucked up, London won't offer that to you. She would rather live with a broken heart then allow you to hurt her and get away with it. She was raised by her cunning aunt, her ruthless uncle, and a bloodthirsty father. She is a product of the way she was raised and we are fucking proud of her for that, but she was also raised by a mother who loves her more than anything in this world, including my son. She has her mother's heart, when she loves someone she is all in and will die for them. If you break that heart of hers, I'll fucking break you so choose wisely." I nod.

"I understand."

"One last thing."

"Yeah?"

"Remember who raised her father, uncle and aunt. I taught them everything they know, if you think going against them is a nightmare, try going against me and you will see the fiery depths of hell if you fuck her over." Bishop stalks back into the house and I slouch back into my chair.

"Well, good luck to you surviving the day, brother. I'm fucking grateful now that London can tell us apart because I would hate to be mistaken for you." I scowl at my fucking prick of a brother as he stands and heads inside.

After Bishop and Royal had a showdown out front about London coming with us, which took at least twenty minutes, for Royal to finally concede when London threatened to follow us and give his new G-wagon away. I'm sitting in the back with Chaos while London sits between Kacey and Royal while Chanel rides shotgun and one of Royal's guys drives. To say the ride is filled with tension is an understatement. I tried to ride with my brothers and Bishop, but Royal threatened to shoot Apollo if I did. Apparently I can't be trusted alone with his father and he blames me for London being here.

I spy Chaos out of the corner of my eye typing away on his computer. Watching him say goodbye to his wife and daughters was strange. The guy looks like he gives zero fucks about anyone, but the moment he looks at his wife or his daughters his whole aura changes. Unlike Royal and Chaos, Chanel's man gets to come along.

"Stop watching me," Chaos growls, breaking the silence in the car for the first time in ten minutes.

"Well, you're doing that wrong for starters," I say. He snaps his head in my direction.

"The fuck did you just say?"

I meet his angry stare with one of my own, I'm tired of them throwing their fucking weight around like I'm nothing. "You're trying to loop the feed on the cameras through Mykonos, you can't because they are all live feed."

"How the fuck do you know that?" I can feel Kacey and Royal staring at me but I keep my focus on Chaos.

"Because I'm the one who updated the system and switched out the old shit so no one would be able to do what you are trying to do."

"What the fuck do you suggest then, dick?" Royal says in a condescending tone. I lazily lull my head to the side to look at him.

"Ask me nicely and I'll shut down the video feed in the area."

"Oh my God, are you gonna make my dad beg too?" My eyes widen as I look to London and shake my head. It takes her a second to catch on to what the fuck she just said.

Royal, of course, is quicker than her. He tries to launch over the back seat to get to me but Chaos and Kacey fight to keep him back. London has no choice but to leap over to where I am in the car or be squashed by her father and uncle. The second she parks her ass on my lap, I throw my head back and groan.

"You really are fucking with my life, you know that, right?" She scoffs and continues to watch her father seethe and fight against her uncles as she answers.

"Nah, I'm testing out my dad's heart to make sure it's strong enough so he doesn't have a heart attack."

"Oh, there will be a fucking attack if you don't get your ass back the fuck over here now!" Royal yells so fucking loud that the driver swerves in fright.

"Calm the fuck down, Royal, we're nearly there," Chanel reprimands him from the front seat. I peer over London's shoulder to see Royal practically frothing at the mouth.

"Move your ass now, London. I'm not fucking with you." The deadly calm tone of his voice alerts me to the fact he is at his wits end.

"Omorfia—"

"If you try to ask me to move, Artemis, I will break your rib then stomp on your dick." I snap my mouth closed and leave her to it. "I am staying right here and you are going to take a chill pill. I'm eighteen, Dad."

"I don't give a fuck if you're forty."

"This is happening!"

"The fuck it is, what comes next is on you." Dread pools inside me, the remainder of the ride spent in silence. Having London on my lap is easier now thanks to Amelia removing my stitches this morning. It's still fucking tender and sore but not as bad. When we arrive at the private airfield, I frown at the sight of four private jets. When I spot the black one, my jaw unhinges.

"You didn't," Kacey says through his laughter.

"He's going to kill you," Chanel says through her own laughter. Chaos just sits there shaking his head smiling.

"After the shit he pulled this morning, he fucking deserves it." The humor is clear in Royal's voice. We pull up next to the other cars that are already parked. London climbs out before me and I go to follow after her but the moment my feet touch the ground, I'm met with a punch to the gut. I drop to my knees in fucking pain. I think Royal just fucking ripped my wound open again.

"What the fuck, Dad!" London screams.

"I told you what comes next is on you, help him and I'll break his fucking nose next time, touch him again after that and I'll blow out his fucking kneecaps."

"You little fucking prick!" Thank you Bishop for interrupting this standoff. While her father's back is turned, she helps me to my feet and I lift my shirt to check my wound, it's not open but it is fucking throbbing now.

"What's wrong, Daddy?" I choke on fucking air hearing Royal call his father daddy. Bishop looks like a bull charging at a red flag as he storms over to Royal, bumping his chest against his.

"You want me to give you an ass whooping, don't you?"

"Make my day and try it, old man." Seeing them facing off against each other is fucking fascinating. They are mirror images of each other except for the eyes and clothes. Bishop peers over Royal's shoulder and winks at London. Royal steps back and darts his gaze between his father and daughter.

"What the fuck did you two do?"

London gasps and tries to look shocked but fails. "Daddy, I

would never do anything to hurt you even after you punched my boyfriend for no reason." Hearing her call me that has a goofy fucking grin stretching across my face.

"Don't fucking call him that."

"You see, you little shit, when you are making phone calls to get my plane painted fucking pink with a chess piece on the side, you should make sure your daughter isn't listening." Royal's eyes widen.

"What the fuck did you do, London?"

"Moi? I did nothing, Daddy." She waves him off and grabs my hand, dragging me toward the plane. "Grandpa may have had your four cars towed to the paint shop to be painted the same color as his plane so you two could match." Laughter bursts out of me, I can hear Bishop and Royal arguing behind us but the moment we enter the jet my laughter dies in my throat at the sight of the rest of the Murdoch brothers and their brother-in-law. All five of their gazes snap toward me and to say the cabin turned chilly is an understatement. It's as cold as a fucking morgue in here!

Chapter Thirty-Three

London

Artemis has been weird and tense since we boarded the plane, he's only spoken to me when I've asked him a question. He's spent most of the time planning an attack with my uncles and dad, his brothers are even included in the conversation but I'm not interested in what they are talking about enough to care to give them my input.

"Why do you look like you're planning someone's murder?" I pull my gaze from Artemis to look over at Uncle Chaos, who sits opposite me.

"He's being weird," I huff out. "Should I punch him in the face to get his attention?"

He smiles. "Not unless you want to make your father happy." I scrunch my face.

"Yeah, okay, fair point." Silence stretches between us as he goes back to typing on his computer while I watch Artemis explain the layout of the cove to my uncles, dad and grandpa.

"He doesn't have a choice, karma."

"What do you mean?" He closes the lid of his laptop and gives me his full attention, making sure to keep his voice low so only I can hear when he speaks.

"He needs to prove himself to your dad."

"No, he doesn't."

"It's not for your dad's benefit, it's for him. He wants to be able to show your father that he can hold his own and play at the big boys table."

"Why?" I ask utterly confused.

"You're London Murdoch, heiress and worth a shit ton of money. He's some random guy with nothing. He wants to prove to your dad he is worthy of his daughter and in my opinion he needs to do it because the fucker had plans to kill my niece. I would have killed him myself if I didn't see how much he meant to you that night."

Hearing the love in his voice warms my heart. "I didn't think you cared, honestly," I say with a shrug. Hurt flashes through his eyes.

"Believe it or not, karma, I have been trying for years to get you to see that I was wrong for blaming you. Every time I have tried to talk to you about it, you'd find any excuse not to be alone with me."

Shame washes over me. "I thought you hated me," I whisper.

"No. I hated myself for a long time, not you. Havoc gave his life for you because he fucking loved you. I have never seen my brother care for anyone as much as he did you."

I blink a couple times and will these fucking stupid tears to fuck off, I'm not a crier. "He's my favorite person." He smiles and nods.

"I have a feeling someone else is coming in a close second to my brother." He flicks his gaze toward Artemis.

"At the rate he's going, he's tied on my shit list with my dad." He laughs.

"Havoc would have approved of him." That shocks the fuck out of me.

"Why?"

"Because he was willing to die just so you could live. Havoc knew before anyone how special you truly are, that dipshit seems to have figured that out pretty quickly as well." Hearing that come from him and knowing he doesn't hate me feels like a weight is lifted off my soul and I can finally breathe. Years have passed and I've harbored so much guilt and shame over Havoc dying, and trying to hide my feelings about that day so it wouldn't upset Chaos, but I didn't have to. Before more can be said, Cronos comes to claim the seat beside me.

"Bestie."

He smiles. "The next time I get on a plane it will be to travel for myself and I can't fucking wait."

I pout. "I'm gonna miss you!"

"You're literally sleeping with my mirror image, you won't miss me that much." I laugh and nudge him with my shoulder, feeling grateful that what happened the other day hasn't affected our friendship.

When we land in Mykonos it's in some private airfield on a cliff that Artemis told my dad about. As we disembark I look around and frown when I don't see any cars waiting for us. Dad marches toward the next plane with Uncle Chaos as they wait for Aunt Sin and Uncle Kacey. I hang back with Cronos. I triplets come to join us and I must say, I don't hate them as much as I used to. I glare at Artemis's back when he descends the steps and doesn't even glance my way as he follows after my dad.

"I'm gonna shoot him," I announce. The triplets chuckle while Cronos remains silent as he stares after his brother. It takes about twenty minutes for Dad to bring everyone up to speed with their plan before he comes to me with his new little tail following after him like a good dog. When Dad stops in front of me, I shoot Artemis a glare, the fucker just stares at me with a blank look. "Do you sit on command when he tells you to?"

"London, cut it out," Dad scolds but fuck him.

"Do you shake hands like a good dog when your master tells you to?" Anger flashes in his eyes. "Or are you a naughty bitch—"

"Cut the shit, we got people to kill tonight and unlike you, killing doesn't come as easy to me." Anger burns inside me at his comeback and before I can utter a single fucking word, he turns and stalks off toward Uncle Rook and Uncle Knight. I turn back to face my dad and of course he looks smug.

"Well done, Dad, you got him under your thumb and away from me. Guess my pussy wasn't that good after all." I don't stick around to hear his tantrum, I head toward the cliff's edge staring out at all the lights. I take a couple deep breaths and channel the emotions raging inside me. I focus all of the anger and hurt into revenge, by the end of the night Costa Argyros will be dead and the Greeks will be no more.

"Here." I turn to see Aunt Sin standing there. She hands me a vest that is loaded with ammo and two guns. When I see what guns they are I snap my gaze back to her. "Your mom wanted you to use her *Pit Vipers*."

"She's never let me use them before."

"I know, don't lose them or she may kill the both of us."

"Yeah, true that."

"Here." She hands me two blades and a strap. I strap each of them to my legs. She checks my vest to make sure it's secure before stepping back and nodding. "You're with me, my dad—"

"I'm not a sniper," I protest.

"I know, there is no vantage point because it's literally in a cave below us."

"Say what?"

"Yeah, that's why we haven't been able to locate the fuckers. You stay with me and my dad, Uncle King is with us and so are Apollo and Ares." I nod my understanding and follow her back to where our group is gathered.

"You ready?" Uncle Vin asks me.

"Yep." He doesn't look convinced. "I swear I'm ready, I know how to do this." He nods and turns back to face Uncle King as they go over the plan one more time.

"You look like a badass," Ares says as I try to tie my hair up, some of the strands are too fucking short and just fall out but I get the majority of it up.

"You're just realizing that now?" I deadpan.

"Nah, we always knew you were a badass from the day you beat the three of us on the trail," Apollo adds.

I decide to throw the idiots a bone and be nice for once. "Stay behind me, only shoot if you have to." All traces of humor vanish from their faces.

"We've killed before," Apollo mutters.

"I know, but that wasn't by choice, this is. Stay behind me

and I'll make sure no one shoots you in your ass cheek." They both scoff and laugh as they nudge me.

"London." Taking a deep breath I slowly turn to face the asshole.

"What do you want, pretty boy, can't you see I'm having fun here being a heartless bitch who loves to kill?" He opens his mouth to speak but snaps it closed. He does the same thing again and I snap, "Say whatever the fuck it is you came here to say."

He snaps his arms out to grip my waist and hauls me into him, covering my mouth with his, kissing me with a hunger I've never felt from him before. I reach up to wrap my arms around his neck but he jerks back and stares down at me panting.

"I'm sorry, I do love you and I would choose you every time, just know that. Please don't fucking hate me." Before I can respond, he kisses me again, robbing me of air once more before he breaks the kiss and stalks away, leaving me standing here utterly fucking confused.

"Did that make sense to you?" Ares asks. I shake my head as I continue to stare after his brother.

"No fucking idea what that was, but this whole boyfriend thing is fucking hard and confusing," I say.

"And that is why we never settle down and share everything because it's easier than dealing with whatever the fuck that was." I pat Apollo on the chest and wink.

"You all share because only one of you is attractive and takes pity on the other two to share the girls." The looks on both their faces is fucking priceless.

Chapter Thirty-four

Artemis

Crouching low, I keep the AK pressed against my shoulder as we drop down behind some boulders. I check through the scope and spot two men stationed at the bottom of the entry. I turn back to Royal and Bishop and hold up two fingers. Royal motions for Chanel to come up. She stays low as she passes by the line of men all dressed in black. She stops in front of Royal who holds two fingers up and then points to where I am. I frown, there is no way she can make that shot from this distance. I switch places with her and watch as she lifts her rifle and sets it up on the top of the boulder. She adjusts the scope and gets into position.

Holy fuck, she is going to attempt the shot!

I watch her exhale and inhale before she squeezes the trigger once and then shifts an inch and fires again. Lifting my own rifle I look through the scope and my jaw nearly hits the fucking floor, she took them both out with a single shot between their eyes. Someone taps me on the shoulder and I look back to see it's Royal.

"She's a dead shot, remember that," he whispers before leading us up the incline. I fall into line behind Bishop as Chanel heads back to her team. As we near the entrance of the cave, I dart forward and tap Royal, he jerks around glaring at me. I point toward the motion sensors on the ground that border the perimeter.

"Wait," I whisper as I crouch low and attempt to pass him but he yanks me back by my shirt.

"Where the fuck are you going?" he says barely above a whisper but his tone is filled with malice.

"To disarm the fucking things, now get the hell off me," I snap and shrug free of his hold. When I'm near the beacon, I drop flat to my stomach and army crawl the rest of the way. I pop the back off the sprinkler looking thing and pull the wires out, the moon casting enough light for me to see the blue wire. I pull the cutters from my pocket and pray they haven't updated the system since I had it installed two years ago. When no alarm sounds, I release a long exhale before gritting my teeth through the pain and army crawling back to Royal.

He says nothing as I reach his side, just jerks his head for me to take the lead. I turn and motion to Chanel with two fingers to head toward the eastern side and do the same to Chaos's team but send them west. I push forward and keep my rifle cocked and ready. As we approach the entrance of the cave I spot four guards. I lift my gun and fire a shot, taking out the first guy. Before I can even shift to take out the other three, Bishop, Royal and Gage have them down. I continue forward on full alert. As we reach the entrance, I slow as this feels way too fucking easy.

"Ambush!" someone shouts. I spin around in time to see Greek soldiers coming up behind us. I duck behind a boulder for cover and then begin to fire, I check around me for Royal and the others but I can't see them.

The entrance of the cave is right there, I could make it if I kept low. Fuck it, I fire two more shots before I dart inside as the gun fight wages on behind me. Being back at the cove feels strange, every time I have come here before it's always been with the dream to overthrow Costa and take over the Godfathers Of The Night to free me and my brothers from his reign but now, I just see it as a curse. I keep flush along the rock wall. As I round the corner, a guard stands there with his back to me. I quietly pull my blade from its sheath and dart forward, covering his mouth with one hand and slicing his throat with the other.

I gently lay his lifeless body to the ground, careful not to make a sound. I creep forward and make sure to keep my head on a swivel, watching my own back. As I round the next corner a shot whizzes past my head and I jerk back, quickly switching out my blade for my Glock. I drop to my knees and wait for a break in the firing then lean around the corner and fire three shots taking down the two men. I take a step forward and another fucking shot rings out, I return fire but miss both fucking shots.

"Give up now, son of Costa, you are surrounded, you won't win," one of the cocksuckers calls out. I recognize his voice as one of Costa's closest guards, he's the one who broke my fucking ribs.

"That's not what your mother said last night while I was fucking her brains out." I stifle my laughter when he begins to hurl insults and curse words at me in Greek. "You sound like your mother," I call out before darting forward and firing two shots. They land in his chest and the look of utter shock on his face is priceless. "Lesson one, motherfucker, never let your emotions distract you." I step over him, making sure to take it slow, they would have heard all of those shots and know I'm coming. I chance a glance around the corner where the entrance to the grotto is and managed to spot a shit load of guards before they began firing. I drop low and cover my head using the rock wall as a shield. When the firing finally stops I stand and wait.

"It's over, Cronos, come out now and I will end your brothers quickly." My nostrils flare at the sound of his fucking voice. The dumb fuck has no idea I'm still alive.

"How about you crawl back inside the cunt you popped out of before I kill you slowly."

"You fucking pathetic fool."

"Before I kill you, I'm going to send you to the underworld deaf, dumb and blind just like your ancestors." I know he's stalling and garnering time for his men to fan out and sneak up on me but there is no way I'm running away like a bitch, if I die here today then so be it. Taking a deep breath, I inch forward ready to go all Bruce Willis, yippee-ki-yay motherfuckers before I'm yanked backward. I stare into the pale blue eyes of Royal.

"Don't be a fucking hero, wait for Chanel to get into posi-tion." I look around him to see Chaos's crew has now joined us.

"There is no back entrance into this place," I grit out.

"There wasn't but in four seconds there will be," he says smugly. Before I can even answer, a loud booming sound comes from inside the grotto, the whole place begins to shake and specks of dust land on us from the ceiling.

"Kill them," I hear someone yell from inside the grotto.

"Move!" Royal shouts. I fall in behind him with Bishop and Chaos on either side of me. Bishop leaps forward and yanks his son back by the hood of his jumper and then fires at the fucker hidden behind a stone pillar on Royal's right.

Holy fuck, he just saved his son's life!

I begin firing at all the guards, taking as many of them down as I can. Chanel and London are on the other side of the room taking care of the men over there. This place is huge, it's like the size of a football field. I dart behind one of the Greek god statues, there's twelve of them in the room, representing each of the gods. I hear the bullets pierce the stone statue, then dart around the other side and fire four shots, taking the motherfucker down. But as I attempt to move into the center of the room, I spy Costa on London's side trying to escape out a side tunnel with two guards. My heart sinks when I spot London chasing after him. I don't think as I rush forward shooting any fucker that comes into view. I spot Royal out of the corner of my eye.

"Royal, London!" He turns toward me and follows the path I'm clearing as he falls into step beside me as we cross the room firing shot after shot. I severely underestimated the number of soldiers Costa had in his employ. I cut in front of Royal and run down the tunnel, following the sound of gunshots.

"Come on you fat fuck, I'm right here."

"I'm gonna fucking rip your cunt apart." I growl low in my chest at his threat of touching her, I push my legs to move faster.

"Come get me then, you fucking cum stain," she screams, then more gunshots are heard. We round the corner and my feet begin to skid out from under me. Royal snaps his arm out, grips my shirt and yanks me upright. We emerge into a secret room I didn't even know existed. I spot the bodies of the two guards first but then I shift my gaze up and I die a thousand deaths at the sight of London on her knees, clutching her arm that is bleeding and Costa holding a gun to the back of her head.

"You pull that trigger and I promise you I won't kill you, but I will promise you will wish I had." The calmness in which Royal speaks is surprising but I can tell from how rigid he is that he is anything but calm. Costa presses the barrel into her head, she locks her gaze with mine for a second and it robs me of air—the resolute look in her eyes freezes my blood. She looks to her father next and the look she gives him will haunt me.

"Drop your guns now or I'll drop her." I do as he says and drop my rifle and Glock, Royal does the same. "Kick them over to me." We do as he says and raise our hands. "Now, before I kill your daughter, should I make you watch as she sucks my cock?"

"You fucking touch her and I'll kill you!" I roar, Costa's eyes widen.

"Artemis."

"In the flesh, you motherfucker," I grit out.

"Take me, let her go and take me. I'm worth more than her," Royal pleads.

"Oh, but she is the heiress and the heart of your pathetic family." London looks at me and the small smirk on her face stumps me until I discreetly follow her gaze to her thigh where she slowly pulls her blade out. I dart forward to distract Costa.

"You let her go and you can have me, I'll fall into line."

"I want you dead!" he roars.

"Then kill me! Kill me, not her. She is worth nothing, she's just some bitch I was fucking." I watch as she finally frees her blade, I just need him to point the gun at me so she can make her move. Royal can't see she is armed from where he stands. I take two steps forward and continue my spiel. "She fell in love with me, we can use that shit, that's what you wanted, right? You want the Murdoch's and *Memento Mori* under your thumb, you can have that with her. She was prepared to move out of her dick of a father's house just so I could fuck her."

"I'm gonna kill you slowly, you little cunt," Royal sneers, if there was a way for me to tell him or show him she is armed I would but I can't. That's when an idea strikes me.

"Before or after I fuck your daughter on top of your rotting corpse?" He turns to me, his eyes burn with the need for my blood, so I keep baiting him. "Do you have any idea how good your daughter can suck dick?"

"You're dead!" he roars as he charges me, I land on the hard ground with a grunt. His right hook cracks across my jaw and has my vision turning blurry. I cover my face trying to block some of his hits but the motherfucker is relentless. "I'll fucking rip you apart, you cunt."

"Enough!" Costa roars but Royal ignores him as he keeps landing hit after hit. I manage to land a few hits on him and fuck it feels good. "I said enough!" Costa screams as he suddenly appears above us and pushes the gun into the side of Royal's temple. I look to the side to see London on the ground.

He knocked her out!

"You will die alongside your father," Royal spits. "I knew you were never good enough for her." His chest rises and falls rapidly. Costas smirks, loving the idea of watching Royal kill me.

"You're going to hell tonight, you worthless piece of shit." Costa sneers down at me. Panic flares to life inside me, I can't allow him to kill Royal. If he does, all of this was for nothing and I will be buried in a hole beside or at the bottom of the ocean with some concrete bracelets. When I spy movement out of the corner of my eye, hope flares inside me.

"Not before you do!" London screams, then plunges her knife into the side of Costa's neck.

Chapter Thirty-Five

London

I rip the knife from his neck and gasp when his blood spurts all over my face and chest. He claws at his throat trying to staunch the blood escaping but fails. I yank him back by his shirt and jump on top of him.

"Before you die, You will feel what he did." I slice the blade across his chest. He tries to scream but it just sounds like he's gargling mouthwash. I do it again but this time dig the blade in so fucking deep I struggle to drag it through him. A haze over-takes me as I continue to slice him, then I go for his fingers and cut off every one on his right hand, the hand he touched me with. "Fucking cunt," I scream, as I begin to stab him,

"Baby, that's enough," I hear Artemis say before he wraps his arms around me and drags me off his father. We fall to the ground with my back to his chest. I hold the blade in a vice like grip as I stare at Costa's dead body. "You're okay, he'll never touch you again, baby, I promise." He places kisses to the side of my head and the feeling of his lips slowly brings me out of my haze as my dad kneels down in front of me. He looks like he's on the verge of passing out. He slowly reaches out and cups my face between his hands, the smile on his face is laced with sadness but it's the sight of the unshed tears in his eyes that worries me.

"You will never put me in a position like that again, that sight will haunt me until the day I die."

"I'm sorry," I murmur.

"Never again, baby girl." He yanks me to him and crushes me against his chest, placing a kiss to the top of my head. "I love you too fucking much to live without you. I won't survive losing you." The watery tone of his voice brings tears to my own eyes. Wrapping my arms around him, I hold him tight.

"I love you, Dad." He relaxes into me and I feel some of the tension leave him.

"I love you too, London, so much." I pull back and smile up at him, he places a kiss on my forehead before resting back on his haunches. Artemis snakes an arm around my waist and draws me back into him, nuzzling his face into the side of my neck, not caring about the blood that covers me. "You knew she had the knife," Dad says, it's not a question but Artemis answers him anyway.

"Yes. You have to know I didn't mean anything that I said about her. I needed him to take the gun off her so she could strike. Easiest way to do that was to get you angry enough to fight me."

Dad snorts. "You just have to breathe to piss me off." I can't help the laugh that slips past my lips.

"Hey, I thought you were on my side?" Artemis tries to sound angry but fails.

"She will always be on my team, dick." Dad's words lack the bite they usually hold.

"From now on I'm team Switzerland!" I say proudly.

"No!" they both shout.

"Why not?" I snap, looking at each of them.

"Because you started this war!"

"You nearly killed me!" they say at the same time, I roll my eyes.

"You both are so freaking dramatic."

"And you're a pain in the ass but we manage to put up with you." I balk at Artemis.

"Ain't that the truth," Dad tacks on.

I pout. "I liked it better when you wanted to kill him and didn't gang up on me."

"Fuck me," Artemis grumbles, I smile and open my mouth but Dad covers it with his hand and glares right at me.

"If you respond to that fucking statement, I will shoot the cunt right here and leave him to rot next to his father." I nod my agreement. He drops his hand but I love the way he eyes me skeptically, like he knows I'm about to say something that will make him wish he never moved his hand.

"I really wasn't going to accept his offer in front of you." Dad slams his eyes closed and looks up at the ceiling.

"It's not okay to strangle your own child, your wife would be very upset," he mutters to himself and I scoff.

"That's fucked up that you have to talk yourself out of strangling me!" I huff as I climb to my feet.

"It's either strangle you or him." I look at Artemis who widens his eyes in warning.

"Don't you fucking dare," he warns.

"Fine. Don't strangle him," I say in a bored tone as I look around for one of the fingers I chopped off Costa. "Oh, there you are!" I say happily as I snag his chubby finger off the ground and slip the lion ring with the stone off his finger smiling to myself. I turn back to my dad and Artemis to find them both gawking at me like I'm a mutant. "What?"

"Nope, I'm not saying a word," Dad says as he climbs to his feet.

"You had to fall in love with a crazy person who gives zero fucks about dead things," Artemis scolds himself as he stands. I make an ugly face and give them the middle finger before tossing Artemis the ring. He catches it and turns it over in his palm a couple times. I can see the relief in his face that his nightmare is finally over but when that relief is overshadowed by a look I don't recognize I begin to worry. He turns to my dad and holds the ring out to him.

"What are you doing?"

"Making a choice," Artemis answers without hesitation.

"What choice?" Dad pushes.

Artemis flicks his gaze to me for a second before turning back to my dad. "You said if I lead I don't get her." I gasp, that motherfucker. That's why he was acting all weird and shit earlier because my dad said something to him. "So, I choose to give up the position of Godfather and choose your daughter."

"Artemis—"

"Quiet, London." I glare at the back of my father's head ready to stab him in the ass until he speaks. "You are willing to give up a role that will guarantee you financial security, status and a position at the head table, as well as places for your brothers at your side for my daughter?"

Artemis takes a deep breath and nods. "Yes. Honestly, it wasn't a hard choice to make. I love her and I know you don't agree with me being with her but with all due respect, I don't give a fuck." I bite my bottom lip to keep from smiling at the fact my dad's stupid ass plan backfired. Dad remains silent for a minute as he stares down at the ring in the palm of his hand.

"What do you plan to do without all of this? You know she will run mine and my father's empires when the time comes, right?"

"Honestly, I have no idea. This is all I have known my whole life. I guess I'll figure something out and yes, I know that and I'll stand by her side and help her, guide her if I can and keep her safe."

A groan comes from my dad. "Fuck." He turns and heads for the exit, but pauses in the threshold looking back over his shoulder at Artemis. "If you impress me over Christmas break you get the ring back, you piss me off you're out."

"Does she come with the ring?" my man asks. Pride swells inside me that he isn't willing to budge on this unless I'm the grand prize. Dad looks at me and sighs.

"You know you could do so much better, right?" I laugh but shake my head. "That's up to her, she knows her place is here with her family when the time comes, but I also won't stop her from forming an alliance with the Greeks through... whatever the fuck it is between you two." I squeal and clap my hands, they both ignore me as they continue to stare at each other.

"If you don't leave in the next two seconds you're gonna see me kiss him."

"Jesus fucking Christ, London," Dad snaps. "You better get a new army because you're going to need the protection from her when she's mad." Artemis laughs at my expense. The moment Dad is out of there, I launch myself at my man. He catches me with ease and I claim his lips in a kiss that sets my blood on fire and has need burning inside me. He breaks the kiss with a groan.

"Now I have to walk out there with a hard-on." I smirk.

"Want me to take care of that?"

He gapes at me. "Seriously? My dad's dead body is right there." I shrug.

"Not the first dead person you've fucked me next to."

"Dear God, you will be the fucking death of me!"

"So, is that a no?"

"London!" I groan at the sound of my dad's shout.

"He so heard you," Artemis teases.

I wink. "I know, that's why I said it. I heard him take five steps before he stopped moving." We both laugh, Artemis locks his fingers with mine and drags me from the room without a glance back at his piece of shit of a father.

"I swear to God I'm gonna fucking murder him!" I scream, my mom chuckles and places her hand on top of my thigh.

"Honey, you can't kill your father." Aunt Sin scoffs, Mom shoots her a scathing look. She slouches back onto the sofa opposite us.

"He took Artemis out before sunrise this morning and I haven't heard from him all day. It's Christmas Eve and my boyfriend isn't here to put the marshmallows in my hot coco!" I whine.

"Want me to do it for you?" Mom offers. I pout and cross my arms over my chest as I drop back into the sofa.

"No. You don't pick out the pink ones and make them into the shape of a heart like he does." I can see my mom trying hard not to laugh, but she loses the battle when Aunt Sin laughs. "I can't wait to go to Grandpa's tomorrow. I'm telling him you've been mean to me and that Dad killed my boyfriend."

"Did not!"

"Did—" I jump to my feet and spin around to see my dad and Artemis standing in the entryway with my Cronos and Uncle Kacey behind. Now that I can see he is alive and not dead my anger spikes. "Where the fuck have you been? Don't you have a phone because you know it has a green button that you push when you need to call someone!" Dad laughs and pats Artemis on the shoulder.

"Goodluck with that one." I shoot my dad a filthy look. In the past few weeks him and Artemis have formed this frenemies type of friendship and I don't like it. They gang up on me, leaving me no choice but to tattle on my dad to Grandpa or fuck with his shit like slashing his tires.

"Omorfia—"

"Don't you fucking *Omorfia* me!" I shout. Cronos steps around his brother followed by Uncle Kacey.

"If you're pissed now, wait till you see what he did without your consent, bestie." Artemis shoots his twin a look that promises he will pay for that comment later.

"Thanks, asshole," Artemis grits out.

"Anytime, Brother," Cronos claps back.

"Did you see your blonde whore?" Artemis balks at me.

"What? No, I was with your dad!" he quickly answers.

"What fucking blonde?" Dad snaps.

"His stupid guy named best friend who is a bimbo," I answer.

"Blake hasn't made contact since you fucking stabbed her!" Artemis shouts.

I shrug. "Shouldn't have been a whore, then I wouldn't have stabbed her, so not my fault."

"Jesus Christ, I wasn't with Blake. I was with your dad getting inked." Suddenly I don't feel so angry and kind of feel like I maybe should have approached this situation a wee bit differently.

"Oh."

"Yeah, *oh*," he mocks me, earning the stink eye. He reaches up and grips the back of his shirt and yanks it off. My eyes widen at the same time my jaw drops open. His whole chest is fucking tatted! My feet carry me across the room to stand before him. I stare at the statues that cover his chest and then it dawns on me.

"Cronos, Apollo, Ares and Adonis." He smiles and nods.

"You got the statues of the Greek gods to represent your brothers?"

"Sure did." A pang of jealousy hits me and I do my best to conceal it but I'm still working on that shit. He turns around to show me his back which is outlined already. "We ran out of time to finish it but it's going to be epic." I don't really take in the design because I'm still salty over the fact I'm not on his chest.

"Yeap, it's pretty, well done and all that shit," I say. He turns around and the smile on his face pisses me off.

"What's wrong?"

"Nothing, I'm tired, night." I try to flee but he grabs my wrist and yanks me back. I refuse to look at him.

"Don't you want to see my favorite one?"

I scoff. "No."

"You sure, because I think she is pretty fucking beautiful."

I snap my head toward him so fast I swear I heard my neck crack. "*Her*?"

He nods. "Yeah, she is fucking amazing."

"Oh well please, do show me the ugly bitch you got

tattooed. It better be in a place where I don't have to see her hideous face." I ignore the laughter coming from the guys behind me as I keep my bored look in place. Artemis holds out his right forearm and I nearly die on the spot.

"Still think she's hideous and ugly?" I swallow loudly and shake my head.

"That's my face!" I screech, he got a portrait of my face on his arm with the London bridge in the background.

"Why is the London Bridge broken?" He grips my chin and tilts my head until I meet his gaze.

"Because London has fallen and I'm lucky enough to say she has fallen for me." My fucking heart jumps in my chest.

"Why did you get my face tattooed on you?"

"It's a picture tatted on my inner forearm to remind me you're not far, literally at arm's reach, it's a new meaning to wearing my heart on my sleeve."

"I love you." He beams down at me.

"I love you too."

"Now is this the part where we sneak out so I can show you just how much I love your tattoo?"

"I'm gonna kill him, he's going to fucking die tonight." Dad seethes behind us. I can't help the laughter that burst out of me, I fucking love pissing my dad off.

Epilogue

Artemis

Six months later...

Sitting here at the table with the leaders of the other families feels surreal, I never thought I would be able to claim a seat here. I had dreamt about it but now to actually be here is fucking everything I wished it would be.

"I vouch for Artemis Argyros to be the new leader of the Godfathers Of The Night, all in favor?" I nod my thanks to Royal, he has helped me more than I ever thought he would with rebuilding my society and making changes for the better of my people. The trials are no longer a thing and we don't deal with any of the skin trade anymore. That caused problems with the other head families but fuck them, I will not have anything to do with that shit.

"Aye," Bishop is the first to answer.

"Agreed," Knox says.

"You have my vote." I nod my thanks to Andreas.

"You cost me a shit load of money but I can't argue against the changes you've made, your casinos are cleaning a shit load of cash for me so, yeah." I expected Karl to fight this but I'm pleasantly surprised at his agreement. Given what is brewing between him and Knox I'm surprised that they haven't taken each other out.

"Karl's right, you've done good, kid, so you get a yes from me." I smile my thanks to Ian.

"Then, I present to you all the new leader of the Greeks and the head of his family." I reach out and offer Royal my hand. He rolls his eyes but shakes my hand.

"Thank you, for everything you have done to help me." The rest of the members call out their goodbyes and congratulations as they leave. I shake each of their hands as they pass by but Knox stops.

"Don't you have four brothers?" he asks.

"I do but three of them are in college back in the US and one of them is traveling the world offering aid to sick children with Amelia."

"So who is your right hand?"

I smile proudly. "My girlfriend." Knox's eyebrows nearly hit his hairline, he darts his gaze to Royal before looking back at me.

"His daughter?"

"Yeah."

He whistles between his teeth and claps me on the shoulder. "You're a lucky man."

Frowning, I ask, "Why?"

"Because you're still breathing." Royal and the rest of his family laugh at my expense. Knox waves goodbye, leaving just me and the rest of the Murdoch and Murelo family behind. I had hoped to get a moment alone with Royal but it doesn't look like that is going to happen so I go for plan B and move to the other side of the room. They all eye me strangely but it's safer this way.

"What the fuck are you doing?" Chaos asks.

"Just to clarify there are no weapons allowed in here, right?" They all frown and share a look before Chanel answers.

"Yeah, why?"

"Good." I take a deep breath and turn to Royal who is standing tall between Chaos and Chanel. I can see from how tense he is that he knows something is about to happen. His father and uncles all reclaim their seats and watch with rapt attention. "Just so we are clear, London is having lunch with her Mom five minutes away and if I don't make it back to her within twenty minutes she will come looking," I warn her father.

His eyes narrow as he places his hands flat on the table and leans forward. "What the fuck did you do, dick?"

"I love your daughter," I blurt out.

"What the fuck does that have to do with anything?" Royal bites out.

"Oh shit, he's going to—" I cut Gage off before he can beat me to it.

"I want to marry your daughter!" I shout. Time stops, I stop breathing for a second and so does Royal. The room is dead silent for a whole minute as we all wait for Royal to come to terms with what I have just asked him. He slowly straightens and brushes off imaginary lint from his shirt. Chaos and Chanel relax and take a step back, the fucker uses that moment to leap onto the table. Chanel and Chaos manage to grab an ankle each and hold him back from crossing the massive round table to get to me.

"I'm gonna fucking rip your throat out!" Royal roars.

"I'm asking you!" I shout back.

"No, no, no, no, no! There is your answer. You are not marrying my daughter." I dart my gaze to his dad and uncles for help but groan at the sight of all six of them covering their mouths with their hands to hide their laughter.

"We live together, she moved to Greece with me, she didn't even want me to tell you because she knew you would act like this and say no."

He stills, his eyes spit hatred at me. "You marry her behind my back and I swear to Christ almighty—"

"Yeah I know, you will kill me and all that shit," I finish for him. "I respect you and I am grateful for all the help you and your family have given me these past months, but I'm going to marry her. I fucking love her and she loves me. Get on board with this idea because she is telling her mother we are getting married right now." His eyes widen.

"You chicken shit motherfucker! You went to my wife?"

"No, I told her not to but you know what your daughter is like when she sets her mind to something, so she made sure she had a backup plan in case I did decide to ask you for her hand."

"You don't marry her until I say."

I cringe. "London has already set a date."

"When?" he grits out through clenched teeth.

I run a hand through my hair knowing this is going to set him off, she knew exactly what she was doing when she picked this date. "December."

"The what?"

I release a whoosh of air. "She set the wedding date for your birthday." Royal loses his shit again and Chanel and Chaos have to hold him back.

Bishop climbs to his feet and buttons his suit jacket with a smile on his face as he says, "I thought him having a daughter was karma biting him in the ass but I see now I was wrong, his karma has only just begun since you came into his daughter's life. Welcome to the Murdoch family and all our fucked up shit."

Thank you!

That is a motherfucking wrap!

This book was a fucking dream to write, I am in love with London and all her smart ass comebacks. I knew from the moment she entered Royal's life that she would get a book. I couldn't not tell her story because she is a badass and needed it.

I cannot thank you enough for reading *London Has Fallen*, it means the world to me that you have taken a chance on reading one of my books!

If you would leave a review that would amazing!

Also by Samantha Barrett

Paranormal Romance

The Dream Series

A Beautiful Dream

A Twisted Fate

A Beautiful Nightmare

Redemption

Anarchy

Brutal Savages

Savage Lies

Brutal Truth

Savage Beast

Brutal Beauty

Mafia Romance

Murdoch Mafia Series

Played By The Bishop

Tormented By The King

Tortured By The Knight

Tempted By The Queen

Turned By The Pawn

Ruined By The Rook

Murdoch Mafia Novella

Stalemate

Memento Mori Series

Reign Of Royal

Broken By Sin

In Havoc Lays Chaos

Fairytales With A Twist

Condemned Beast

SPORTS ROMANCE

Playing For Keeps

Offside

Touchdown

End Game

Hail Mary

Blindside

RH SPORTS

Hate Us Like You Mean It

MM

Love Me Like You Mean It

ACKNOWLEDGMENTS

Marky Beez, my ride till the fucking wheels fall off, my booty call, my disco stick. Thank you for being a fucking champ and taking shit loads of cold showers because I was working late. I'll pounce on the D after I finish writing this, you dirty man!

Leah, I can't say thank you enough for everything you have done for me babe. These covers and graphics are everything and because of you, these books capture the attention of my readers thanks to the stunning covers, I love you!

Jaye-*the bitch from Waterford,* I should just not mention you here but then I would have to deal with you adding shit to my books and me publishing them without checking! Thank you for helping me plot this book and reading over it and forcing me to keep going when I wanted to tap out!

My babies, God I love you both so fucking much. If you ever turned out to be anything like London I would be requesting a fucking refund! Shine bright my babies because you both are my light at the end of dark tunnel, Mummy loves you!

My alpha's, Debbie, Clare and Sarah, you ladies have no idea how much I love you, these books would not be what they are without you. Each of you plays a role in keeping me on track and pushing forward, without my Three Musketeers none of these books would be here, thank you my loves.

My Army & my beta girls, you ladies are the core of this

whole book journey, without your hype, love and constant support I don't think I would be where I am today. I love each of you so fucking much for all you have done and continue to do for me.

Lizz, I can't thank you enough for putting up with me and my release schedule! I know I have thrown so many books at you over the years and you never complain, you smash them out and always make them ten times better. Thank you my friend xxx

My darling dark delicious readers, you are the most amazing bunch of humans I have ever had the chance to interact with and also be able to meet some of you has been the highlight of my year. Thank you so much for taking a chance, reading these crazy motherfuckers and loving them as much as I do.

Sam xxx

About the Author

Samantha Barrett is a dark romance, PNR author who loves to write out-of-the-box stories. She is originally from the land of the long white cloud, New Zealand. She is totally fluking her way through this whole author gig, if she isn't writing you can find her kicking back with her kids and husband with a bag of chips and a glass of wine in her hand.

Sam loves Twilight and is a TWIHARD proudly.

Made in the USA
Columbia, SC
12 December 2024

49031566R00207